A Student's Guide to Literature / Classics

学科入门指南
文学·经典

[美]R.V. 杨　[美]布鲁斯·S. 桑顿　著

高　睿　译

ZHEJIANG UNIVERSITY PRESS
浙江大学出版社

目　录

文学入门指南

经典入门指南

CONTENTS

A Student's Guide to Literature

A Student's Guide to Classics

文学入门指南

引　言：文学的矛盾

　　文学的本质是矛盾的，同时文学对于读者的影响也是矛盾的。书面文字或口头发言都是承载文学作品的媒介。但是，书面传播也好，口耳相传也罢，它们并不能代表文学作品本身。读者会被优秀的诗歌小说吸引甚至为之着迷，是因为这些作品看起来很真实。哪怕他们心里清楚，这种真实感即便基于史实，也不过是作者刻意营造的结果，是虚构的产物。经久不衰的文学作品都蕴含某种深意，亟待人们理解、思考与阐释。当然，形成这样认知的原因在于这种吁求并非显而易见，而是很含蓄。济慈曾说："诗歌过于直白，并不讨喜。"文学在社会中的功能定位同样不甚清晰。它可以单纯地作为娱乐消遣的方式，毕竟无论男女都会通过讲故事或唱歌自娱自乐，消磨时间，或是缓解"现实生活"的压力。与此同时，在整个西方文明的发展过程中，文学也占据了教育和文化传播的中心地位，成就了共同身份感，促成了个人和社会对人类体验的理解。文学在文化传统中扮演着重要角色，从柏拉图以来的道德家和改革家到今天的媒体批评家和文化多元论者都非常关注。

　　对待文学，必须既谨慎又宽容。文学研究的主要目的在于学习如何批判地阅读，以及在面对充满魅力甚至蛊惑的作品时能够保持谨慎客观的态度。但是，文学作品和任何艺术作品一样，比如一首交响乐，一幅画作，一篇小说或一部史诗，读者只有心悦诚服，才能领略个中三昧。正因为如此，文学研究是一种人道主义或人文主义的学科，而非精确的实证科学。一名合格的物理学家，只要能坚定地遵循科学规律就能保持绝对客观，他的人道主义观点对他以何种方式进行研究或得出何种结论没有影响。医学家并不会将人体视为装载着灵魂的肉体加以研究，其兴趣仅仅在于人体的生物机理。当然，文学研究者必须保持客观，仿若其研究的对象与其毫不相干；解读作品时也必须摒弃个人因素。不过，批评家在看《李尔王》时，代入感固然没必要强烈到把自己当作主人公，却还是应该对这个悲剧人物的困难处境感同身受才能做好评论。与此相对，对患者的同情或许是癌症研究人员工作的动力，却绝不是他研究的内容，也不是这门科学的要素之一。因此，理科学习并不能作为文科学习的参照。诚然，所有艺术都包含某些真实的、"科学的"因素。比如，对伊丽莎白时期舞台布景和印刷业的了解能够提供大量有用的信息，有助于我们理解当年人们是如何观赏《哈姆雷特》，以及剧本是如何保存的。可是，这些事实无法解释这部作品的魅力与意义。文学作品不是自然现象，也不是标本，而是我们赖以栖身的这个世界的文化成分。华兹华斯曾说过，诗歌"即是与人对话"。我们不能像昆虫学家研究蚂蚁和蚁穴那样研究诗人和诗歌。

　　文学博大而精深。这本短短的指南只能勾勒出该门学科最基本的概况。笔者只是希望简单地描述文学的本质与宗旨，向读者介绍学习文学的最佳途径。书中可能提及文学类别或文体的概念，也会谈到文学如何伴随西方文明而发展。但是，不会涉及跟其他文明相关的文学。这主要是因为笔者才疏学浅，同时也因为笔者认为"文学"一词虽然早已不限于西方世界，但在本书中还是被视为一个完全西方的概念。最后，文末会附上西方传统经典作品，受过良好教育的人都应该有所了解。此外，有些作品声誉或许稍逊，却同样优秀、影响深远，引人深思。不过，并非所有的优秀作品在本书中都有所收录，因为本书面向的不仅是文学专业的本科学生，还有希望具备高中毕业水平文学知识的各年龄段学生。本书当然无法取代这些文学作品本身，不过笔者仍然期望这本指南能帮助同学们自信、谨慎地制定合理的文学学习计划，或者，可以进一步增强他们的文学意识。

文学导读

　　我们在尝试明确文学的本质和宗旨时面临的第一个问题，就是关键概念的语义含混。"文学"一词有很多意义，有时甚至彼此矛盾。就辞源学而言，该词源于拉丁文中的"littera"；与英文的"letter"一样，这个拉丁文词汇既指代表发音的图形符号，也有公文或信函之义。而与英文的"literature"以及欧洲其他各种语言中相应的同源词一样，拉丁文 litteratura 最重要的一个含义也是构成通识教育主要元素的那些书面作品。因此 litteratus 意即知识渊博教养出众的人；在此基础上产生了"文人"这个说法。"文学"（literature）一词解释为"书面艺术作品"，也就是韦勒克和沃伦所说："文学性的艺术作品"。此概念源起于19世纪。在此之前，人们惯常使用的词汇是"poetry"，但是今天这个词基本上只用于韵文而非散文。也就是说，poetry（诗）的语言符合一定韵律，分割成一个个"音步"，或者至少按行自由排列。所以，19世纪大半时间，各大学英语系都开设了"文学"导读课程或在相关基金支持下编纂介绍性的丛书——分为"诗歌"、"小说"和"戏剧"。

　　文艺复兴及以前的批评家并不认为散文和韵文分家有任何实质性的意义。不过，过去两三百年中，这种分家的趋势随着散文小说的发展逐渐强化。讲故事基本上完全采用非韵文体或散文体，只有抒情诗和讽刺诗还坚持使用韵文。叙事体散文现在已乏人问津。当代戏剧如果以韵文创作难免流于矫揉造作。据笔者所知，18 世纪晚期出版以英雄双韵体写成的《植物园》一书（作者伊拉斯谟·达尔文是著名的进化论之父达尔文的祖父）是史上最后一部以韵文创作的科技说明文。因此，20 世纪中短篇抒情诗、自省诗或讽刺诗被视为单独的文学门类也就不足为奇了。它们与小说和戏剧差异巨大，后者通过叙述和舞台表现讲述故事。[1]下文提及"文学"时，会时而使用其通行的含义，时而强调其历史内涵（即，诗歌）——人类想象力的产物。

本书采用的文学含义始于柏拉图和亚里士多德。他们认为文学的本质就是模仿，即模拟或再现现实，或人类对现实的体验。柏拉图的这一观点遭到苏格拉底的反对（见《理想国》），而亚里士多德则表示认同（见《诗学》）；无论如何，古典学者大都已认同文学的模仿功能。不过，这个基本事实很难被精确验证，因为这是人类的本能反应，不证自明。譬如，知道友人最近读了本小说或看了部电影，我们首先会问"它是关于什么的？"我们最关注的就是角色如何行事，彼此之间的关系如何。我们期望通过作品了解人生该如何度过。文学作品虽然再现现实，但其本身是作者创造出来的。"诗人"一词源自希腊文动词 poieo，意即创造。同样，"小说"一词则来自拉丁文 ingo，即"做成"、"假装"或"形成"。由此可知，文学（或诗歌）的中心是口头创作，通过这种创造性活动实现对某些人生体验的模拟或虚构。

亚里士多德在《诗学》一书中为分析悲剧创造了很多分类，经过必要的修改后在很大程度上完全可以适用于所有文体。其中，情节亦称故事或事件安排，是主要元素。亚里士多德指出，

---

[1]诚然，20 世纪有很多长篇诗歌，但是，我认为没有人能够从庞德的《诗章》和大卫·琼斯的《咒逐》中读出连贯的故事。

虽然性格成就一个人，他的幸或不幸却是自己行动的结果。第二个元素——人物的塑造——与情节密不可分。它决定各人的行事方式。遣词造句，又称语言，抑或更准确些，风格，是第三元素。这一元素与思想（或主题）或谈话中不时出现的想法紧密相连。最后两个元素——场景和音乐（或歌曲）——严格说来是古希腊悲剧的特点，不过时下的其他艺术形式甚至也有同样的应用，比方说现代电影中的"特效"和"原声音乐"。即使是纯文学体裁也含有类似元素：哈代的很多小说都以威赛克斯郡为背景，逼真的再现更有助于体现小说的主旨和效果。此外，亨利·詹姆斯的小说以及丁尼生的诗歌，无论是风格还是结构都带有"音乐"感。

有些原本非文学性的作品，随着时间推移早就不再具备最初的实际功能，但也常被视为文学，仍然历久不衰，原因在于作者对那些相对次要的元素非常注意——措辞精辟，描写生动，场景再现栩栩如生，语言韵律优美动人；这些都是文学的魅力所在。卢克莱修的《物性论》若仅仅是对享乐主义的论述，则其充其量不过是哲学史上的一个注脚。然而，丰富的比喻、六音步韵文的节奏感却使其魅力在诗歌中凝固，余韵不止。同样，爱默生的很

荷马，依据传统被一致认为于约公元前 700 年在民间口头传诵的故事基础上创作了《伊利亚特》和《奥德赛》。荷马可能出生于巧斯岛或士麦那，他也很可能的确是一名盲人（在一个武士社会中，吟游诗人的确是适合失明人士的最佳职业）。很可能与荷马同时代的人将这两首传唱史诗记录了下来；而当时正在向腓尼基人学习他们文化的希腊人也将其继承下来。

多散文都能让人领略到震撼的精神体验——即使有些读者认为他作为道德家并不称职。约翰·多恩的布道词也一样，即使不是高教会派的信徒也会为之心驰神往。有些作品最初很难说是否属于文学。柏拉图的《对话录》作为西方哲学奠基作品的地位不可撼动，但是其中有几篇，如《会饮篇》和《斐德罗篇》完全可以视作戏剧。而如何对托马斯·莫尔的《乌托邦》进行解读，很大程度上取决于是把它当做政治哲学的论述还是文学作品。但是，这并不意味着小说与非小说，诗歌与论说文之间的区别可以忽略不

维吉尔（普布利乌斯·维吉利乌斯·马洛，前70—前19），出生于曼图阿附近一个乡绅家庭。在接受过当时标准的演说教育后，他没有成为庭辩律师，而是到那不勒斯师从伊壁鸠鲁学派的西洛学习哲学。内战结束后，他父亲的土地被没收用于犒赏屋大维的军队老兵；后来经朋友说项——这是当时的传统，虽然令人难以置信——屋大维（后来成为维吉尔的庇护者）又将土地还给了他的父亲；《牧歌·之一》中维吉尔对此表示得非常欣喜。毋庸置疑，维吉尔对为他说项的这位朋友梅赛纳斯（深得屋大维的宠信）的友谊和庇护深受感动，梅赛纳斯还将他引荐给屋大维。尽管维吉尔是一名宫廷诗人，但是他在叙述埃涅阿斯缔造罗马帝国的经过时毫不避讳"一将功成万骨枯"的惨烈，而弥漫在整部《埃涅阿斯纪》中的忧郁氛围也说明诗人对帝国建立并非一味鼓吹毫无疑义。博斯威尔曾写道，塞缪尔·约翰逊博士"常常满怀激情地引用"《农事诗》（卷三，第66—68页）中的句子——喟叹美好时光从指缝中匆匆溜走，生老病死难以避免。维吉尔并不是一位为政客摇旗呐喊的诗人。

计，而是说文学与其他学科之间其实存在着广阔的灰色地带。正如人人都知道日夜有别，但它们的交替却始终是个渐进的过程，并不能截然分开。

人类想象的核心就是摹写（或模仿），即再现生活——或更确切地说，再现生活的体验。人类天生具有好奇心；与猫或猴子不同，人类的好奇源自意识；意识到自我存在必然就会意识到其他人、其他灵魂的存在。诗人通过自我表达向读者敞开自己的心灵和精神世界。对自我与他人之间异同的认知，对自我认识至关重要。人只能存在于与他人的联系中，也只有通过这种联系才能自我定位。因此，文学既是作者的自白，也是读者内心的呈现。如果诗人完全从自我出发，只表现自己的才能，那么他的作品就无法为人所理解。同理，纯粹主观性地解读一部作品，忽略其结构风格上的特点，完全不理会文字背后隐含的作者意图，也不可能真正读懂该作品。文学源自语言，和语言一样，它以共同文化为先决条件，而共同文化则源于共同的人性。

了解人性，了解文学作品展现的人类状况是文学实现其教育功能的基础。诗歌或小说有助于读者形成道德观与社会观。不过与其说是通过说教，不如说是促使读者想象何为公民的义务与权利。由此说来，文学不是直言什么是对什么是错，更多的是促使人们自行体会何谓善恶。在《李尔王》中，莎士比亚并没有明言埃德蒙是个恶棍，而是一层层地揭示这个反面人物的傲慢与自怜、野心与嫉妒，甚至在这一过程中观众还可能对埃德蒙心生同情甚至好感。这也是文学的陷阱之一：观众可能会罔顾整部戏的主旨，如同埃德蒙宣称的那样将他视为受害者。还有个更有趣的例子：有些倾向于浪漫主义的读者原本喜爱布雷克和雪莱，可是读了弥尔顿的《失乐园》后为其中至恶的化身撒旦所迷，竟然转而青睐燕卜荪了。不过，与说教相比，文学固然可能引人误入歧途，却也更有循循善诱的魅力。虽然知道欺骗、背叛和谋杀不可原谅，但是读了《李尔王》或者看过这出戏，人们却能更深刻地体会这一点，会自然而然地对干巴巴的借口和政治谎言背后的邪恶产生厌恶，从心里排斥与现实中埃德蒙式的人交往，也能抵制住内心深处邪恶因子的诱惑。

"诗人的愿望应该是给人益处或乐趣。"这是贺拉斯在《诗艺》中的名言。后来西德尼爵士对这句话加以提炼，指出诗歌的教育和娱乐功能相辅相成："然而，唯有通过其塑造鲜明的善、

贺拉斯（昆图斯·贺拉提乌斯·弗拉库斯，前65—前8），与友人维吉尔相比出身低贱，他的父亲曾经是一名奴隶，后来获得自由并发迹。他父亲让他在罗马和雅典先后接受了良好的教育。贺拉斯在雅典时加入布鲁图斯的军队，后来布鲁图斯在腓立比战败（莎士比亚在《裘利斯·恺撒》中对他战败自尽进行了戏剧化的描述）。贺拉斯在此战后返回家乡时，他父亲的财产几乎被抄没殆尽，但他还是获得了一份公职。后来他的诗歌引起了梅赛纳斯的注意，后者将他引荐给仁慈的奥古斯都皇帝。贺拉斯的性格同忧郁的维吉尔相反，纵览他的作品——无论是机智诙谐的《讽刺诗集》和《书札》，抑或是优美细腻的《颂歌》——贺拉斯表现出的是怀疑一切的宽和与疏离，以及丰富的幽默感。他乐于接受奥古斯都和梅赛纳斯的恩惠，却拒绝参与政事；他更喜欢呆在位于萨平的农场（正是他的田园诗歌使这座农场声名显赫）。贺拉斯对欧洲诗歌最重要的遗产就是"宁可退耕南阳也不愿闻达于诸侯"这一思想。

恶诸象，寓教于乐，才能最好地了解一个作者……"贺拉斯或西德尼都不否认文学教育"披着美好的外衣"，但正如后者所言，两人都本能地认识到，寓教于乐之所以可行，正是因为"塑造鲜明的善、恶诸象"就是诗歌本身。西德尼强调，文学有教化之力是因其可以再现人生体验，因为人生是有意义的。"好的诗人"，他写道，就像"超凡"的画师，"他们以心灵作画，不墨守成规；他们以色彩呈现给观众的都是最赏心悦目的画面，就像瑠克利希娅为他人之过而自责时那专注而又哀伤的目光；画家描绘的并不是从未见过的瑠克利希娅，而是这一美的具象"。文学之所以能打动人心，即在于能让我们在想象中体味善与美，于虚构中见到真实。

我们应该时刻牢记，除了戏剧，文学的再现都是通过文字完成的。文学对语言有巨大的压力，不过也因此促使语言朝更广博、更丰富、更优雅的方向进化。很难想象人类没有语言会怎样，因此与其将语言视为人类的一项成就，更应该将其视为人性的一个必要条件。然而，语言并非只会进化，同样也可能衰落。莎士比亚戏剧之所以魅力恒久，与 15、16 世纪英语更加完善细腻是分不开的。文学阅读与创作推动了语言的迅猛发展，同时也因此受益。文学就是高度浓缩的语言，它将意义、表达方式推向极致，又促成新的意义和表达方式的产生。因此，拉丁语在中世纪早期的没落，很难说是因为这种语言本身过于简单、有失高雅，还是因为以拉丁语创作的文学作品逐渐流于粗俗且殊少新意。可以确定的是，文学研究离不开语言学习，而学习语言归根结底依赖于对文学的了解，因为文学的语言是反复推敲的结果。伟大的文学作品构成了一个社会的语言文化，批判、反思、自信的阅读必须"读书破万卷"，而"下笔如有神"则更需要借鉴凝结于文学作品中的语言精华。

　　不同语言、文化，不同时代的文学之间密不可分，说明了历史和文学的关系。作者难免受到所处社会政治条件的影响，但其创作最关键的语境还是文学本身。撇开个人动机和外部压力不谈，创作的最终目标很明显是成就文学作品。斯威夫特从未说过《一个温和的建议》仅是部讽刺作品，并不是真的计划将爱尔兰的婴孩做成盘中餐。他也从未提到格列佛只是个虚构人物，所谓的《格列佛游记》不过是他丰富想象力的产物。同

　　奥维德（普布利乌斯·奥维狄乌斯·纳索，前43—17），没有维吉尔和贺拉斯的谨慎（或是人脉，抑或是那份幸运）；后两者都能既保持独立又能保有君主的青睐。奥维德的早期情色诗歌，于露骨的情欲描绘中处处夹杂着作者的自嘲，注定为正统所不容。《埃涅阿斯纪》在维吉尔过世后因其宣扬的为国捐躯而获得普遍赞誉之时，奥维德却暗示能够引诱别人的妻子——破门而入，与情敌斗智斗勇，与佳人深夜幽会——也不窗为一种另类的战场得意（《爱经》卷一，第九章）。这种"做爱不作战"的口号注定激怒奥古斯都，因为其统治要求复兴爱国主义和洁身自好的传统。后来奥维德卷入了一场官司丑闻（很可能和皇帝那放荡不驯的孙女有关），被终身驱逐到帝国边境、黑海之滨荒凉的本都。后来，即便创作了对希腊神话的盛大演绎——《变形记》——和庆祝罗马宗教节日的《日历》也没能使他回归帝都。奥维德借最后的作品《哀怨集》和《黑海书简》请求奥古斯都的仁慈，但在奥古斯都皇帝（及其继任者提比略皇帝）处却如石沉大海。最终罗马这位最欢快、最富魅力的诗人只能悲惨地客死他乡。

样，莫尔在《乌托邦》里说自己从始至终只是个无所适从的看客，倒显得拉斐尔·希斯拉德对那个千里之外秩序井然的国度的描述十分可信。可是，只有最天真的读者才会认为这些故事是真实的，而非作者借此抒发自己的胸臆，或是对他人的作品进行回应。文学与真实的历史（包括作者自己的传记）关系密切，但这并不是种直接的关系。因此，文学之于教育意义特殊——文学涉及大量人物、地点、事实、具体日期等等，但是，这些知识对属于精神领域活动的文学研究本身不是第一位的。甚至，正如一部分文学作品是作者与读者、语言形式与文学语言学传统之间的张力结构一样，文学（和所有的精神世界产物一样）是人类历史的一个组成部分，而不完全是这一过程的展示台。

因此，追溯文学历史的最佳途径是考察各种文体（即文学"门类"）的出现、发展和变迁。不过，"文体"和"文学"一样也不是个明确的概念，这给我们的考察造成了障碍。史上曾根据不同原则将文学作品分门别类，只是各个时期的认知之间存在一定出

但丁·阿利吉耶里（1265—1321），出生于佛罗伦萨，1301年在罗马作为外交使节服务于教皇时被卷入政治斗争遭到流放。但丁无论在爱情还是政治上都是个理想主义者，所以他宁可毕生无法回归佛罗伦萨也不愿意妥协或认罪。《神曲》是他在流亡过程中创作的，他对他人的疾苦感同身受（《天堂篇》第十七章，第58—60页）。但丁意识到人世就是一段流亡之旅，真正的归处在天堂。在佛罗伦萨的圣十字教堂里，不仅有米开朗基罗、马基雅维利、伽利略和罗西尼等名人的遗骸，还专为但丁保留了一座空坟和纪念碑；而但丁本人的遗体则葬在异乡拉文纳。

入。大部分作品都遵循一定的传统，可是几乎没有哪部经典作品能够完美地契合学者为文体所下的定义。这恰恰是文学之伟大的又一个证明——文学，就是不断挑战既定文体的界限。由此可见，传统并非无足轻重。即便是阅读"现实"小说，读者会下意识地接受旁白无所不知、逻辑严密——那是因为我们了解白话小说的传统。大胆创新，甚至颠覆传统的作者实则最为倚仗传统。具有一定文学素养的读者能够在阅读过程中理解维多利亚时期小说的传统。可是，除非读者经验丰富，能够清楚意识到作者舍弃了常规的叙事手法而独辟蹊径，否则很难理解采用意识流写作的《致灯塔》，或没有明确情节的《等待戈多》。

在西方文学的发展过程中，文体的演化不仅仅在于形式，也在于作品的风格和内容。因此，这个概念既可以指某一特定的文学形式，也可以代表某类主题或对象。只是，严格契合某一特定文体的作品非常少见。例如，罗伯特·弗罗斯特的大部分诗作都可以归为"田园诗"，但他并没有以忒奥克里特斯的《田园诗集》或维吉尔的《牧歌》为榜样创作正规的田园诗，也不是严格模仿文艺复兴的作品——如彼特拉克的《牧歌》。事实上，很多伟大的作品都脱胎于作者对形式的再想象，和对前人的精神描摹。《白鲸》或《战争与和平》等"史诗"小说，其实就是对荷马与维吉尔等人开创的古代史诗中诉求与冲突的重新演绎。文体这个重要的文学概念不仅适用于作品的形式，也适用于文学传统的历史演化。不过将特定的诗歌、戏剧和小说硬套入某一文体就过于迂腐了，毕竟削足适履是行不通的。一部文学作品，可以看成作者向文学传统及自然限制妥协的结果。然而，正如西德尼所言，这种妥协"并没有触及作者的底线"。又或者如 T.S. 艾略特所说，文学体现了"传统与个人才能"的冲突与融合。

西方文学的本源乃是史诗，即描述英雄如何不断突破自我局限的故事。西方文学（甚至西方文化与教育）可以说是源自史诗《伊利亚特》和《奥德赛》。传统上认为这两部作品是盲人诗人荷马所作，成形于公元前8世纪。从公元前5世纪起，荷马史诗由雅典和希腊的其他城邦传遍整个西方世界，并对后世的文化、教育和文学产生了深远影响。可与之媲美的还有《圣经》，尤其是其中的《创世记》和《出埃及记》（传说为摩西所作）影响同样巨大。这几卷书的问世比公元纪年还要早一千两百多年，就其主题、规模以及恢弘的气势而言均属于当之无愧的辉煌巨著。书中希伯来人逃离埃及、摆脱被奴役的身份最终抵达理想家园的过程是当之无愧的史诗。不过，《圣经》一向被奉为神圣的历史（或被披露的真相），而不是诗歌。的确，古典文学——以及那些充斥着盲目崇拜又无多大教育意义的神话故事——之所以在基督教盛行之后还能存在，很大程度上应归因于古希腊罗马人对于神祇的态度：他们从不会像基督徒与犹太人那样执

杰弗雷·乔叟（约1340—1400），出生于富裕的葡萄酒酒商人之家，不过因为受过良好的教育，又天资聪颖，结交的都是贵族和王族。年轻时乔叟就是宫廷宠儿，他曾于军中服役，并在百年战争中被俘，但在交纳赎金后被释放。此后，他担任过外交官和政府公务员，先后受到冈特的约翰、理查二世和亨利四世的庇护。他的经典作品《坎特伯雷故事集》是其一生丰富经历和对人性深刻洞察的结晶。从表面上看，全书带有怀疑一切的疏离、宽容和幽默，但那绝不是愤世嫉俗；这个作品展示的是智慧，以及一种悲天悯人的情怀。

着于追寻真相、苛求真实。尽管《圣经》对西方文化的影响只有将整个希腊罗马文学加在一起才能等量齐观，但两者性质不同。在两三百年以前几乎没有人会将《出埃及记》视为与《伊利亚特》一样的"诗歌"。

《伊利亚特》以希腊围攻特洛伊的第十年（也是最后一年）为背景，围绕阿喀琉斯的雷霆之怒展开，而《奥德赛》叙述的则是英雄奥德修斯突破万难历经十年艰苦返乡的故事。这两部作品确立了西方史诗的特质。只要在文学丛书中看过《奥德赛》、《神曲》或《失乐园》的节选，我们就会熟悉这些特质。史诗，以诗歌的形式记叙艰苦的远征或大规模的冲突，一般都会涉及几个国家的命运，人物个个威武不凡，既有神祇也有英雄，以天界和人间为背景，风格恢宏壮丽。史诗一般都会运用荷马式比喻等特定的技巧，出场人物众多，等等。以上描述无一例外适用于所有史诗，不过并没有提及叙事的节奏，简洁明快的风格（因为气势"磅礴"势必不能"笨重""拖沓"），"英雄"人物的鲜明人性，以及最重要的一点——史诗情节紧凑，着重于人物之间的激烈斗争而不是他们各自的命运。如《伊利亚特》选取的是特洛伊战争的第十年。故事以争夺被俘姬妾所引发的龃龉开篇，却并未终结于木马计和特洛伊之劫，而是以赫克托尔惨遭杀戮作结，紧接着当然就是大败赫克托尔的阿喀琉斯很快便步其后尘英年早逝。奥德修斯的故事同样也是"直入中段"，其十年漫漫旅途始于大战的最后一年，故事焦点是他在大战后急于回归家园与妻子团聚。荷马史诗文字优美，凸显了坚定的道德追求，时至今日还能引起读者强烈的精神共鸣。其恒久的魅力即在于此。

除了荷马史诗，还有另三部史诗也不可不读——维吉尔的

《埃涅阿斯纪》、但丁的《神曲》和弥尔顿的《失乐园》。尽管荷马史诗历史最悠久，但毋庸置疑维吉尔对文学传统发展的直接影响更大。罗马帝国逐渐分裂之后，西欧普遍不了解希腊，对荷马的作品也仅有耳闻。然而，整个中世纪都在阅读维吉尔；此后两千年他的影响无远弗届，至今不衰。与《伊利亚特》、《奥德赛》不同，《埃涅阿斯纪》是一首自省诗，反映了英雄回归自我的历程。主人公"埃涅阿斯"并不好武，他笃信神明，顺从地接受自己的命运，可他也忠于职守。维吉尔固然为一个伟大国度（即后来的罗马）的诞生而欢呼，却也不无叹息地承认为了赢得战争胜利，付出的生命代价太过惨重，令人痛心。维吉尔深刻理解人性的弱点，不吝笔墨地刻画英雄遭受的精神淬炼，难怪长久以来一直被视为半个基督徒。这部西方主要的传统史诗充满了对杀伐的怀疑，这暗示了欧洲文化并不像很多人

米盖尔·德·塞万提斯（1547—1616），一生命途乖蹇。在堪称基督教对抗土耳其转捩点的勒班陀一役（1571）中，他失去了自己的左眼，左臂也丧失行动能力。1575年他被柏柏尔海盗俘虏，苦熬了五年才被赎回。他的余生作为一名小小的政府官吏以写作艰难维生。《堂吉诃德》（1605）的第一部分取得成功时他已经年逾五旬；此书前两部分（第二部分1615年问世）并未改善他的经济状况，与其此时的显赫文名全不相称。与维吉尔和贺拉斯不同，塞万提斯在挑选庇护者上运气糟糕：他将自己的作品献给一些贵族，但显然是明珠投暗。这部西方世界最有影响力的小说虽然给它的作者带来了不朽的声誉，却并没能给他任何世俗的成功。

猜测的那样总是为了争霸轻启战端。维吉尔在西方文学、文明中的地位由另一部必读史诗《神曲》可见一斑。诗中人物"维吉尔"是"我"的导师，"我"在其引导下穿越地狱和炼狱的情节占全诗的三分之二。"我"对于文学风格的理解以及文学抱负

威廉·莎士比亚（1564—1616），无疑是自己作品的真正作者；目前对莎士比亚真实身份的最热门猜测是第十七任牛津伯爵爱德华·德·维尔。绝大多数作家虽然天资不俗，但通常并没有接受过正统教育，更鲜有贵族——拜伦和托尔斯泰是极罕见的例子。莎士比亚受到的教育，他的经历都完全可以保证他在文学上的成就，正如亨利·詹姆斯所言，他"得天独厚"。基本可以确定莎士比亚从小就接受天主教教育，虽然当时信奉旧教逐渐受到伊丽莎白女王政府的迫害。越来越多的证据表明，他在16世纪80年代后期曾担任过英格兰北部的小学校长和流浪演员；17世纪晚期一名英国国教的牧师报告（也可以说"控诉"）说莎士比亚"到死都是一名天主教徒"。我们可以假设莎士比亚的剧作和诗歌——特别是神秘的《十四行诗集》（1609）——脱胎于他的经历、兴趣和理想；不过，这些作品与其生活究竟有何关系尚无法确定。莎士比亚超越了以往任何一位诗人，他在环球剧场（一个恰如其分的名字）营造出了一个无比深邃丰富的平行世界。他的作品与伟大的创作过程一样，清楚地向人民展示了一个才华横溢的作者；但人们对其本人却近乎一无所知。很难确定我们的世界如何出现，又为何存在，但是世界的消失却是不可想象的；同理，很难理解莎士比亚如何构建自己的戏剧世界，但人们同样无法想象这个世界有一天会不复存在。

的形成都离不开维吉尔。但丁直白地表明将维吉尔与其前人在以文化为基调的诗人哲人这个小圈子中合而为一的意图。如果说荷马代表了希腊英雄主义时代,维吉尔代表了罗马帝国时期,那么但丁体现的就是中世纪的世界观,特别是托马斯·阿奎那的神学综合法。以上类比固然有其真实成分,但仍然流于肤浅老套。但丁的《神曲》当然鲜明地呈现了他所处世界的政治、宗教和社会的各个方面,以及他得自于同时代思想家(包括阿奎那)的哲学观念和其自身苦难的经历,但作品首先还是关于一个人发现自我、寻求救赎——即回归自我——的过程。在这一发现之旅中,"我"曾直面原罪,也曾诚心忏悔,并且光荣地与神达成了和解。诗中用语是不折不扣的基督教语言,否则便无法解读。尽管如此,这部作品仍然能让信奉其他宗教或根本不信奉任何宗教的读者产生共鸣,因为《神曲》激发了学者的兴趣,触动

约翰·多恩(1572—1631),母亲是托马斯·莫尔的侄孙女。他的两个叔叔都是耶稣会会徒,在他们的教导下,虽然当时的宗教迫害越来越严重,他从小就被教育拒不加入国教。类似于奥维德对于所处时代正统的叛逆,多恩的早期爱情诗(以及讽刺诗)言辞大胆、诙谐幽默,也极大地挑战了新教的权威。多恩笔下的人物往往风流不羁,他本人也抛弃世俗追求和一名富绅17岁的女儿私奔。在雅各宾派统治时期度过了十年困苦的生活后,多恩终于找到了一条良心和生存之间的中间道路。他成为一名教士,最后还成为圣保罗大教堂的教长。他的心灵挣扎成就了最具震撼力的英语宗教诗歌。他的布道词和《突发事件的祷告》也是英语散文中的瑰宝。

了他们的心灵。但丁和同时代年幼于他的彼特拉克以托斯卡纳土语创造了一种风格，与维吉尔的拉丁文分庭抗礼，奠定了现代意大利语的基础。这一过程足以显示语言与文学之间密不可分的联系。同时这对于文艺复兴时期的人文学科至关重要——通过文学创作，一门语言、一种文化可以达到永恒，实现完满。英语在成为世界通用语言的同时，也像拉丁语在罗马帝国时代后期一样开始出现糟粕甚至衰退。然而，只要莎士比亚和其他伟大的英语作家的著作还存在于世，英语的高明之处——即灵动的具化想象的能力——就能得以存续。

西方最后一部伟大史诗的作者弥尔顿，和其他作者一起拓展了英语语言的能力。与但丁一样，从弥尔顿的作品也可以明显看到维吉尔的影响。六音步诗《埃涅阿斯纪》的魅力在非拉丁语世界中就只有无韵体《失乐园》可以媲美。没有哪一首英语诗可以更好地在恢宏格局中再现英雄的尊严。更令人叹为观止的是，他竟是以英语按照拉丁语的规则写作。弥尔顿凭借自己的洞察力与品位精准地知道可以在多大程度上将英语韵文和拉丁语风格的措辞与句法完美结合，从而达到了"散文与韵文未曾达到的境界"（卷一，第16页）。弥尔顿对题材的处理同样令人心情复杂。《失乐园》无疑是一部古风古韵、气势磅礴的史诗巨帙，但它不仅是最后一部史诗，甚至可以说也为这种体裁画上了句点。《失乐园》的主要出场人物是一群坠落的天使，而言行态度始终如一、充满英雄气概的却是撒旦一角。最有意思的是，因为飘渺的本质令天使连重伤也无法承受，更不用说死亡，因为天使并不具备实体，所以无法承受重伤，更不用说死亡，故而全诗唯一一场宏大的战争（即卷六的天堂之战）结果无疾而终，有时更几乎是场闹剧。学者们至今还在争论弥尔顿究竟是借《失乐园》给人们提供一个弥尔顿（1608—1674），真正的饱学之士，而且经历丰富，参与了那个时代重大的政治和宗教事务。自然，弥尔顿的主要作品也都和当时的社会问题有关。如果当初莎士比亚也能接受正统教育，也能享受世俗特权，那么他应该也会创作出类似于弥尔顿的作品，因为有些人瞧不起这个"斯特拉特福人"，认为他不具备以上两个条件，不可能创作出那些诗歌和戏剧。事实上，莎士比亚的作品很受欢迎，而且与弥尔顿的学院派风格相比，莎士比亚走的是大众路线。弥尔顿的作品表现出了一个激进学者终极的乖僻，比如他的圣诞诗《基督诞生的清晨》，几乎完全抛开马厩降生一幕的温情，而将这个婴孩比作被巨蛇缠绕的大力神赫拉克勒斯；他的这首作品也因此被称为"史诗圣诞颂歌"。在《酒神之假面舞会》中，弥尔顿使用假面戏（一种体裁，因其可以充当歌曲、舞蹈、奢华的舞台剧或精致的舞台布景而受欢迎）宣扬朴素的基督教新柏拉图主义。尽管弥尔顿是17世纪最重要的诗人，但其鼎盛时期却几乎全部致力于政治宗教散文的创作。他因为严厉抨击英格兰教会的礼拜仪式和主教团的等级制度赢得清教徒的崇敬；不过后来又因他支持离婚的合法化（他的初次婚姻是与一名17岁的皇室成员，很不幸福）而失去了他们的青睐。弥尔顿强烈要求处决查理一世，给克伦威尔留下深刻印象，后来弥尔顿在摄政王政府担任了几年公职。查理二世和英格兰教会的主教复辟后，弥尔顿对政治失去了希望，他的社会地位一落千丈，就连眼睛也看不见了，这时他以圣经为主题创作了一系列古典作品——《失乐园》、《复乐园》以及《力士参孙》——奠定了他在世界文坛的不朽地位。

欣赏英雄式武德的新视角（一种内在的精神力），抑或是单纯对其不以为然。无论如何，自弥尔顿以来，西方世界再没有真正的史诗问世，就连可以算得上史诗的作品也没有。

当然，不少作品很容易让人联想到史诗——讽刺史诗，像是德莱顿的《麦克·弗莱克诺》、《押沙龙与阿齐托菲尔》，以及蒲柏的《夺发记》和《群愚史诗》。这些作品都是将史诗的传统应用于琐碎、荒谬的事件以达到讽刺的目的。浪漫主义史诗，如华兹华斯的《序曲》，拜伦的《恰尔德·哈罗德游记》和《唐璜》，以及惠特曼的《自我之歌》（事实上是整部《草叶集》），都是以类似史诗的手法处理性格复杂的主人公主观体验的例子。

还有些古代的长篇作品也值得找来一读，如前文提过的卢克莱修的《物性论》。另外还有一篇绝对不容错过——奥维德的《变形记》，这是一部对大量涉及变形的希腊神话进行重新演绎的杰作。该作品语言洗练、情感真挚，是中世纪及文艺复兴时期作家引用古代神话最主要的灵感来源。中世纪的重要长篇诗作，除了但丁的《神曲》外当属乔叟以同韵偶句创作的幽默故事集《坎特伯雷故事集》。另外，还有一部中世纪幽默故事集的杰作——薄伽丘的《十日谈》。拉伯雷的《巨人传》是散文叙事作品，文体很难界定，书中展现的人性中恶作剧、讽刺的一面也可见于伊拉斯谟的《愚人颂》及莫尔的《乌托邦》。

戏剧是最具有社会性或群体性的艺术，因为剧作家必须依靠一群合作者"看"着自己的作品实现。可想而知，一段时间内戏剧佳作不断涌现是很罕见的。公元前 5 世纪雅典举行的酒神祭祀是西方戏剧无可争议的源头。从那时流传至今的剧目——埃斯库罗斯、索福克勒斯和欧里庇底斯的悲剧，以及阿里斯托芬的喜剧——是最早的戏剧作品，也有人认为是最好的。与之媲美的创作直到两千年后才出现：文艺复兴晚期，16、17世纪英格兰、法国、西班牙迎来了第二轮辉煌。其中最伟大的，当然也是史上最出色的剧作家，就是莎士比亚。最好每个学习英语的学生都能通读他所有的作品，包括戏剧和诗歌。退而求其次的话，可以选读以下作品：《亨利四部曲》（其中的《理查二世》卷一和卷二、《亨利四世》以及《亨利五世》），一系列成熟的浪漫喜剧（《威尼斯商人》、《皆大欢喜》、《第十二夜》），晚期的浪漫作品《暴风雨》以及最伟大的几出悲剧：《罗密欧与朱丽叶》、《哈姆雷特》、《奥瑟罗》、《李尔王》、《麦克白》和《安东尼与克里奥佩特拉》。与莎士比亚同时代的英国人克里斯托夫·马洛的作品《浮士德博士》，还有本·琼生的几出喜剧，如《狐狸》和《炼金术师》，都不容错过。17世纪法国出现了一批伟大的剧作家——悲剧作家高乃伊和拉辛，以及喜剧作家莫里哀。高乃伊的《熙德》、拉辛的《安德洛玛克》和《费德尔》、莫里哀的《愤世嫉俗》或《伪君子》无疑中选。塞万提斯所处的年代也是西班牙戏剧的黄金时代，但大部分美国人了解不多。洛佩·德·维加虽然并没有特别出众的作品，但素以多产著称。同时代的后辈卡尔德隆同样著作等身，他的《人生如梦》可能是最出色、最具代表性的

约翰·班扬（1628—1688），其父亲是一名补锅匠，他在乡村小学学会了读写。内战期间，班扬曾参加国会军，后来在17世纪50年代加入非国教的浸礼会并成为加尔文派的一名掌权传道教士。1660年查理二世复辟后，班扬因为无证传道两次入狱，第一次入狱长达十二年。他在第二次入狱过程中完成了《天路历程》，这是一本讲述原罪和救赎的寓言体作品，打动了无数基督徒的心。

巴洛克式戏剧，而《天才魔术师》对浮士德神话的演绎也令人目眩神迷。莫利纳因为一部魅力巨大影响非同凡响的《塞维利亚的骗子》而出名，该剧是最早把唐璜的故事搬上舞台的作品。

还有几位剧作家值得一提，其中有复辟时期的康格里夫，18 世纪的谢立丹、博马舍和席勒。而歌德创作的《浮士德》是文艺复兴以来无可争议的经典。《浮士德》更像一部戏剧式史诗，而不是传统意义上的舞台剧，它可能是浪漫主义和德国文学最伟大的一部杰作。之所以说《浮士德》是世界文学的巅峰之作是因为它以独特的方式将风格、人物塑造、哲学深度完美地融为一体。挪威人易卜生是近现代早期不可多得的剧作家，其他杰出的剧作家还包括萧伯纳、布莱希特、贝克特、尤金·艾里斯柯和路易吉·皮兰德娄。

20 世纪见证了散文小说——特别是长篇小说——的崛起。虽然塞万提斯的《堂吉诃德》并不是第一部长篇散文小说，但它是公认的鼻祖。《堂吉诃德》成书于 17 世纪早期，叙述的都是普通人日常生活中的小事，和浪漫冒险故事的魔幻风格相比独树一帜。书中描写主人公竭力想要到达自己憧憬的梦幻之地却始终无法实现，这无形中给小说这种新形式引为创作背景的客观世界划定了现实的界限。小说（包括长篇小说和短篇小说）的现实主义即在于描写平凡人在普通世界里的生活，具体又准确，令人信服。即使是科学幻想小说（与纯幻想小说相比较）也总是尽量以当时的科学事实和理论为基础，使构建出的想象世界真实可信。幻想小说——从《贝奥武夫》到《仙后》再到《指环王》——都含有纯粹想象的元素，如被施了魔法的湖泊、龙、精灵，但同时也可能是道德现实主义和精神现实主义的作品（后面的"现实主义"并不是解释文体特征的纯粹文学用语）。《堂吉诃德》的天才之处就在于，故事虽然以现实主义为背景，却执着地怀抱着对理想中骑士王国的憧憬，从而将文学的"理想主义"与道德的"理想主义"完美结合。

塞万提斯之后不断有人将小说这种现实主义体裁发扬光大。早期最有影响力的作家出现在18世纪的英国，最重要的作品或许就是笛福的《鲁滨逊漂流记》、菲尔丁的《汤姆·琼斯》及斯特恩的《项狄传》。之后19世纪迎来了小说的辉煌时代，英国文坛可谓群星闪耀。简·奥斯汀在19世纪初创作了六部言辞辛辣、

亚历山大·蒲柏（1688—1744），自出生起就是罗马天主教徒。他出生的这一年恰逢"光荣革命"驱逐了詹姆二世，将威廉三世迎上皇位，并且完全断绝了天主教复辟的可能。蒲柏原本可以表面归顺国教从而获得一些好处（比如在政府挂个闲差），但他还是坚持住了自己的信仰。他幼年罹患结核性脊椎炎，造成驼背，身高不到四英尺。长期的病痛让他写下"我的一生，缠绵病榻"（《致阿巴思诺医生书》，第132页）的语句。不过，虽然健康不佳，蒲柏却是首位依靠出版作品而衣食无忧的英语作家。他成功地将《伊利亚特》译成英雄双韵体，从此实现了经济上的独立，并得以在一座乡间小屋终老。人们常常认为蒲柏的英雄双韵体是以诗歌形式诠释启蒙运动理性主义，但是，威廉·韦姆萨特却雄辩地证明——诗歌的韵律完全是凭借发音来排布文字，其本质就有违理性。而蒲柏的作品因其诙谐之处与16、17世纪的诗歌更为类似，反而同伏尔泰和狄德罗的怀疑论殊少共同之处。因此，蒲柏位于特威肯汉姆的乡间小屋舍弃了法国人重形式的对称风格而选择清新"自然"之风就不足为奇了，这预示着浪漫主义的来临。

涵义隽永、风格独特的喜剧小说。《傲慢与偏见》和《爱玛》是其最重要的作品；相比之下，后者催生了一系列优秀的荧幕改编作品，前者稍显不及。维多利亚时期的其他经典还包括狄更斯的《大卫·科波菲尔》、《荒凉山庄》和《远大前程》，萨克雷的《名利场》，乔治·艾略特的《米德尔马奇》和《弗洛斯河上的磨坊》，以及特罗洛普的《巴彻斯特大教堂》和《红尘浮生录》。而在美国，梅尔维尔的超长篇《白鲸》和超短篇《比利·巴德》、以及马克·吐温的《哈克贝利·弗恩历险记》也是同时期的杰作。玛丽·雪莱的《弗兰肯斯坦》和霍桑的《红字》虽然很难界定究竟算长篇小说还是哥特式传奇小说，但的确值得一读。法国 19世纪出了三大文豪：维克多·雨果（代表作《悲惨世界》）、巴尔

　　塞缪尔·约翰逊（1709—1784），其父亲是一名书商，1731年父亲去世后全家陷入了贫困；当时，约翰逊还未能完成在牛津的学业。幼年的困乏导致约翰逊一生病弱，但即便如此，凭借自身的努力坚持，他还是成为 18 世纪晚期最伟大的英国文人。他的声名并非来源某一部作品，而在于他一生的总体成就。他编纂了史上第一部英语字典（1755），对散文和期刊文学的发展影响巨大，创作了一系列优美的诗歌和一部引人入胜的哲学浪漫小说（《雷塞拉斯》，1759），与詹姆斯·博斯韦尔共同创作了一部重要的游记，他编辑的莎士比亚作品集（1765）是文本编辑和阐释性评论的里程碑式作品，他的《诗人列传》（1779—1781）是传记文学的扛鼎之作。约翰逊本人也成为传记作家的灵感来源，博斯韦尔的《约翰逊传》（1791）记录了他那严肃的表象下的智慧、诙谐和同情心。

扎克（代表作《高老头》）和福楼拜（代表作《包法利夫人》）。而俄国，因为拥有了托尔斯泰的《安娜·卡列尼娜》和《战争与和平》、陀思妥耶夫斯基的《罪与罚》和《卡拉马佐夫兄弟》、以及屠格涅夫的《父与子》，或许最有资格以史上最伟大的长篇小说的祖国自居。

　　20 世纪初涌现出了一批旅居国外的作家，如居住在英国的波兰人康拉德（代表作有《黑暗之心》等），美国则以亨利·詹姆斯（尤其是他的晚期小说）为代表。20 世纪上半叶的三大"高峰现代派"小说的代表是爱尔兰人乔伊斯的《尤利西斯》，法国人普鲁斯特的《追忆似水年华》和德国人托马斯·曼的《魔山》。这几部小说写作手法新颖，刻意将主观意识抽离，因此读者往往认为它们很难理解，甚至根本无法理解。乔伊斯之后，20 世纪最伟大的长篇小说作家之一，福克纳的代表作有《喧嚣与骚动》和《我弥留之际》。温塞特虽然没能得到学术界的肯定，但以其多卷历史小说《劳伦斯之女克丽斯汀》及《欧拉夫·奥当逊》可以算是 20 世纪最具生命力的常青树。除了她之外或许再也没有一个作家更好地继承 19 世纪俄国作家的遗志，完成小说家的天赋使命——即创造错综复杂、引人入胜的情节，安排真实可信的角色，并赋予其深刻的寓意使其得到升华。

　　除了史诗、戏剧和小说以外，各种文体的短篇诗歌——田园诗、讽刺诗、讽刺短诗、抒情诗——也值得一读。长篇叙事文体，如史诗和小说，都是以第三人称叙述不同人物的故事；戏剧则是各角色之间的对话；而短诗就像是诗人的自白，以韵体或无韵体抒发自己的胸臆。显然，抒情诗和讽刺诗的效果部分在于可以和诗人亲密接触，通过文字这扇窗得以窥见诗人的心灵世界（虽然事实并非如此）。而读者对历史上真实存在的诗人过分执着就会分散对诗歌本身的注意。诗歌无非是一种再现，是虚构的产物。诗人一旦试图作诗，必然会务求真实自然。但是，哪怕诗歌取材于诗人的亲身经历，诗人在作品中也只是在扮演一个角色。他创造出一个人物形象，并借这个角色之口说话。人物形象在拉丁语中指罗马戏剧中演员戴的面具，这个艺术名词表明诗人其实是躲在一张"面具"或"脸孔"后面，使角色成为自己情感和想法的载体，从而尽可能使该角色脱离个人体验，引起读者共鸣。所以，即便有人可以用无可辩驳的证据证明"W.H 先生"的身份，或是证明"黑夫人"确有其人，读者还是会继续对《十四行诗集》进行解读。

正因为短诗比戏剧和故事更依赖风格的细微之处，抒情诗、讽刺短诗或讽刺诗一经翻译就会失去效果和美感。尽管如此，鉴于某些诗人于西方文学，甚至整个文化，都不可或缺，因此哪怕只有翻译版本，他们的作品也不能错过。其中值得推荐的

简·奥斯丁（1775—1817），生于一个英国国教牧师家庭。一生未嫁，和家人一起过着平静的日子，从而打破了人们对优秀作家必定经历丰富、受过良好教育、叙述的是大人物、大事件（奥斯丁的作品从不提及法国大革命或拿破仑）的常规理解。在她的笔下，读者只能读到寻常人的平常生活和再普通不过的愿望。她曾经这样形容自己的作品："我就如在（两英寸宽的）象牙上精雕细刻，观众如果不仔细就会忽略。"奥斯丁捕捉到平凡生活中的点点滴滴，再以或冷淡、或讽刺、或辛辣的口吻叙述出来。C.S.刘易斯曾道，可以说奥斯丁更像约翰逊博士一脉相承的晚辈，而不是亨利·詹姆斯的长辈，她是浪漫主义时代的古典文学大师。

包括萨福现存于世的抒情诗、加塔拉斯的一部分抒情诗、奥维德的《爱经》，还有其中最值得一读的是彼特拉克写给劳拉的十四行诗，即使到现在这些十四行诗对我们理解复杂而模糊的性爱观念也很关键。贺拉斯的《歌集》同样重要。这部作品是理解朴实美好、遗世独立的乡间生活（英美文学的永恒主题）的主要凭借之一。贺拉斯的讽刺诗不但对无法排遣的乏味做了经典刻画，还是乡下老鼠和城里老鼠故事的蓝本。朱文诺尔的讽刺诗大肆挞伐城市生活的腐败，影响非常深远。他提出"人类欲望之虚荣"（据约翰逊的英语改编版本）这一理念和一个非常生动的说法——"野性的义愤"。

中世纪产生了众多优美的抒情诗。不过英语抒情诗传统始于16世纪早期，鼻祖是华埃特和萨里，代表作有西德尼的《爱星者

塞缪尔·泰勒·柯勒律治（1772—1834），和其友人华兹华斯一样，自青年时期就充满浪漫主义和洞察力，深受法国大革命鼓舞，深信世界即将迎来变革。但是，当他们合作的《抒情歌谣集》于1798年出版时，两个人却都对大革命的矫枉过正幻灭了，其后他们逐渐趋于保守。《抒情歌谣集》收录了柯勒律治的主要作品《古舟子吟》，这是英语诗作中的精品。1802年，柯勒律治出版《悲戚颂》，哀叹自己江郎才尽。有趣的是，这部作品本身却才气洋溢。然而，先后经历与萨拉·弗里克的不幸婚姻以及与华兹华斯的嫂子（也可能是弟媳——译者注）之间无疾而终的爱情，诗人的才华的确在渐渐远离柯勒律治。为了治病，他还曾一度鸦片成瘾。不过，失之东隅，收之桑榆，柯勒律治最终成为继约翰逊之后最伟大的英语批评家。他的主要批评理论作品有《文学传记》（1817）。

与星》，斯宾塞的《爱情小诗》（他的作品还包括《婚曲》，这是以各种语言创作的婚乐中的佼佼者），以及最好的英语十四行诗集——莎士比亚《十四行诗集》。17 世纪是抒情诗歌佳作辈出的时代。约翰·多恩的《歌与十四行诗》、《讽刺诗集》、《圣十四行诗》和《赞美诗》，以及弥尔顿的"短诗"都是个中翘楚。本·琼生、罗伯特·赫里克和安德鲁·马维尔以细腻的抒情诗和自省诗著称；乔治·赫伯特的《圣殿诗集》是最优秀的英语宗教抒情诗合集；不过，克拉肖的《圣十字架赞美诗》以及亨利·沃恩的《闪耀的火石》比之前人也毫不逊色。德莱顿的《平信徒的信仰》收录了史上最佳的两部宗教政治讽刺诗，还有始终没能得到应有肯定的《牝鹿与豹》也十分优秀。德莱顿为 18 世纪讽刺诗和讽刺史诗第一人亚历山大·蒲柏的不世成就奠定了坚实的基础。

西格里德·温塞特（1882—1949），挪威人，父亲是一名考古学家——或许正是由于家学渊源，温塞特描述中世纪挪威的历史小说中总是异常精确。她的一生充满悲伤：和艺术家丈夫离婚、一个儿子在第二次世界大战初期因反抗纳粹而牺牲；她的小说以严苛审慎的视角，看待人类的原罪和与欲望的斗争。她对现代生活的描述特别灰暗，不过，她的文名之确立却是因为两篇以中世纪挪威为题材的小说——三部曲《劳伦斯之女克丽斯汀》（亦称《新娘·主人·十字架》，1920—1922）以及四卷本历史小说《欧拉夫·奥当逊》（1925—1927）。《劳伦斯之女克丽斯汀》出版后，温塞特于 1924 年加入天主教。她于 1928 年获得诺贝尔文学奖，主要是因为她的历史小说，不过，她的以现代为背景的小说同样十分优秀。同时，温塞特还是出色的历史、社会以及宗教题材的散文家。

新一轮的抒情诗高潮伴随着浪漫主义运动而来。威廉·布雷克的《纯真之歌》与《经验之歌》、柯勒律治的《古舟子咏》、雪莱和济慈的颂歌都在经典诗歌之列。前文曾提到对史诗进行过改革的华兹华斯和拜伦也创作了不少优秀的抒情诗。以丁尼生、白朗宁和马修·阿诺德为首的维多利亚时代浪漫主义诗人的诗作都很值得一读。《尤利西斯》、《我已故的公爵夫人》和《多佛海滩》都是耳熟能详的名字。霍普金斯是继乔治·赫伯特之后

T.S.艾略特（1888—1965），美国人，生于圣路易斯的一个显赫家庭，祖先是新英格兰的早期定居者。艾略特的家族可以追溯到都铎王朝的幽默作家托马斯·艾利奥特爵士。艾略特曾经为了完成在哈佛大学的哲学博士论文而游历英格兰和法国，但最终却弃哲学而选择诗歌。他于1915年永久定居英格兰，终生未获得博士学位。1922年《荒原》出版，其对20世纪文学影响之深远足可比拟斯特拉文斯基的《春之祭》之初演，或是毕加索的立体主义画作的问世。《荒原》精于用典，充斥着令人费解的意识流，艾略特借此一举奠定了其文学地位。他在诗中大肆抨击现代工业社会的人情淡漠，生活在其中的人们感到深重的孤独。1928年艾略特刚刚加入英国国籍时宣称自己是文学古典主义者、政治保皇派以及英国天主教信徒，这对当时的整个文化界不啻为一记响雷。接下来的几十年，艾略特更成为英语世界最重要的现代文学批评家，以及宗教和文化事务的保守派评论家。他在戏剧《大教堂中的谋杀》以及《鸡尾酒会》中使用韵文的尝试毁誉参半。不过，他的其他作品，如《圣灰星期三》和《四个四重奏》则是20世纪最出色的宗教诗歌。

最伟大的英语宗教诗人——尽管其诗作在他过世三十年后才得以出版。美国的杰出诗人出现在 19 世纪晚期，他们中有终生未嫁的隐士诗人艾米莉·狄金森和傲慢自负、自学成才、生性浮夸的惠特曼。20 世纪杰出的英语诗人有叶芝、弗罗斯特、T.S. 艾略特和华莱士·斯蒂文斯。

以上推荐的所有作者及其作品都有很高阅读价值，具备一定教育背景的读者至少都该对其中大部分有所了解。当然，这些作品需要仔细、反复地品评——读者一定会收获不菲！大部分人阅读都是因为兴趣，所以很可能因为作者的哲学政治观点而对作品和作者产生兴趣，这种兴趣值得鼓励。不过，如果能够通盘了解整个西方文学及其中里程碑式的经典作品，于个人也将益处良多。读者，和作者一样，都需要反思历史从而充分把握当下，同样他们也有必要通过欣赏他人的长处从而发现自身的优点。

附　录：参考书目

　　本附录由四部分组成：首先，也是最重要的，是按照字母顺序收录的作者及他们最主要的作品。除了文中提及过的，还增补了一些；第二部分围绕西方文学知识和评论的传统及其奠基之作，及 20 世纪最有价值的相关作品；第三部分讨论后现代比较激烈的文学批评家；最后一部分介绍几本挑战后现代主义理论在学术文学研究领域统治地位的书籍。

主要的文学作品

　　企鹅经典和牛津世界文学经典以大量出版价格适中的平装文学经典著称。这些书一般都有确切的简介、详实的注解，而且翻译优质可靠。这两家出版社都是对古典文学感兴趣的读者的首选。不过，如果读者懂得希腊语和拉丁语，或哪怕仅仅是略懂，就可以选择哈佛大学出版社的罗勃古典文学图书馆系列。诺顿评注版多年以来也出版了很多作品，文本准确、译文忠实，并且还提供详实的背景信息。不过，最近的版本提供的信息越来越注重政治正确性而非学术和阐释价值（参见下文塞万提斯条目）。幸运的是，坊间还能找到很多早期的优秀版本。

　　埃斯库罗斯（前 525 或前 456），《俄瑞斯忒亚》(《阿伽门农》；《奠酒人》；《善好者》)。这部三连剧有很多译本，保罗·罗什的版本最值得推荐。

阿里斯托芬（约前 445—约前 385），《云》;《蛙》;《利西翠妲》。本杰明·罗杰斯的版本被广泛认为是个中典范。

马修·阿诺德（1822—1888）。其大量诗歌，特别是《多佛尔海滩》《被隐藏的生命》《恩培多克勒斯在埃特纳火山》以及《色希斯》都很有阅读价值。

简·奥斯丁（1775—1817），《傲慢与偏见》;《爱玛》;《劝导》。

巴尔扎克（1799—1850），《高老头》;《欧也妮·葛朗台》。

博马舍（1732—1799），《塞维亚的理发师》;《费加罗的婚礼》。

塞缪尔·贝克特（1906—1989），《等待戈多》;《剧终》。

威廉·布莱克（1757—1827），《纯真之歌》;《经验之歌》。他的"预言"作品更是受人疯狂追捧。

乔万尼·薄伽丘（1313—1375），《十日谈》。

贝托尔特·布莱希特（1898—1956），《母亲的勇气》;《高加索灰阑记》。

罗伯特·勃朗宁（1812—1889），《男男女女》;《剧中人物》;《指环与书》。

约翰·班扬（1628—1688），《天路历程》。

乔治·戈登·拜伦，拜伦勋爵（1788—1824），《恰尔德·哈罗尔德游记》、《唐璜》。

卡尔德隆（1600—1681），《人生如梦》。

加塔拉斯（约前 84—前 54），《诗集》。世界文学经典还出版了盖伊·李的经典双语版。

塞万提斯（1547—1616），《堂吉诃德》。塞缪尔·普特南的译文和注释仍是最佳选择。最近诺顿批评版出版的伯顿·拉斐尔的版本，相比之下较为平淡，也有些许错误；另外该出版社还出版了一系列强调"性别"和某些特定性概念的散文。

杰弗雷·乔叟（1340—1400）。《坎特伯雷故事集》最好阅读中世纪英语版本。目前有多种版本可供勤奋的学生学习。

柯勒律治（1772—1834），《古舟子吟》；《克里斯特贝尔》；《忽必烈汗》；"对话"诗歌；以及《悲戚颂》。

威廉·康格里夫（1670—1729），《如此世道》。

约瑟夫·康拉德（1857—1924），《吉姆老爷》；《黑暗之心》；《诺斯特罗莫》；《胜利》。

高乃依（1606—1684），《熙德》。

理查德·克拉肖（1612/13—1649）。克拉肖以《泣者》中丰富的奇思妙喻而闻名。他为特蕾莎修女所作的诗和关于耶稣诞生、主显及圣名的赞美诗属于最杰出的英语宗教诗。乔治·瓦尔顿·威廉的《理查德·克拉肖诗歌全集》是优秀编辑的典范。

但丁（1265—1321），《神曲》。艾伦·曼德尔鲍姆的三卷双语平装版提供了翔实的介绍和注释，是读者的好选择。查尔斯·辛格尔顿的三卷大部头版本评注精妙，是学习的典范。多萝西·莎耶的译文则以其评论著称。

丹尼尔·笛福（1660—1731），《鲁滨逊漂流记》；《摩尔·弗兰德斯》。

查尔斯·狄更斯（1812—1870），《荒凉山庄》；《大卫·科波菲尔》；《远大前程》。

艾米丽·狄金森（1830—1886）。托马斯·约翰逊的版本最为标准。

约翰·多恩（1572—1631）。C.A.帕特里德斯和约翰·肖克罗斯的旧式拼写版本各擅胜场。A.J.史密斯的现代版本（企鹅出版）则以出色的注释见长。A.L.克莱门斯的诺顿批评版非常有用。牛津出版社出版的安东尼·拉斯帕的精编版《突发事件的祷告》，还有艾芙琳·辛普森（十卷标准版的编辑）的平装布道词精选集。

费奥多尔·米哈伊洛维奇·陀思妥耶夫斯基（1821—1881），《地下室手记》、《罪与罚》、《卡拉马佐夫兄弟》。

约翰·德莱顿（1631—1700），《押沙龙与阿齐托菲尔》；《麦克·弗莱克诺》；《平信徒的信仰》；《牝鹿与豹》。

乔治·艾略特（原名玛丽·安·伊万斯，1819—1880），《弗洛斯河上的磨坊》；《米德尔马契》。

T.S. 艾略特（1888—1965）。平装版《精选诗集》包括《J. 阿尔弗雷德·普鲁弗洛克的情歌》、《枯叟》、《空心人》、《圣灰星期三》、《荒原》、《四个四重奏》（也有平装版）之外最重要的诗歌，以及最主要的韵体剧作《大教堂中的谋杀》。

爱默生（1803—1882）。《散文集》，第一、二系列，包含他最重要的作品。

伊拉斯谟（1466—1536）。《愚人颂》的最佳译本是克莱伦斯·米勒的版本，但是罗伯特·亚当的译文（诺顿批评版）比之前者在背景信息方面更有优势。

欧里庇底斯（约前485—约前406），《阿尔刻提斯》；《酒神的女祭司们》；《希波吕托斯》；《美狄亚》。

威廉·福克纳（1879—1962），《喧嚣与骚动》；《我弥留之际》；《押沙龙，押沙龙！》；《八月之光》。

亨利·菲尔丁（1707—1754），《约瑟夫安德鲁斯》；《汤姆·琼斯》。

福楼拜（1821—1880），《包法利夫人》。

罗伯特·弗罗斯特（1874—1963）。他的诗歌朴素平实，带有鲜明的美国风。不过别人为他写的传记都可以略过。

歌德（1749—1832），《浮士德》，路易·麦克尼斯译。

托马斯·哈代（1840—1928），《远离尘嚣》；《还乡》；《无名的裘德》。

霍桑（1804—1864），《红字》。

乔治·赫伯特（1593—1633），《圣堂》。对于学生而言最有用的是路易·L.马尔兹的版本，牛津作者系列将他的作品与亨利·沃恩的诗歌并列刊印。

罗伯特·赫里克（1591—1674）。《西方乐士》和《雅歌》都是迷人的诗歌；J.麦克斯·帕特里克出版了精美的平装版本。

荷马（约公元前700年）。罗伯特·费格斯、罗伯特·菲茨杰拉尔德和拉蒂摩尔都创作了《伊利亚特》和《奥德赛》的优秀现代版译文。不过伊丽莎白时期乔治·查普曼的《伊利亚特》译本以及18世纪蒲柏的译本目前坊间都能有平装本（普林斯顿和企鹅出版），都值得细细品味。

G.M.霍普金斯（1844—1889），凯瑟琳·菲利普斯的牛津作者版和W.H.加德纳的企鹅版都值得推荐。

贺拉斯（前65—前8）。詹姆斯·米切翻译的《颂歌》非常出色；帕尔默·博伟翻译的《讽刺诗集》与《书札》很不错。大卫·费里的《颂歌》译文也获得了不少赞誉。

维克多·雨果（1802—1885），《巴黎圣母院》；《悲惨世界》。

易卜生（1828—1906），《玩偶之家》；《人民公敌》；《海达·高布乐》；《培尔·金特》。

尤金·艾里斯柯（1912—1944），《秃头歌女》；《犀牛》。

亨利·詹姆斯（1842—1916），《一位女士的画像》；《鸽翼》；《大使》；《金碗》。

本·琼生（1572—1637），《狐狸》，《炼金术士》；《沉默的女人》。

詹姆斯·乔伊斯（1882—1941），《都柏林人》；《一个青年艺术家的肖像》;《尤利西斯》。

济慈（1795—1821）。有很多版本都很好。他的作品中几首颂歌不可不读:《夜莺颂》、《希腊古瓮颂》、《致秋天》;短篇叙事诗《圣阿格尼斯之夜》;以及一些十四行诗,特别是《初读查普曼译荷马有感》。

卢克莱修（约前94—约前55),《物性论》。

托马斯·曼（1875—1955),《托尼奥·克勒格尔》;《威尼斯之死》;《魔山》。

克里斯多夫·马洛（1564—1593),《马耳他岛的犹太人》;《爱德华二世》;《浮士德博士》。

安德鲁·马维尔（1621—1678）。读者可以阅读乔治·洛德和伊丽莎白·邓诺的平装版;前者将很多优质争议的诗歌都划入马维尔名下。

赫尔曼·梅尔维尔（1819—1891),《白鲸》;《书记员巴特比》;《比利·巴德》。

弥尔顿（1608—1674）。梅里特·休斯的一卷版《弥尔顿诗歌散文全集》是读者的好选择。朗文出版的约翰·卡利和阿拉斯泰尔·福勒版本评论非常精辟。

莫里哀（本名为让·巴蒂斯特·波克兰,1622—1673）。理查德·威尔伯翻译的《伪君子》和《愤世嫉俗》精彩绝伦。

托马斯·莫尔（1478—1535）。对学生而言,诺顿批评家版《乌托邦》最有用,由罗伯特·亚当翻译。企鹅出版的保罗·特纳译本意图使之现代化,但有欠考虑,可读性低。《关于苦难之慰藉的对话》有耶鲁出版的平装版。

弗兰纳里·奥康纳（1925—1964),《好人难寻》;《慧血》。

奥维德（前43—17）。鲁尔夫·亨弗雷和贺拉斯·格里高利以韵体翻译的《变形记》非常精彩；盖伊·李的双语版《爱经》也很出色。彼得·格林翻译的《情色诗集》（包括《爱经》、《爱的艺术》等）以优秀的介绍和评论见称。

彼特拉克（1304—1374），罗伯特·德龄翻译的《歌集》有哈佛出版的平装版本，提供原文本、清晰的白话译本以及精辟透彻的评论，是读者独一无二的选择。

路易吉·皮兰德娄（1867—1936），《六个寻找剧者的角色》。

亚历山大·蒲柏（1688—1744），《批评论》、《夺发记》、《群愚史诗》以及韵体书札是他最重要的作品。由约翰·巴特编辑、Twickenham 出版的一卷本是读者的最佳选择。另外，小威廉·韦姆萨特和奥布雷·威廉姆斯等学者编辑的选集也相当不俗。

马塞尔·普鲁斯特（1871—1922），《追忆逝水年华》。

拉伯雷（1494？—1553），《巨人传》。

让·拉辛（1639—1699），《安德罗玛克》；《费德尔》。

萨福（生于约前612）。现存的残篇是西方世界爱情诗歌的主要来源之一。

弗里德里希·冯·席勒（1759—1805）。席勒最出名的就是他的《欢乐颂》，后被贝多芬天才地融入自己的第九交响乐。《华伦斯坦三部曲》、《玛丽亚·斯图亚特》、《奥尔良的姑娘》以及《威廉·退尔》（后被罗西尼借鉴创作出同名歌剧）都是他的重要剧作。

莎士比亚（1564—1616）。最好的一卷本是 Riverside 的版本，总编 G.B. 埃文斯。诺顿版加入了历史学家的评论。雅顿版将戏剧和诗歌分卷出版，一般被视为标准；不过 Signet 版价格更低廉，质量也不错。雅顿版的《十四行诗集》由凯瑟琳·邓肯－琼斯编辑，企鹅版的编辑是约翰·凯利根，这两个版本都以现代化的文本和精彩的评论著称。不过，最好的版本可能还是史蒂芬·布斯的耶鲁版，其中含有编者所著的现代版本，以及 1609 年四开对面排版的版本，后者附有相当完整翔实的评论。

萧伯纳（1856—1950），《圣女贞德》;《武器与人》;《人与超人》;《卖花女》。

雪莱（1792—1822），《解放的普罗米修斯》;《西风颂》;《致云雀》;《阿多尼》。

谢立丹（1751—1816），《情敌》;《造谣学校》。

西德尼爵士（1554—1586），《爱星者与星》;《阿卡狄亚》

斯宾塞（1552—1599）。《仙后》读者可以选阅托马斯罗什编辑的平装版，该版本注释非常详尽。至于短诗，《牧人月历》是文艺复兴时期最重要的一组田园牧歌。而《爱情小诗》和《婚曲》则是对爱情和婚姻的完美礼赞。

劳伦斯·斯特恩（1713—1768），《项狄传》。

华莱士·史蒂文斯（1879—1955）。《诗集》有平装版本;《心底的棕榈》平装版中也收录了斯蒂文斯的大量诗歌和散文。另外，对他感兴趣的学生会发现美国图书馆系列的《诗歌和散文集》卷也很值得一读。

斯威夫特（1667—1745），《一个温和的建议》;《格列佛游记》;《澡盆的故事》。

丁尼生（阿尔弗雷德，丁尼生勋爵，1809—1892），《悼念》;《尤利西斯》《提脱诺斯》;《玛丽安娜》。

萨克雷（1811—1863），《名利场》;《亨利·埃斯蒙德》;《巴利·林顿的遭遇》。

忒奥克里特斯（约前 300—约前 260），《田园诗集》。

莫利纳（1580—1648），《塞维利亚的骗子》。

J.R.R. 托尔金（1892—1973），《霍比特人》;《指环王》。

列夫·托尔斯泰（1828—1910），《战争与和平》;《安娜·卡列尼娜》。

特罗洛普（1815—1882），《巴彻斯特大教堂》;《首相》;《红尘浮生录》。

屠格涅夫（1818—1883），《父与子》。

马克·吐温（本名塞缪尔·克莱门斯，1835—1910），《哈克贝利·弗恩历险记》。

温塞特（1882—1949），《劳伦斯之女克丽斯汀》;《欧拉夫·奥当逊》。

亨利·沃恩（1622—1695），《闪耀的火石》。

洛佩·德·维加（1562—1635），《羊泉村》;《愚妇》。

维吉尔（前70—前19）。罗伯特·菲茨杰拉尔德和艾伦·曼德尔鲍姆的《埃涅阿斯纪》平装版各有千秋，都是不错的选择。盖伊·李的双语版《牧歌》（世界文学经典）可能是其优秀拉丁译诗中的精华。而 L.P. 威尔金森则创作了非常出色的《农事诗》译本，介绍和评论都很精彩（企鹅经典）。

惠特曼（1819—1892），《草叶集》。

维吉尼亚·伍尔芙（1882—1941），《达罗卫夫人》;《到灯塔去》。

华兹华斯（1770—1850），《序曲》;《丁登寺杂咏》;《不朽颂》;组诗《露茜》。

叶芝（1865—1939），《库利的野天鹅》;《基督重临》;《丽达与天鹅》;《在学童中间》;《驶向拜占庭》;《班磅礴山麓下》。

文学批评研究溯源

柏拉图（约前429—前347）是最早的文学批评家，他在

《伊安篇》和《理想国》中最早就文学的形式及其伦理性和知识性提出哲学层面的疑问；《会饮篇》和《斐德罗篇》则因为对爱情的不同表现形式（诗歌的永恒主题之一）的探讨而为人称道；而《斐德罗篇》和《高尔吉亚篇》中对修辞的简介也非常深刻。亚里士多德的《诗学》是第一部系统研究文学理论的著作，他和柏拉图一样认为诗歌自成一体，对社会意义重大。至今《诗学》中的用语和概念还在沿用。贺拉斯的《诗艺》（确切地说是《书札》卷二之三，"致比索贤父子"）既是优美的诗作，又对一系列诗歌话题进行了广泛讨论。《论崇高》据传为公元 3 世纪的修辞学家朗吉努斯所作。但是，很可能它实际成书时间为公元前 1 世纪末。

第一部英语文学批评作品是西德尼爵士的《诗辩》，该书一一梳理了 16 世纪意大利人文批评家，对亚里士多德/柏拉图传统进行了充满智慧和创新的反思。本·琼生戏剧性的序言和《木材：或发现》一书也作出了不朽的贡献。德莱顿开创了一种文学批评传统，使文学评论如同文人在与一群高雅世故的听众对话一般。除了为自己作品写的序，德莱顿的《论戏剧诗歌》同样意义深远。德莱顿的批评风格在艾迪生（1672—1719）和斯梯尔（1672—1729）处得到了继承。此二人都曾为早期高雅期刊的典范《闲谈者》和《旁观者》撰稿。亚历山大·蒲柏仿效贺拉斯的《诗艺》而作的《论批评》同样既是优秀的诗歌，也是对文学关键问题的深入讨论。塞缪尔·约翰逊博士是最早的英语词典编纂家、优秀的诗人和散文家，同时也是以英语写作的最伟大的批评家。他的杰作除了《漫步者》和《环球纪事》中的随笔以外，都收录在他编辑的莎士比亚作品集及他自己的《诗人传》中。

　　1800年版的《抒情歌谣集》收录了华兹华斯和科勒律治的诗，其"序言"为华兹华斯所作，是最早阐明浪漫主义原则的作品。浪漫主义文学最伟大的批评家——同时也是最伟大的英国批评家之一——柯勒律治，除了最重要的作品《文学传记》之外，其批评理论也零星见于他对莎士比亚和17世纪诗歌的评论。雪莱的《诗辩》是一部修辞学杰作。济慈的信件中也包含了大量引人深思的评论。维多利亚时代的主要文人马修·阿诺德尽管饱受同时代后现代主义当权派的抨击，但他的确是个一针见血、眼光犀利的文学和文化批评家。而切斯特顿（1874—1936）的评论则以幽默隽永见长。

　　20世纪是学院派批评家大行其道的时代。出名的评论作者往往是大学的教授而非诗人或文人，不过很多诗人文人通常也选择在大学里栖身。百年中文学评论多在学术领域内展开。这里向同学们推荐几位当代评论家，他们对文学的评价和阐释是很好的指导。这些批评家不一定家喻户晓，只是笔者根据个人的爱好和经历做出的选择。

　　T.S.艾略特虽然曾遭到学术界几十年的冷遇，但仍是20世纪最重要的诗人和批评家。《论文选集》忠实地展现了他的文学思想，还包含有他最重要的一篇论文《传统与个人才能》。艾略特的诗歌和评论对20世纪30年代源自南方重农派运动的新批评主义产生了巨大的影响。诗人兼批评家克劳·兰赛姆（1888—1974，代表作《世界的肉体》）和艾伦·塔特（1899—1979，代表作《四十年论文集》，1999年由ISI出版社再版）都是其中代表人物。兰赛姆的学生布鲁克斯（1906—1993）则通过介绍性文选——如《理解诗歌》（与罗伯特·华伦（1905—1989）合著）及《精制的瓮》——对文学教学及文学研究产生了深刻影响。在耶鲁大学，布鲁克斯有很多志同道合的同伴：雷内·韦勒克（1903—1995）和韦姆萨特（1907—1975）。布鲁克斯与韦姆萨特合作出版了《文学批评简史》，该书结构紧凑，可读性极强。韦姆萨特的一系列论文——《语言偶像》《可恨的矛盾》以及《猎豹之日》阐述并捍卫了新批评主义的道德和美学原则。韦勒克与奥斯丁·沃伦合著的《文学理论》探讨了 20 世纪中期文学的本质和宗旨。

在同时对文学的普遍本质和具体文学作品进行阐释的批评家中，笔者要特别推荐艾布拉姆斯（1912— :《镜与灯》、《自然的超自然主义》）、奥尔巴赫（1892—1975 :《摹写》）、布斯（1921—2005 :《讽刺的修辞》、《小说修辞》）、路易斯（1898—1963 :《爱的比喻》、《弃置的形象》）、麦克（1920—2001 :《大家眼中的莎士比亚》）、马尔兹（1915—2002 :《冥想的诗歌》）以及特立琳（1905—1975 :《自由的想象》、《对立的自我》）。

后现代主义的攻讦

上文提及的批评家虽然观点不一，却都认为：文学艺术作品旨在再现道德的现实影响，具有内在的整体性。20 世纪 60 年代出现了一场广泛的简约主义运动，该运动在 90 年代达到高潮，即后现代主义。简约主义运动尝试将文学的地位降至一种文化现象。该主义认为文学作为一种意识的产物理论上完全可以简化至其物质根源。后现代主义的渊源可以说贯穿了整个现代哲学史，它源于认识论上的疑惑，之后经历了中世纪的唯名论，其主张来源于德国哲学家尼采（1844—1900）和海德格尔（1889—1976）。尼采最初是一名极为出色、深富创新精神的古典语言学家，后成为存在主义的先驱。他因罹患梅毒变得疯狂，致使其后的作品逐渐陷入虚无主义。海德格尔将胡塞尔的现象学发扬光大。不过，他逐渐认为自柏拉图以来整个西方传统殊多缺漏，于是立意将其彻底重建，为此他还曾尝试将前人的著作全部销毁。海德格尔也是一名纳粹，并且"至死不渝"，这使得他的追随者无比头疼，使出浑身解数为其辩护。

很难界定这些德国哲学家对后世造成了何种影响。不过，因为三名法国人——德里达（1930—2004）、福柯（1926—1984）和拉康（1901—1981）——的缘故，他们受到了美国大学文学系的高度重视。有人认为巴尔特（1915—1980）也应属此列。不过，或许因为他的作品并没有以上三人那么晦涩难解，又或者因为其不乏幽默诙谐的笔调，学术界普遍认为他的深度和影响力不及前三位。必须要指出的是，德里达是学哲学出身，福柯的专业是哲学和心理学，拉康学的则是精神病学和精神分析。即是说，他们无一人是文学科班出身。然而，他们的影响却遍及英美各大英语系。此三人的风格都是刻意艰深，其原因就在于故意使用神秘、不为大多数人所知的术语，句法异常，并伴有大量逻辑跳跃。有鉴于此，德里达最容易读懂的作品当算《声音与现象》，该书的美国译本（大卫·埃里森译）还包含德里达的一篇重要论文《书写与差异》。另一篇较易理解、同时也很重要的文章是《柏拉图的药》，此文在《撒播》中再版。福柯最重要的作品是《何为作者》，在《阅读福柯》中再版。他的《性史》、《罪与罚：监狱之诞生》以及《疯颠与文明》在英语系的影响无人可出其右。由此可知文学学术研究的大体现状。对社会历史的专注表明文学学者已经不再将文学本身当作值得耗费心力研究的领域。至于拉康，他将弗洛伊德的精神分析与语言学嫁接在一起。以上三人都抬高了语言本身，他们认为语言决定思想和思维活动（而不是正好反过来）。不过，他们彼此相轻，并不信服。拉康的作品基本上都很晦涩，不过从朱丽叶·米切尔与杰奎琳·罗斯共同编辑的《女性性欲：拉康与弗洛伊德学派》可以了解他的大体观点。

德里达是解构主义之父。他在美国最大的支持者就是保罗·德·曼（1919—1983），后者最主要的作品是《洞见与不察》，一本驳杂的论文集。德·曼死后被发现年轻时曾在纳粹占领的比利时为一合作报社撰写过反犹太文章（难道有什么规律？）。耶鲁"四人帮"（实在很难想象在不到十年时间里耶鲁的改变竟然如此之大）的哈特曼（1929—）和米勒（1928—）替他解了围；"四人帮"的最后一人布鲁姆（1930—）在《影响的焦虑：一种诗歌理论》和《竞诗：写给文学修正主义》中以活泼的爱默生笔法宣扬了弗洛伊德观点。不过最近几年，他逐渐成为当代学术界眼中的保守派，开始为莎士比亚和西方文学经典辩护。拉康受茱莉亚·克里斯蒂娃（1941—）和简·盖洛普等激进女权分子中影响巨大。女权分子认为人性和所谓"性别角色"都是"社会决定的"，根本没有人性基础。相比德里达与拉康，福柯的影响最大。他的作品不仅为英国的文化唯物论和美国的新历史主义奠定了学术基础，也催生出许多的旁枝，如酷儿理论。新历史主义和其变体传播之广、名目之多，令人叹为观止。一旦听到诸如"在分性别化的机构进行论战"或"对现有秩序进行大胆的改变"之类的话就知道必定有人希望谋得职位或升迁。另外还有一些自诩为马克思主义者的学者，如英国的伊格尔顿（1943—）和美国的詹姆逊（1934—），后者是毛泽东和斯大林的忠实拥趸，也是美国为人引用最多的批评家。最后，我们再来看看费什（1938—）。此人很难定位，因为他的立场时常改变。

他以痛斥诡辩而成名，而其作品中唯一始终不变的就是学术和道德的相对主义，他称之为"反基础主义"。费什仅仅执着于维护教授群体的地位和特权，他似乎就是为了坚持这一观点而坚持。公平地说，我们必须注意，费什作为批评家是以清晰活泼的文风取胜，但其作品之实质总结起来，就是今日的一则头条：哪有什么"言论自由"？！没有也好。

对后现代主义攻讦的回应

后现代主义和政治正确性在美国的高等教育，特别是英语和外国语言学系占据了主导地位，其霸道和压抑远远超出媒体承认或意识到的程度。然而，也不是没有反对的声音。下面以一些（主要是）文学领域的重要作品为例：埃利斯的《反解构主义》和《失落的文学：社会议程和人文科学的堕落》、赫什的《文学解构：奥斯维辛后的批评》、雷曼的《时代的征兆：解构和保罗·德·曼的灭亡》、斯图尔特的《文艺复兴漫谈：通俗语言和关键问题的神秘》、韦勒克的《文学攻讦和其他论文》，以及杨的《向文字宣战：文学理论和文理教育》（由 ISI 出版）。

经典入门指南

序　言

政治学、哲学、历史、史诗、诗歌、喜剧、悲剧、修辞学、民主、美学、科学、自由、参议院、共和国、司法、总统、立法——以上所列词汇不多，不过足够引起注意。它们有两个共同点：首先，它们的所指对象是构成西方文明政治、学术和文化基石的主要元素；其二，它们都源于古希腊语和拉丁语。

古典文学这门学科研究的是古希腊和古罗马的语言、文学、历史和文明，西方世界大部分的学术、政治和艺术泰半源自这两种文化。几个世纪以来西方教育就是研究希腊语、拉丁语以及以这两种语言创作的不朽典籍。了解古典文学就能够理解西方文化的源头、核心的理想、理念、人物、故事、形象、门类以及概念。这就是所谓的通识教育，即训练学生的思维，使之具备作为自由公民生活在自由国度所需的独立批判意识。

不过，时代在改变，希腊语和拉丁语研究已不复当初执牛耳的地位。今天的古典文学日渐式微，只有得到了足够财力支持的学校才会保留这门课（更多是基于传统而保留，并非因为坚信古典文学对通识教育和西方文明具有基础意义）。然而西方文明及其价值观正受到冲击，因此现如今古典文学之意义并不逊于以往。再说目前人们对古老事物的兴致依然不减：各种名著的译本仍然大卖，热门影片如《角斗士》，也证明古希腊、古罗马的魅力历久不衰。希望这本小书能鼓励你们更深入地学习这些"高尚的奢侈品"（杰斐逊语）——即古希腊和拉丁的语言和文学。

什么是古典文学？

古典文学这一学科由不同的研究领域组成，这些领域都植根于希腊拉丁语言。学习古典文学的首要任务就是具备希腊语和拉丁语的阅读能力，即必须掌握词汇、语法、句法和词形变换。[1] 对这些语言的研究（也称为"语言学"）主要是通过学习古希腊罗马文学作品中的原句或对这些句子的改写。

从一开始，古典文学的学习对象就是古代的伟大作家和经典作品，而不是如何问路这类日常事务。即便是学习希腊拉丁语的词汇、语法都能让我们接触到史上最杰出的文学作品、作者及其理念。古典文学和其他人文学科有个很大的区别：古典文学在很大程度上将语言学习和文化、历史、哲学及希腊罗马文学的学习融为一体，但前提还是必须先学会这些语言，之后才能阅读希腊语和拉丁语的作品。

学完基本语法之后，学生可以选择一个特定的研究领域。不过在此之前，大多数人往往已经阅读过大量文学、历史、哲学的古代文本。这也是学习古典文学的又一益处：学生不得不广泛涉猎古希腊罗马文化而不会囿于某一领域。另外，为了理解古代语言而着意培养的分析和精读能力也可以推及其他领域。

---

[1] 拉丁语和希腊语都是屈折语言，即名词、代词和形容词都会根据在句中的不同功能而变形。研究这些形式变化的学科就是形态论。

由此，同学们就不大容易受到带有明显意识形态偏见的思想吸引，自己做出有失偏颇的诠释的可能性也会大大降低（虽然并不能完全消除）。因为归根结底，无论个人的理念如何，古希腊拉丁文本都必须正确地解读。这种实证的具体的方式极大地限制了含糊、偏颇的诠释。

古典文学的研究涉及所有人文社会学科：历史（包括宗教史、社会史、学术史）、哲学、艺术（包括花瓶制作、镶嵌工艺和雕塑）、建筑学、文学批评（韵律学和诗学）、语法、修辞学、考古学、地理、政治科学，以及科学史、医学史、工程学史、战争史、数学史和几何史。而且古典文学也是研究基督教历史、《新约》文本的形成和传播、早期基督教神学家及其著作的基础学科。

除上述方向以外，还有些技术性较强的基础学科：

金石学。这门学科研究的是镌刻在石头、陶器、（有时包括）木器之上的铭文（刻在钱币上的属于钱币学范畴）。古代流传至今的铭文达数千件，其中有些保存完好，有些则已残破不全。铭文被发掘出来之后，再由金石学家清理并解读，整个过程无比艰难。这不仅是因为镌刻着铭文的石头长年累月多半已经破损，也是因为古代文字往往没有断句，也没有小写字母。另外，随着时间推移，一些字母的书写发生了变化，还有一些字母为了美学需要笔画进行过变形。铭文对于各类史学家而言都至为宝贵，因为它们主题丰富，涉及社会、政治、宗教、法学、文学等各方面，既有政令，也有为已逝爱侣爱子所作饱含深情的悼文。

这里有一则关于铭文的小趣闻涉及罗马的斗兽场：有一段时至今日仍清晰可辨的铭文谈到了公元5世纪的一次大修。砖石上面有很多小孔，是以前镌刻铭文金属字母的地方。1995 年，海德堡的艾尔福迪分析了小孔排列的规律后复原了这段铭文。铭文可以上溯至韦斯巴芗皇帝时期，是专为纪念约公元 79 年斗兽场的建造告一段落所作。由这段铭文可以得知，斗兽场是"用战利品"建造的。这一时期唯一可能的战争就是公元 66 至 70 年的犹太人起义；起义的结果是耶路撒冷的圣殿被毁，所有珍宝被劫掠一空。换言之，圣殿中的金银财宝都充作了斗兽场的修建经费。

纸莎草学。古代书面文字一般是写在莎草纸（以埃及特有的一种草制造）上。莎草纸在潮湿的气候中会腐烂，但是埃及和中东地区（古代很多希腊罗马人先后在此居住了几个世纪之久）气候干燥，纸莎草文书因而得以保存。纸莎草学的研究对象主要是书写在纸莎草上的文字，也包括在同一地点发掘出土的黏土板（陶片书）和木板的残片。迄今为止，约有三万份纸莎草文本付梓，还有更多保存在世界各地的收藏家手中。纸莎草学者必须解读不同风格的手写体，在对错误和拼写进行更正之后再将文字转录。这些文书的原本经常遭到破坏，有孔洞或撕裂的痕迹，所以纸莎草学家有时不得不进行猜测将缺漏补全，或者就只能任其保持这种状态。很多古希腊文学经典都只有纸莎草版本存世，其中包括米南德的几出喜剧、白话叙事诗中的重要片段，以及如公元前 4 世纪讨论雅典政府的《雅典宪法》之类的哲学著作，还有各种各样文件，例如信札、诏书、请愿书、契约和收据。和金石学家一样，纸莎草学家也为文学、哲学、政治、法学、宗教和民生史学家提供了原始信息。

纸莎草学的一个分支是古文字学，即研究文字和字母是如何书写在莎草纸上。考古学关心的是古代手迹的解读、它们的发展、变迁以及书写工具（如莎草纸、墨水等）。

文本批评。文本批评以所有流传下来的文本（包括手稿、其他作者的引用、莎草纸和陶片的残存）为基础确立尽可能准确的文本。大多数古代文本都历经数代，几经翻录，抄写时的错误在所难免。现代文本批评必须衡量所有现存版本，以决定哪一个更可靠。查漏补遗、更正笔误、辨别不符合作者风格、韵律或文体之处，林林总总都只为尽可能贴近原文。现在刊印的希腊拉丁文本通常会以脚注形式加入"注解"，列明所有的版本和更正（即"校订"）。

了解不同版本的文本对解读古代文学很重要。古罗马诗人加塔拉斯（下文还会提及）给友人凯利乌斯的信中谈到一位名叫莱斯比娅的女性，她曾与加塔拉斯过从甚密，写信的时候正在与凯利乌斯交往。在一个文本中，他称她为"我们的莱斯比娅"，意指两人同时在与之交往。但在另一个版本中，他却又称呼她为"您的莱斯比娅"，暗示自己和她已经结束了。读者如何解读该诗，又如何理解作者对莱斯比娅的态度必然会受到阅读版本的影响。

很明显，这些技术性学科多少都有重叠之处，彼此联系也甚为紧密。多数古典文学家对这些技能都了解一二，平时工作中也都会运用很多、甚至所有这些技能。例如，对斗兽场感兴趣者需要了解建筑学、工程学和金石学，同时也必须熟悉诸如马休尔对斗兽场举行的运动会的描述或苏东尼斯的《恺撒众皇生平录》一类著作的文本和手稿传统。当然，最重要的是，从事这一技术性工作的学者为每一个研究历史、艺术、文本批评、哲学或社会史的古典学者提供了基础材料（特别是文本）。

大多数从事古典文学研究的人接触的主要都是文本，即在过去两千五百年里影响了西方文明的伟大典籍——虽然多数是译本。下面我们将按照不同文体向大家介绍书面文本。如此一来，古代文化中很重要的一个部分，特别是艺术和建筑，很遗憾只能略过不谈。若读者想了解更多古代哲学知识，可以阅读本丛书中麦克伦尼所著的《哲学入门指南》。

这里还要请读者注意以下几点：其一，现在人们阅读时都是不出声的默诵，但是在古代，文学却往往采取在公开场合宣讲的形式。所以文学在当时并非自娱自乐，而是一种社会性、政治性很强的活动。换言之，文学在当时更受重视，其道德、政治和社会意义也更为人所接受和肯定。

其二，我们现在拥有的仅是古希腊拉丁文学的一小部分，而且多是残本，余者皆已遗失在漫长的历史洪流中，其数量之大，可以以悲剧为例说明。如今现存完整的希腊悲剧仅有三个作者的三十三部作品。但在将近一个世纪的悲剧黄金时代（约前500—前400），大约有数十位作者创作了约有一千部作品。今天我们仅仅知道他们的名字，看到的也多是残破不全的文本，有些甚至仅剩只字片语。因此，在对古代文学进行概括时，必须谨记，这种概括不过是立足于残存的古籍。

史　诗

　　西方文学现存最早的作品即荷马（约前 750）所作的《伊利亚特》和《奥德赛》这两部史诗。学术界始终在质疑（"荷马之迷"）是否真有个名叫荷马的人存在过并创作了这两部史诗，抑或荷马其实是个虚构人物，两部作品其实是由几个人将口头流传的史诗进行汇总的结果。今天多数学者认为这两部史诗为一到两名作者所作。

　　《伊利亚特》和《奥德赛》均是扬抑抑格六音步诗———种诗歌韵律，由六音步的扬抑抑格（一个长音节后接二短音节）或扬扬格（每音步包含二长音节）组成。诗中第五音步总是扬抑抑格，第六音步由两个音节构成，最后一个音节长短皆可。起初，史诗由吟游诗人表演。他必须熟记数千种传统"格式"、整句整句的诗或惯用语（如"长发的亚该亚人［即希腊人］"或"（有着）粉红（指尖）的曙光（女神）"，然后将这些元素组合成前后连贯的故事表演出来。荷马创作之前史诗吟唱的传统已延续了多久？荷马是亲自记录或是口述给书记官？他的史诗有多少来自传统，又有多少是个人原创？这些问题令人心驰神往，却永远也不可能得到解答。

　　史诗的主题包括一段段冒险故事、不同的价值观还有贵族勇士的经历，他们生活的世界神祇频频光顾，还会和凡人结交。荷马史诗以公元前 12 世纪的特洛伊战争及其后续（英雄返乡或回归）为背景。现代考古学的发现证实曾经有个叫做迈锡尼的文明（因其最重要的废墟在希腊中部的迈锡尼发掘而得名）存在过，它在很多方面，特别是物质文化上，与荷马的描述颇为相似。不过，荷马讲述的是公元前9至8世纪的事，那时城邦和人民授权的政府正在崛起，贵族世家的地位受到了冲击。

两部史诗中，较长的《伊利亚特》或许成书更早。故事发生在特洛伊战争第十年的几个星期之中；主人公阿喀疏斯是"亚该亚第一猛士"，他与阿伽门农（希腊远征军统帅，其兄弟墨涅拉俄斯的妻子海伦与特洛伊王子帕里斯私奔导致战争爆发）大吵一架怒气勃发。《伊利亚特》就是以阿喀疏斯的愤怒为线索展开故事，一直写到他的至交好友帕特罗克洛斯之死，还有特洛伊勇士赫克托尔命丧他手——后者昭示着特洛伊的陷落。

在诗中，荷马对贵族英雄的荣誉感和复仇心的毁灭力量进行了精彩绝伦的刻画，说明逞一时意气的后果就是牺牲所有人只为成就个人荣光。荷马向我们展示：一个以通过暴力实现个人荣誉为理念的政体是无法存在的。人类之所以存在皆因"彼此之间有所牵绊"，或者说人人都对他人存在义务，而英雄却往往会为了自己的荣誉舍弃这些义务。

《奥德赛》讲述的是特洛伊陷落以后英雄奥德修斯返乡的故事。这个故事读来比《伊利亚特》更亲切。其中写到很多迷人的

荷马（约前750），生活在公元前8世纪，但是几乎没有关于他的可靠信息。他的诗歌暗示他对于东爱琴海有一定了解，一些古代资料表明他的故乡在艾奥尼亚——今土耳其西海岸。荷马很可能出生在巧斯岛或士麦那城。其他关于荷马的信息，例如他是个盲人，都是人们的猜测。

场景、妖娆魅惑的女性和凶残恐怖的怪物，同时对奥德修斯长时间缺席给其家乡和家人造成的影响也做了生动的描绘。奥德修斯比阴郁、自我又理想化的阿喀琉斯更具有吸引力。首先，奥德修斯年纪更长，妻儿俱全。他为人更加实际，也比阿喀琉斯更加圆融宽和，后者在生活的种种不尽人意之前总是碰得头破血流。

除了睿智的奥德修斯之外，《奥德赛》还塑造了几位非凡的女性角色，特别是奥德修斯那同样机智的妻子佩内洛普。他们两人的结合是因为拥有相似的性格、品德和价值观。这反映出社会风俗在成就个人身份、维护社会秩序上所起的关键作用。自然世界严酷而危险，人类之所以能够生生不息是因为和奥德修斯一样，我们会运用智谋渡过难关，同时也因为人类社会有共同的价值观、风俗习惯和行为准则，可以抵消自然力量和人类自身毁灭性的欲望与激情造成的负面影响。

荷马在两部诗歌中都探讨了人类行为和动机不可思议的多样化和深刻性。他也肯定了人生在世必然受到各种局限，而灵魂却又是极端矛盾与复杂的。荷马的写作功力更是非同凡响，优美的辞藻、丰富的比喻、生动的描述及简洁的叙述，在两千七百年后的今天仍然逸趣横生、无比鲜活。

荷马之后的史诗主题不一，有写特洛伊战争及其起源的，有讲述俄底浦斯之子的底比斯之争的，也有关于希腊英雄返回家乡的。这些史诗（合称为"史诗集群"）现在仅存残本或后人的概述。公元 3 世纪，士麦那的昆图斯（生卒年不详）从《伊利亚特》的结尾处写起，讲述了阿喀琉斯之死、木马计和特洛伊之劫及其他冒险故事。另有一种以史诗风格创作的六音步诗——一度认为是荷马所作——合称为"荷马式赞美诗"。这些诗写于公元前 8 至 6 世纪，现存三十三首，长度不一，都是关于神祇的历险和品性。最有意思的是第二首，它讲述的是德墨忒尔和女儿佩尔塞福涅（被冥王哈得斯抢走）的故事。还有第五首，是关于阿芙罗狄忒与凡人男子安喀塞斯相恋的故事。

荷马在希腊文学、文化中的地位等同于莎士比亚在英语国家的地位，都是无与伦比的。公元前 3 世纪早期，罗得岛的阿波罗尼乌斯（生卒年亦不详）出版了极具争议的《阿耳戈英雄纪》（约前 270—前 45）。这部诗歌描述了伊阿宋和阿耳戈英雄寻找金羊毛的故事；其中使用了很多荷马史诗的传统和风格元素，如"扩展比喻"（这是一种详细的比较，可以长达数行）。但此诗同时也反映了更多阿波罗尼乌斯所处时代关注的问题，如性欲的心理、魔法和幻想、科学和地理，以及对宗教、仪式起源的兴趣。阿波罗尼乌斯很清楚自己的诗歌同文学的伟大传统之间是不可分割的，这也是其作品引人入胜的一个原因。

《阿耳戈英雄纪》深受罗马人喜爱，其影响在维吉尔（前70—前 19）的《埃涅阿斯纪》中可见一斑。在维吉尔之前，恩尼乌斯（前 239—前 169）的《编年纪》（约前 169）曾以拉丁六音步将罗马史写成荷马式史诗。可惜如今只有些片段留存于世（恩尼乌斯的灵感来自罗马每年公布大事记的做法）。而维吉尔的《埃涅阿斯纪》则被很多人视为西方古典文学最有影响力的作品（有几百年的时间荷马史诗在欧洲相当沉寂）。《埃涅阿斯纪》的主人公"虔诚的埃涅阿斯"，在故土特洛伊陷落后逃离并建立了罗马城。这一路上，他和奥德修斯一样饱尝艰辛，在到达意大利后又被卷入了《伊利亚特》式的战争，但《埃涅阿斯纪》绝不只是荷马史诗的罗马版。

维吉尔借鉴了恩尼乌斯的史诗传统，向荷马、罗得岛的阿波罗尼乌斯以及欧里庇底斯等希腊的悲剧作家取经，创作出一部在神、自然、心理学、艺术、能力和政治各层面上探寻秩序可能性的杰作。他并不像有些人误解的那样一味地对奥古斯都皇帝歌功颂德或仅仅是模仿荷马。他肯定秩序(包括政治秩序)的必要性，但同时也承认为了建立秩序有时必须付出沉重的代价。维吉尔眼中的宇宙，秩序和混乱交缠不休。他认为在这场秩序和混乱的交战中，凡人有自己的责任和负担，往往需要付出巨大代价。这种乐观与悲观、希望与绝望、理想与现实的交织使该书别具一格。另外，《埃涅阿斯纪》也反映出作者成熟圆融的文学技巧，他的人物个性鲜明，描述栩栩如生，语言精雕细琢，一千年来几乎每个受过良好教育的人都将其视为文化珍品。

维吉尔(普布利乌斯·维吉利乌斯·马洛，前70—前19)，来自曼图阿附近的一个村庄，在米兰接受教育；这说明他家境富裕。他曾经在那不勒斯居住过一段时间，学习伊壁鸠鲁哲学，该学派鼓吹遗世归隐，只与志同道合者来往。公元前40年，依照一项传统，维吉尔的父亲被屋大维和马克·安东尼没收了所有土地，以作为酬金支付给自己的兵团。但是，这一点——连同后来屋大维归还土地一事——似乎只是人们对《牧歌》第一首和第九首内容的推测。写完《牧歌》之后，维吉尔投效了梅赛纳斯，此人是屋大维之友，对诗人相当慷慨。维吉尔很快成为最出名(最富有)的诗人，其他诗人对他也屡有提及；例如，贺拉斯就曾经赞赏过他的"温文儒雅"，普洛柏修斯对他也非常称道。维吉尔在赴希腊途中发烧，在布林地西姆去世；其时，他的经典作品《埃涅阿斯纪》基本完成(没有证据表明他曾经委托朋友将自己的手稿付之一炬)。维吉尔被安葬在那不勒斯。

奥维德（前43—17）的《变形记》（约公元8年）是一部很有影响力的拉丁语作品，因为也是扬抑抑格的六音步诗，所以被归为史诗。但是这十二卷诗歌舍弃了常见的武士英雄主义和战争场面，开篇就是创造世界，最后以恺撒成神结尾。奥维德在此诗中以身体外形的变化为主线穿插了数十个小故事，其中包括著名歌手奥菲斯勇闯冥府解救自己的妻子尤丽狄丝，以及阿拉克涅挑战女神米涅娃的纺织技艺最终被变成蜘蛛的故事。在这首诗中，奥维德有意识地对希腊罗马著作和神话旁征博引，

奥维德（普布利乌斯·奥维狄乌斯·纳索，前43-17），来自阿布鲁奇（即意大利地图中靴跟之处），父亲祖上曾是骑士。奥维德在罗马接受教育，并游历过希腊，这是当时那个阶层的年轻人的普遍做法。他在法院做过几个小吏的工作，此后开始致力于诗歌创作。在声誉鼎盛时，被奥古斯都自罗马驱逐到荒凉的黑海小城托弥斯。奥维德说其流放乃是因为"两宗罪"：一首"诗歌"及一个"错误"。这首诗歌就是《爱经》，这是一首笔调诙谐的打油诗，也是一本猎爱指南，只是偏偏与奥古斯都复兴罗马昔日道德观的意图背道而驰。而所谓的"错误"，很可能指奥维德曾无意间撞破某些皇室成员的丑闻——奥维德曾言及阿克特翁的典故（阿克特翁是个猎人，他无意中看到处子女神狄安娜的躶体，因此被他自己的猎犬撕成了碎片【故事源自希腊神话，狩猎女神阿耳忒弥斯在罗马神话中被称为狄安娜。原为阿克特翁偶然窥见阿耳忒弥斯在沐浴，女神因此把他变成了一头鹿，被他自己的五十只猎犬撕碎——译者注】）。奥维德死于托弥斯，留下遗孀、一个女儿和两个外孙在罗马。

独具匠心地加入叙事成分和生动的细节，让读者不由联想到现实主义风格的长篇小说。《变形记》对文艺复兴时期的文学影响巨大，诗中故事为大量绘画、雕塑和文学创作提供了灵感。莎士比亚当年阅读的就是戈尔丁翻译的版本。

维吉尔之后存留下来的史诗再也无法达到《埃涅阿斯纪》在诗歌、哲学上的高度。斯塔提乌斯（公元 1 世纪）的《底比斯战纪》讲述了俄狄浦斯的几个儿子争夺底比斯统治权的故事。该诗在中世纪和文艺复兴时期人气很高，其中毋庸置疑有圣保罗劝说斯塔提乌斯皈依基督教的原因。另一部深具影响的史诗是卢坎（39—65）的《内战记》，该诗以史诗体裁详尽地叙述了罗马共和国的毁灭，以及公元前 48 年恺撒与庞贝大战以后自由的丧失。到了 18 世纪，卢坎更因为塑造了乌提卡的加图（前 95—前 46）而颇受共和政体倡导者的追捧。加图宁可自杀也不投降恺撒，因此成为支持自由而非独裁统治的共和主义者的象征。

诗　歌

　　古希腊罗马时期的很多诗歌都得以保存，它们的时间跨度超过一千年，遵循的风格和韵律也多种多样。其中历史最为悠久的门类是说教诗（亦称教化诗）。赫西俄德（约前700）常被归为史诗作家，因为他是以六音步和荷马的风格创作，不过主题却殊为不同。

　　赫西俄德的《神谱》叙述了宇宙的诞生、众神的出生及家系，尤为重要的是普罗米修斯偷取火种拯救人类的故事。同样的六音步诗《工作与时日》融格言、谚语、语言、譬喻和神话于一体，探讨了勤奋工作的意义和游手好闲的危害。该诗是写给诗人的兄弟珀西斯的，后者很显然骗走了赫西俄德的一部分遗产并将之挥霍殆尽。此外，《工作与时日》还包含很多农业和航海的实用知识，并附有一份黄历，注明所有吉日和不吉的日子。其中

　　赫西俄德（约前700），与荷马差不多是同时代的人。他的诗作提供给我们很多关于诗人的信息：如，他的父亲放弃经商，移居至雅典西北的波奥提亚；又如，他曾经在一次歌唱比赛中赢得一只三角鼎；再如，他被自己的兄弟珀西斯和当地官僚勾结，骗去了一部分遗产。赫西俄德的诗歌暗示他怀有小农价值观和世界观，对城市和贵族充满了不信任。

尤其值得一提的是关于潘多拉（第一个人类女性，她的好奇心释放了各种灾厄）、另一个版本的普罗米修斯以及五个时代（始于天堂般的黄金时代，逐渐堕落到现在灾难、困苦、疾病丛生、道德沦丧的黑铁时代）的神话故事。

赫西俄德之后，道德、哲学训诫仍是说教诗的重要主题。恩贝多克利（约前492—前432）和巴曼尼底斯（约前450）等哲学家在诗歌中阐明自己关于"世界如何运作（物理学）"、"存在的本质（本体论）"以及"获取知识的方式（认识论）"的观点。其后约公元前300至100年（即希腊化时期）涌现出了更多专精的主题，比如尼坎德（约前130）关于蛇、蜘蛛和毒虫的诗歌（《底也伽》），关于毒药的论说文（《解毒药》），以及阿拉托斯（约前315—前240）探讨星座的《物象》——此书在古代很受欢迎，后被译为阿拉伯语。

抒情诗本是伴七弦琴而唱的诗歌，曾一度被叫做 *melic*，即希腊语的"歌曲"。抒情诗有单人表演，也有一群人身着戏服边唱边跳的。最早的抒情诗可以上溯至公元前7世纪，如今仅剩残本，不过从残留的片段中仍清晰可见荷马对其意象和措辞的影响。就主题而言，抒情诗通常关注诗人的个人经历，同时引用传统的神话故事。这种诗体涵盖了爱情、政治、战争、友情、饮酒以及向宿敌复仇等主题。

很多抒情诗人的名字得以留存，但其作品多数已经残破不全。其中有两名来自莱斯博斯岛的独唱诗人非常重要。其一是阿西奥斯（生于约前625—前620），他的诗歌残本中写到了友情、莱斯博斯岛上抗击独裁统治的几次斗争、流放、海难及饮酒，以上主题都伴有详尽的描述和神话的原型。"国家有如航船"的比喻也是在他的诗中最早出现的。另一位诗人萨福（生于约前650）更具影响力，在古代被誉为"第十位缪斯"，她的诗歌充满着音乐之美。但是只有两部诗歌完整保存至今，其余都只剩残本。不过，从保留下来的文字中可以看到萨福的诗作话题相当广泛，其中涉及她的兄弟和女儿、诗歌、美、神的赞美诗、神话以及莱斯博斯岛上的政治斗争。萨福的诗歌最突出的特点是描述了作者深受女子的强烈吸引，她以震撼人心的意象生动地描绘了自己的感情。不过，这种情感往往被她努力克制住了。

　　合唱抒情诗通常是公共仪式或庆典的一部分，神的赞美诗就是其中之一：例如献给阿波罗的"赞美歌"和为酒神狄奥尼索斯所作的"敬酒歌"，由妙龄女子合唱的少女之歌，以及婚礼歌等等。到公元前6世纪，世俗话题逐渐进入合唱抒情诗。诗人会为庇护自己的君主和贵族歌功颂德。在公共运动会，如奥林匹克运动会，取得胜利的贵族也会委托诗人为自己创作"凯歌"。合唱抒情诗遵循严谨的韵律，往往将某一特殊情境扩大至人类的普遍体验，歌曲的核心多是对神话故事的叙述。古代经常举行合唱抒情诗大赛。

　　萨福（生于约前650），公元前7世纪后半叶出生在莱波斯岛，这是一个接近今天土耳其北部海岸的小岛。关于萨福个人的传言自古以来就没有停止过，比如说她是个同性恋，妓女，生得又丑又矮，经营一家女子培养学园，后来因为求爱不遂跳崖自尽。比较确定的是，萨福作为一名贵族，参与了莱波斯岛上的政治斗争，后曾一度被流放到西西里。根据她的作品片段（现存九卷莎草纸卷诗集中的一首），她已婚，有一名叫克蕾丝的女儿，唯一的兄弟是个为高级交际花一掷千金的纨绔。

在此特别推荐两位诗人：西蒙尼底斯（生于约前556）和品达(约前518—前430)。西蒙尼底斯创作了大量凯歌和敬酒歌，后者曾赢得了五十七次大赛胜利。可惜，没有一首诗歌保存下来。品达的合唱诗歌风格非常多变。他为在奥林匹亚、德尔菲（皮提亚运动会）、尼米亚和科林斯（伊斯米亚运动会）举行的四届泛希腊运动盛会的冠军所作的四十五首凯歌幸运地流传至今。品达创作的凯歌细腻而高雅，以繁复而精致的手法描述了运动员的成就，并对其家族不吝溢美之词，诗中还常常援引和其家庭及所属城市相关的神话故事。他的诗作总是从更广泛的人类生活和道德教化这个视角去刻画运动员的体验。

还有一种颇具影响力的诗体叫做挽歌（因其遵循的韵律而得名）。这种诗由六音步和五音步扬抑抑格的对句组成，长短不一，话题广泛。因为挽歌均是在葬礼悼词和墓志铭中使用，故而今天"elegia"一字带有忧郁的涵义。

雅典政治家梭伦（卒于约前560）在挽歌中对雅典宪法的改革（极大地推动了雅典民主进程）进行了阐发，为其辩护。阿齐罗库斯（活跃在约前650）的主题——友情、爱情、政治和战争——与抒情诗相仿。他有一首极其著名的诗歌谈到自己如何在一次战斗中弃盾而逃。他满不在乎地写道："大不了再买一面同样好的。"泰奥格尼斯（活跃在约前550—前540）是挽歌产量最为丰富的作者，一生共创作了一千四百行诗歌。泰奥格尼斯是旧式贵族，他对"一度命如草芥"的人有钱优势之后就认为自己可以与贵族平起平坐甚为不满。他的诗也有对年轻的友人（也可能是情人）库尔诺斯的道德劝诫和实用建议。到了公元前5世纪，挽歌常常和"论坛"或酒会联系在一起。其时宾客会朗诵诗歌，进行哲学讨论（如柏拉图的《对话录·会饮篇》）。

因此，很多挽歌都以饮酒和爱情为主题。

讽刺短诗是另一种主要的诗体，因为同样是以挽歌对句创作，因而常会与之混淆。最初讽刺短诗是刻在物品（如坟墓）之上的。很多早期的讽刺短诗都没有署名。前文的西蒙尼底斯就是一位讽刺短诗作者。他的关于波斯战争（公元前490以及前480或前479）的讽刺短诗最为出名——虽然有人对他是否真的是这些诗歌的作者表示怀疑，其中以三百斯巴达勇士在色摩比利山口被屠杀殆尽的这首为最："去告诉斯巴达人，过路人，说我们忠于职守，力竭而死。"

到希腊化时期（即从亚历山大大帝［前323］死后到罗马统治［前30］之间的希腊文学），讽刺短诗已不再是单纯的铭文，而是演化成一种文学形式。它的主题多种多样，既有献给猎户、妓女等普通人的，也有为死去的宠物而作的悼词。它们通常涉及政治、家庭、友谊、饮酒、爱和性。这个时期讽刺短诗很强调风格和自我意识，同时也秉承了对言简意赅的一贯重视。埃斯克勒皮亚底斯（约前300—前279）和卡里马科斯（生于约前310）是其中的代表人物。前者诗作中对性欲的丰富描写极大地影响了后世的爱情诗，而后者据说创作了八百多首不同风格的作品。现存的除了神的赞美诗，还有六十四首讽刺短诗，其中最优美的当属为其逝去的友人赫拉克利特斯所作的动人诗篇。

大多数希腊诗人都不局限于某种风格，到了希腊化时期诗人已经留意到此前数百年的文化积淀。他们不满于风格的局限和批评的束缚，开始有意识地尝试不同的形式和主题，他们既尊重传统又努力打破传统。卡里马科斯的《起源》长达四千行，现在仅剩下一部分。全诗以挽歌的格式呈现了众多的文学主题，既有关于坟茔和塑像的长篇讽刺短诗，也有神话故事的叙事诗，再以对"起源"的浓厚兴趣将它们穿插在一起。这个时期的另一位诗人忒奥克里托斯(活跃在约前270)除二十四首讽刺短诗外,还创作了《田园诗集》(书名"Idylls"在希腊语中的意思近似于"小品")。《田园诗集》都是些完成度极高,以错综手法描绘生活各阶层人民的画卷,从西西里牧羊人到亚历山大港的中产阶级家庭妇女不一而足。他那些描述西西里乡村生活的作品开创了经久不衰的田园诗派,作品以牧羊人的生活喻指对爱情、艺术、闲适、自由、政治和自然的探索。凯里马科斯和忒奥克里特斯都创造性、有意识地改革了诗歌艺术,对罗马诗人产生了重要影响。

这一部分讨论的诗人和诗作仅是希腊数百年历史中创作群体的一小部分,可惜大多数作品即使保存下来也都已残缺不全。但可喜的是,从现存于世的典籍中我们仍可一窥当年的高超技艺、多样的韵律、主题、风格,这些都推动了西方文学的形成,也成为西方文学无法割舍的宝贵财富。

罗马诗歌最早从中受益。罗马诗人对之前几个世纪的希腊诗歌,以及希腊化时期创作的有关诗歌的学术著作烂熟于心。公元前2世纪末、1世纪初的罗马创新诗人的作品或已失传或仅剩残本。但是,我们的确知道他们"师从"希腊化时期的作品,在公元前一世纪早期被称为"新诗人"。

罗马文学中有两大杰作属于说教诗。卢克莱修(约前95—前55)的《物性论》阐述了伊壁鸠鲁哲学。伊壁鸠鲁认为现实世界是物质的,不过是随机运动的原子集合;灵魂随身体的死亡而消逝;神祇对凡人的行为漠不关心;至善乃是超脱于忧虑、痛苦的灵魂解脱。卢克莱修以六音步格式解释伊壁鸠鲁的思想,其中饱含才华洋溢的意象,以及一些固定的内容,如对阿伽门农牺牲伊菲革涅亚的描述；卢克莱修在结尾处使用的句子后来常被启蒙运动用来引用，一呼百应——"如此大恶，宗教竟不以为忤！"

另一篇是维吉尔的《农事诗》（约前29），和卢克莱修相比青出于蓝而胜于蓝。该诗探讨的是在严酷的自然世界中建立人类秩序的可能性。此前农业耕种始终是说教诗的主题，如瓦罗（前116—前27）的《论农业》（前37）和大加图（前237—前149）的散文论说文《农业志》。但在维吉尔的作品中，农业是个贯穿全诗的比喻，用来说明人类同自然世界、神明的关系，并探寻政治统治的价值观与农业价值观之间的关系。一边是人类能够缔造秩序的乐观情绪，一边则是人类囿于自身欲望而导致脱序的悲观情绪。两种矛盾情感和谐交织，一如其后的《埃涅阿斯纪》。《农事诗》对农耕与政治统治之间关系的探讨是后世18、19世纪平均地权论——特别是大部分美国缔造者信奉的农业社会哲学——的重要先驱。

维吉尔以后最好的拉丁语说教诗是打油诗，奥维德的《爱的艺术》和《爱的补救》。前者看似在教读者如何寻花问柳、豢养情妇，其中有大量的神话故事和对罗马社会现实情境的生动描述。后者与前者风格类似，传授的则是如何摆脱露水姻缘的经验。《岁时记》是奥维德的另一部说教诗，全书十二卷，现仅存六卷，每卷对应罗马历中的一个月，注明了宗教庆典的日子。

拉丁语抒情诗的早期创新作品或失传或残缺不全。但加塔拉斯（约前84—前54）有一百一十四首诗保存至今。这些诗韵律不一，主题多样，有讽刺短诗、赞美诗、叙事短史诗，以及为有过露水之缘的有夫之妇莱斯比娅所作的挽歌。在这些挽歌中我们可以看出作者已经超越了希腊化时期诗人对性欲的轻描淡写，他触及了这种不安于室的蠢动心理的矛盾和纠结——灵魂在责任与激情、愉悦与羞耻之间摇摆不定。但是，和他的"导师"萨福一样，即便是在深刻详尽地叙述自己如何既痛恨莱斯比娅的无耻又欲罢不能的同时，加塔拉斯也在字里行间体现出了对主题很强的驾驭能力。

事实上，为了实现这样的心理分析，加塔拉斯已经成功地将讽刺短诗拓展到新的领域，衍生出了新题材——有时被称为"主观情色挽歌"，因为这种诗以挽歌对句创作，关注性欲对诗人意识的影响。这种风格的诗歌现存于世的还有普洛柏修斯（约前50—前2），狄巴拉斯（约前55—前19）和奥维德。普洛柏修斯写到了他和名为辛西娅的女性之间的暧昧关系。诗歌以大量神话例子和错综复杂的暗喻说明，当时偷情泛滥已经取代了罗马政军界传统的"荣誉之道"。他的最后两本书主题更丰富，其中包括模仿卡里马科斯风格的关于"起源"的诗歌。与普洛柏修斯一样，狄巴拉斯也是位情场"勇士"，同时也是他的情妇黛丽娅的"奴隶"。他在诗中记录了日常生活的细节，以及这种情事经历对自己心理的影响。最后，从奥维德的《爱经》我们可以看出爱的挽歌不再温情脉脉，作者以凝练、辛辣、睿智的语言，毫不掩饰地点明婚外不伦之恋对传统家庭观的破坏。此前的诗作相形之下着意刻画婚内婚外的矛盾紧张，显得戏剧化十足。

傲立于罗马诗人顶峰的还有维吉尔和贺拉斯。维吉尔的第一部诗作是《牧歌》，其中收录的（多称为）田园诗以扬抑抑格六音步格式描绘了忒奥克里特斯《田园诗集》中的农民和牧民所处的乡村景致。忒奥克里托斯笔下落英缤纷、小河潺潺的乡村似乎遗世独立，不受政治、国家的干扰。而维吉尔的"世外桃源"却笼罩在政治的阴影之下，种种社会变革已经威胁到田园式生活的自治、自由、闲适和惬意。这一冲突由《牧歌·之一》开篇即可看出：牧羊人提屠鲁"在树荫下小憩"，而梅利伯则因为土地被一名罗马士兵强占而不得不流亡。《牧歌》——特别是《牧歌·之一》——对后世西方文学影响之大，文学史学家库尔修斯一度断言："不熟悉这首小诗就缺少了打开欧洲文学殿堂大门的钥匙。"

　　除了维吉尔以外，对欧洲诗歌影响最深远的另一位诗人就是贺拉斯（前65—前8），他有很多不同风格的作品留存至今，其中包括有意识地模仿早期希腊抒情诗（特别是阿西奥斯的作品）的四卷《颂歌》。贺拉斯的诗歌涵盖了早期抒情诗的所有主题：爱情、饮酒、友情、政治。其中有一篇庆祝埃及艳后克里奥佩特拉之死，非常出名。他的作品沿袭了希腊化时期复杂成熟的风格，并对他人的诗作、地域和神话大肆引用，知识相当渊博。他的有些诗歌也从哲学层面探讨了如何生活，包括"人生苦短，

　　贺拉斯（昆图斯·贺拉提乌斯·弗拉库斯，前65—前8），生于意大利东南部的阿普利亚。他的父亲曾经是个奴隶，获得自由后成为小农场主和拍卖人。他的父亲显然经营有方，因为有能力将他送到罗马和希腊；在希腊，他结识了布鲁图斯，此人后来刺杀了恺撒。贺拉斯在对屋大维和安东尼的斗争中站在布鲁图斯一边，因此布鲁图斯失败后贺拉斯的家族失去了自己的土地。不过，贺拉斯还是获准回到意大利成为领政府俸禄的公务员。此后他开始创作诗歌，并且遇见了维吉尔；维吉尔将他引荐给梅赛纳斯（前38）。梅赛纳斯在罗马东北的萨平赐给他一座农场，使得贺拉斯得以有足够的时间和财力继续诗歌创作。

过好每一天"这样让人记忆犹新的观点。几个世纪以来,有识之士都曾学习贺拉斯诗歌中的某些名言。他推崇行事有度的"中庸之道";他赞赏为国捐躯的行为;他还认为应该"把握当下"。这些都是《颂歌》中的语句。

贺拉斯是拉丁语抒情诗的巅峰。自他以后,虽然也有抒情诗见诸文字或者保存下来,有些抒情诗人的名字也为人们所知,但在基督教抒情诗大放异彩之前这种体裁再也不曾辉煌过。

拉丁语讽刺短诗最早都是作为名人的墓志铭,例如恩尼阿斯在公元前 2 世纪为西比奥将军(罗马人,于公元前 202 年扎马一役中击败了汉尼拔)所作的讽刺短诗。虽然很多保留下来的作品都暗示在加塔拉斯以前讽刺短诗很流行,但不作为墓志铭的讽刺短诗很少留存于世。加塔拉斯的作品谈到了爱情、政治、

加塔拉斯,盖尤斯·瓦勒里乌斯(约前 84—约前 54),出生在维罗那附近一个的显赫家庭,不过他的大部分时光是在罗马度过的。如果他的诗歌记录的都是事实,那么在公元前 57 至 56 年,他曾是比西尼亚总督的随从人员。很有可能在他去比西尼亚的途中,他曾经去特洛伊附近给自己的兄弟扫墓。似乎加塔拉斯曾经反对恺撒,但是后来又接受了恺撒的友谊。有证据表明,加塔拉斯参加过一次社会艺术运动,主张放弃罗马文化理念,代之以希腊文明的价值观,即更注重个人的感性和经验而非对国家的责任。如果加塔拉斯的诗歌如实地反映自己的生活,那么他和一名富裕的贵族女性——很可能是克洛蒂亚·梅特鲁斯,一名执政官夫人——有私情。加塔拉斯无疑英年早逝。和萨福一样,关于他一生的流言不断,大多是基于对他作品的猜测。

友情、作诗、复仇，其中有一篇是作者对自己兄弟的凭吊，感人至深。和从琐事着眼、言语睿智的希腊讽刺短诗不同，加塔拉斯的作品讲述了诗人的日常生活，是复杂深刻、完成度极高的艺术作品。

马休尔是加塔拉斯之后的一代大师（约40—104），他生于西班牙，但一生中大部分时光是在罗马度过的。马休尔的讽刺短诗有些是典型的希腊风格，包括墓志铭和为某些大事件而作的应景诗。不过他的绝大多数作品不论是用韵还是成熟的风格都秉承贺拉斯之风。马休尔对日常生活的描绘辛辣睿智，带有社会、心理现实主义色彩。尤其值得称道的是其敏锐的观察力。两千年后的今天，他诗中所述人性的弱点、矛盾以及荒谬之处仍能引起读者的共鸣。马休尔的作品往往在结尾处峰回路

马休尔（马库斯·瓦勒里乌斯·马提亚利斯，约40—约104），公元1世纪活跃在罗马的很有影响力的西班牙人之一（小塞尼加和昆体良也在其中）。马休尔得到图密善皇帝的庇护，为赏识自己的大贵族歌功颂德。因为文名赫赫，他得到委任以诗歌庆祝斗兽场的揭幕（公元80年），并为此获得三子权，这是由奥古斯都皇帝赐予为人父母者的一种荣誉，通常是一种豁免权，如可以免于成为监护人（因为担任监护人很可能所费不菲）。他结识的人非富即贵，因此他为帝国写了很多宣传作品——尽管他本人抱怨自己所得物质补偿有限。他是其时最炙手可热的诗人，罗马以外各省都传诵他的作品。图密善去世以后，他的运势急转直下。马休尔以98岁的高龄返回故乡西班牙，居住在一名富孀提供的小农场，在101至104岁之间辞世。

转，出人意料，很有特色。比如他曾这样评论一个由医生转行的丧葬师："他成了丧葬师，不过是换行不换业。"——言下之意，其人医术太差，闹出过不少人命。

讽刺诗是诗歌的一种，其题材与有些讽刺短诗类似。按照罗马修辞学家昆体良（约35—90）的说法，讽刺诗是罗马人的发明。在拉丁语中 satire 意为一盘装着各种食物的大餐。因此，讽刺诗也有不同的风格，对应不同场合，探讨不同问题。但其主要特点在于以辛辣睿智的语言抨击虚伪做作，旨在"于笑声中揭露真相"（伟大的讽刺诗作者贺拉斯语）。

尽管起源于罗马，讽刺诗其实有其希腊文学的渊源。希腊有种叫"抑扬格"（因其所用韵律而得名）的诗，专门痛斥社会腐败或敌人的恶行。贺拉斯的《抒情诗集》（约前30）是第一首尝试"抑扬格"的罗马诗。但并非所有的诗歌都抨击社会腐朽、道德沦丧。"骂倒之词"对讽刺诗的形成也有影响。这是一种哲学家旨在惩恶扬善的公开演讲，通常以口语体创作，穿插以笑话，甚至故意使用下流语言以达到目的。愤世嫉俗的哲学家美尼普斯（活跃于约前300—前250）为一种同时使用韵文和非韵文的讽刺诗冠上了自己的名字。佩特罗尼乌斯（见下文）的《萨蒂利孔》就以美尼普斯式的讽刺揭露了罗马帝国暴发户式的粗俗。

这些希腊文学的渊源在贺拉斯之前的早期讽刺诗作中可以看到，但可惜的是这些诗作一般只剩几行或一些片段。贺拉斯的十八首《讽刺诗》（约前30）都是之前共和国时代影响的具体实例，因为采用口语体和在不同话题间流畅的转换，贺拉斯称之为《布道词》或《谈话录》。在这些诗中，贺拉斯引用自己的生活体验及他人的恶形恶状，告诫读者应该时时涵养德行。与他的模仿对象卢西里乌斯（生于前180）相比，贺拉斯在选择目标时更加谨慎有节制，或许这也反映出共和国风雨飘摇之态和其后奥古斯都大帝治世的特点。因此贺拉斯更关注的是某类人而非某个人。他有一篇著名的讽刺诗讲述了城里老鼠和乡下老鼠的寓言，以此谴责罗马统治阶级的骄奢淫逸。

朱文诺尔（约60—130）有十六首诗怒斥恶行和愚蠢，不过他后来的作品都更加节制、超脱。另外，朱文诺尔倾向于史诗和悲剧的恢弘的格局，而不是卢西里乌斯的下里巴人或贺拉斯的时髦谈话风格。朱文诺尔的诗歌取材都是在他看来罗马腐败的典型：统治阶级的堕落，廷臣的阿谀奉承，同性恋者的肆意滥交，贪婪、汲汲营营往上爬的人，外国人，皇帝和他的马屁精近侍，阴柔的男人，放荡的女人。其中声名最为卓著的是描绘罗马苦难生活的第三首，和关于在吞噬一切的时间面前人类渺小的第十首。塞缪尔·约翰逊曾仿照这两首诗进行创作。朱文诺尔这种"野性的义愤"（叶芝形容斯威夫特讽刺诗的原话）的语气对西方讽刺文学影响深远，他的作品经常被人引用，如"有健全的身体才有健全的心灵"，以及"由谁来对监管者进行监管？"

最后一种值得一提的诗歌体裁是书信体诗歌，即书札。和一些希腊化时期的书信格式创作的诗歌不同，书札完全是罗马人的创新。卢西里乌斯的书札有残片幸存，加塔拉斯的一些诗作也是书信体。贺拉斯的《书札》（约前20）是现存最早的书札体诗，都是六音步，以正确的生活方式为主题。我们所知的第二本书信著作为《诗艺》，下文还会有所提及。

奥维德也曾创作过书信体诗歌：《哀歌》（9—12）是作者因某些不为人知的理由触怒奥古斯都皇帝而遭流放之后完成的。诗人详述了谪居在黑海之滨的穷乡僻壤那种凄凉，同时借此诗传达出返回国都罗马的强烈愿望。为此他还创作了《黑海零简》。

　　现存的拉丁语诗作都担负着将希腊传统传播到欧洲的功能，因为有数百年时间欧洲对希腊一无所知，而很多希腊文本都遗失了。但是很多拉丁诗都超越了对希腊前辈的单纯模仿。希腊风的影响在维吉尔、贺拉斯、加塔拉斯和奥维德这里已经演化出鲜明的罗马风格。同样，后世的欧洲文人也会在将希腊罗马传统发扬光大的同时衍生出一种全新的文学传统。

戏　剧

或许，希腊人创造的影响最为深远的艺术形式是悲剧和喜剧。公元前 6 世纪晚期雅典城盛行的宗教庆典演变为这两种艺术形式：悲剧源于春季举行的城市酒神节；喜剧则源于冬季的勒奈亚节（悲剧在这个场合也会表演）。后来雅典城诞生的这种戏剧节传遍了整个古代希腊。

雅典戏剧是一种市政宗教仪式，因此实质上属于城邦的"政治"事务。所有剧目都在卫城山坡上面对约一万五千名市民上演，由雅典城邦对剧目进行监管，并由市民推举代表评选出获奖选手和作品。因此，悲剧关注的是整个社会共同关心的问题，如人类存在的基本条件和各种局限，以及个人和城邦之间的矛盾关系、家庭与政治权利、激情、理性和法律。我们还要注意，

埃斯库罗斯（前 525—前 456），雅典剧作家。他曾参与马拉松战役（前 490），可能也参加过萨拉米斯战役（前 480）。他的第一部悲剧创作于公元前 499 年；他曾荣获十三次戏剧大赛的第一名，第一次是在公元前 484 年；他的最后一次创作是公元前 458 年的《奥瑞斯提亚》。埃斯库罗斯在西西里逝世。他的墓志铭是自己撰写的，对自己多达九十部的戏剧只字不提，只谈到自己曾在马拉松一役中同波斯人战斗。他的两个儿子和一个外甥都追随他的脚步成为剧作家。

当时的剧作家拥有很大的自主权，可以自由选择主题，因此戏剧就演变成了政治评论和批评的载体。

悲剧结合了史诗的宏大场面，将英雄和神祇的故事配以音乐、舞蹈和韵律感十足的歌唱抒情诗。一般而言，三位参赛的剧作家每人都要创作三部悲剧和一出"山羊剧"（这是幕间表演的粗俗搞笑作品，主要表现沉迷于酒色的半兽人和其父神西勒努斯的冒险）。到了5世纪早期，这三部悲剧必须构成围绕一个主题展开的三连剧。表演结束后，十名市民组成的评委会将评出第一、二、三名。悲剧对集体的意义从合唱部分就可以看出：合唱既要应答，也要评论，还会和角色进行互动，因此通常充当观众在舞台上的代表。

阅读希腊悲剧的译本与亲历现场的感受不可同日而语：观众置身露天剧场，耳中听着合唱的颂歌，眼里看的是精心编排的舞蹈，会为昂贵的戏服、演员的面具和美轮美奂的布景而惊叹。但即使到了两千五百年后的今天，读者也依然可以从译本中感受到悲剧情节的魅力，剧中人物也依然可以打动我们的心。对于古希腊人而言，他们的感受是政治性的，舞台上下同时体会着人类面临的主要矛盾和问题。援引亚里士多德的话，这种共同体验会唤起强烈的同情和恐惧，因而希望能得到"情感净化"，避免这些情绪在政治体制内孳生。

现存最早、保存最完整的悲剧作品属于埃斯库罗斯（约前525—前456）。他创作了七十到九十部悲剧，十三次独占鳌头。埃斯库罗斯的作品有七部完好地保存下来，[1]其他都只剩残本。

---

〔1〕除了《俄瑞斯忒亚》（包括《阿伽门农》《奠酒人》《善好者》（或称《复仇女神》））以外，还有《被缚的普罗米修斯》（约前478）、《七将攻忒拜》（前467）、《哀求者》（年份不详，是作者的早期作品），以及描述萨拉米海战的《波斯人》（前480）。

他的作品中，人类的苦难是源自人性；欲望膨胀催生出傲慢自矜，人类失去节制，最终招致神明的惩罚。悲剧观点认为人活一世处处受限，妄图突破这些局限就会遭到厄运。不过，埃斯库罗斯认为人类社会及其政治价值观还是有希望的，因此才可以建立更稳定的秩序，将激情导致的混乱降至最低。在其作品——也是现存唯一一部完整的希腊三连剧——《俄瑞斯忒亚》（前458）中，埃斯库罗斯追溯了雅典民主的演化历史——从以阿伽门农国王的家庭为代表的充满家庭暴力、背叛、杀戮以及复仇的黑暗迈锡尼时代，到阳光灿烂的民主雅典时代。剧中各种冲突皆因理性、言语和法律的力量得到解决；一头蛇发、充满血腥与罪恶的复仇女神臣服于雅典娜（智慧女神，雅典城也因其而得名）。

除埃斯库罗斯外，索福克勒斯（约前496—前406）的作品也流传至今。他创作了超过一百二十部作品，赢得约二十次冠军。我们现在能看到其中的七部，其中包括希腊最负盛名的悲剧《俄

索福克勒斯（约前496—前406），创作了超过120部作品，公元前468年获得第一次戏剧比赛优胜。他曾和埃斯库罗斯和欧里庇底斯同台竞技，公元前406年欧里庇底斯辞世时，索福克勒斯专门让合唱团服丧致哀。他总共赢得过二十次胜利。和埃斯库罗斯一样，索福克勒斯也曾参政：公元前443至442年他任财政官，约公元前441至440年则是伯里克利麾下的一名将军。在公元前413年西西里的灾难（在争夺西西里的战役中，雅典惨败于叙拉古——译者注）之后，他被委任为处理危机的"十人委员会"一员。他同时还担当英雄哈隆的祭司，死后他被尊为"德克西翁"，被当成英雄享受后人献祭。

狄浦斯王》（时间不详）。弗洛伊德对此剧作了严重误读。[1]该剧并不如弗洛伊德所认为的是一部"家庭情感剧"，它其实是在说明人类执意要了解真相并没有多少道理，因为人类本身的欲望和时运难以把握，真相却并非确定不变；这一主题是索福克勒斯戏剧的一个代表性特点，被亚里士多德称为"发现"——即在某一个时间节点，主人公会发现自己误判或误解了真相而反受其累。不过，索福克勒斯也承认虽然人类有各种弱点，却仍然会积极追寻真相，哪怕为此而招致厄运，因为这就是人类生存的动力。

最后一位作品侥幸得以保存的悲剧作家是欧里庇得斯（约公元前 5 世纪 80 年代—公元前 407 年或 406 年），他名下有大约九十部戏剧，流传至今有十九部（不一定都是他本人的作品），[1]还有九部大部分得以保存。欧里庇得斯只荣获过四次桂冠，但后来他成为 5 世纪最受欢迎的悲剧作家。今天普遍认为欧里庇得斯比埃斯库罗斯和索福克勒斯两人更加现实。他笔下的人物不光有激情和欲望，同时也暴露了更阴暗、更复杂的心理，从而拉近了与现代读者间的距离。由《希波吕托斯》中的菲德拉或《美狄亚》中的女主角美狄亚可以看出，欧里庇得斯特别留意性欲对心灵的腐蚀。他的作品也描绘了战争的残酷。《特洛伊女人》和《赫古巴》证明戏剧创作者在雅典享有极大的自由，因为这两部作品创作于与斯巴达人的伯罗奔尼撒战争期间，直

---

[1]《阿尔刻提斯》（前 438）、《美狄亚》（前 431）、《希波吕托斯》（前 428）、《安德洛玛克》（约前 426）、《赫古巴》（约前 424）、《特洛伊妇女》（前 415）、《腓尼基妇女》（时间不详）、《海伦》（前 412）、《俄瑞斯忒》（前 408）、《酒神的女祭司们》和《伊菲革涅亚在奥里斯》（前 405）、《瑞索斯》（时间不详）、《埃勒克特拉》（时间不详）、《赫拉克勒斯之后裔》（时间不详）、《赫拉克勒斯之疯狂》（时间不详）、《祈援人》（时间不详）、《伊翁》（时间不详）、《伊菲革涅亚在陶里斯》（时间不详）和山羊剧《独眼巨人》（时间不详）。

指雅典人在战争中不时出现的残虐行为。

除了前面提到的三十三部悲剧，其他剧作家也有数百部作品有残本流传至今，令我们得以一窥这个人们所知甚少的世界。同时，从这些残余的片段，我们完全可以领略到希腊悲剧的辉煌成就及其对后世的恒久影响。

和悲剧相比，喜剧流传至今的更少，仅有阿里斯托芬（约前450—约前386）一人的十一部作品，其他作者就只剩残本。阿里斯托芬创作于"旧喜剧"晚期，所谓"旧喜剧"是和后来的新剧种相对的概念。[1]阿里斯托芬的作品中政治的影响十分

欧里庇底斯（约前5世纪80年代—前407或406），于公元前455年——即埃斯库罗斯逝世的翌年——创作自己的第一部戏剧。他在公元前441年赢得了第一次比赛胜利,最后一部戏剧《酒神的女祭司们》在他逝世后声誉大噪。不像埃斯库罗斯和索福克勒斯那样受人欢迎，他虽然创作了约九十部作品，但一共只获得了四次第一名。他离开雅典来到马其顿，并创作了关于马其顿国王阿克劳斯祖先的一出戏剧，最后死在马其顿。没有证据表明他离开雅典是因为他在戏剧比赛中没有获得大成功。无论如何，欧里庇底斯在雅典之外声名卓著:据说，逃离叙拉古灾难（参见"索福克勒斯"注——译者）的雅典人只要能背诵他的作品就可以获准在雅典城生活。

---

〔1〕《阿卡奈人》（前425）、《武士》（前424）、《云》（前423）、《黄蜂》（前422）、《和平》（前421）、《鸟》（前414）、《利西翠妲》和《特士摩》（前411）、《蛙》（前405）、《妇女大会》（前392）、《财神》（前388);除此以外，还有近千份残本。

明显：绝妙的情节、粗俗的幽默、污言秽语、打油诗、明嘲暗讽以及夸张的角色，很明显是为了评论或抨击雅典的民主、政客、领袖及哲学家，这些人物甚至会被标上姓名在众目睽睽之下顶着枷锁出场。

阿里斯托芬借助作品说明人类的各种欲望，特别是性欲，都会造成社会动荡、统治混乱，因而亟需监管与控制，而这是极端民主所无法保证的。不过，和雅典民主一样，他的喜剧在某种意义上也崇尚平等，因为他笔下的人物无论是否煊赫，是否高贵都有无法避免的缺陷和弱点。他固然抨击人性，但是对于人类的生命力与多样化，和追求自由与彰显自我的本能又不无敬仰。这种颠覆的本质或许在《吕西斯特剌忒》中最是表露无遗。该剧讲述希腊女性如何通过拒绝履行夫妻义务而迫使男人们终止了与斯巴达之间的战争。结尾处，男人对女人的偏见（例如，男人认为女人无法控制自己的性欲，不适于参政）最终苦了他们自己，因为是男人最终屈服于性欲，而女人们则赢得了这场政治斗争的胜利。

阿里斯托芬的最后两部作品《财神》和《公民妇女大会》被视为"中喜剧"的早期例证。"中喜剧"是盛行于公元前4世纪的一种新式喜剧。不过，因为阿里斯托芬以外八百多部作品几乎都没有保存下来，所以很难界定这个剧种的特点。由上述两部作品看来，似乎合唱的戏份被删减了，也有证据表明同时删减的还有政治评论和不雅语言。后来，"中喜剧"常以普通人平凡事为主题，包括爱情小伎俩和各式各样的欺诈招数。

到了公元前3世纪，"新喜剧"占据统治地位。幸运的是米南德（约前344—前292）的《恨世者》和另几部作品的部分得以保留至今。米南德创作了大约一百部喜剧，在其中看不到政治批评、污言秽语和荒诞不经的情节，合唱也只出现在幕间。他的情节涉及几种固定角色，如夸夸其谈的士兵、游手好闲的寄生虫、道貌岸然的伪君子、机智出众的奴隶，英俊迟钝的爱情中毒症患者。阿里斯托芬的大部分作品都围绕爱情、身份误会、遗失的宝藏和棒打鸳鸯这些主题，不过通常结局都是真爱至上，有情人终成眷属，就像时下的爱情喜剧一样。

古罗马戏剧受希腊影响很大，但也有自己的传统。拉丁语悲剧如今仅存帕库维乌斯（前220—约前130）和阿克齐乌斯（前170—约前86）等人的作品片段。这两位作者从罗马历史中取材，并对希腊神话中的小故事进行改编。小塞尼加（约前4—65，斯

小塞尼加（卢西乌斯·阿奈乌斯，约前4—65），生于西班牙北部的一个富裕骑士家庭。父亲是史学家、雄辩家大塞尼加；侄子则是史诗作家卢坎；唯一的儿子英年早逝。在十几岁的时候，他到罗马学习雄辩，后来追随斯多葛派教师和犬儒学派的德米特里乌斯学习哲学。在埃及短暂逗留一阵后，他坐船返回罗马，途中遭遇一次海难不过侥幸得存。回到罗马后，小塞尼加成为一名财务官。他是罗马最著名的演说家之一。有一则轶闻说到他的口才触怒了盖乌斯皇帝，还差点为此送命。后来他因为通奸罪被克劳狄乌斯皇帝驱逐到科西嘉，后被尼禄的母亲阿格里庇娜召回并任命为执政官，掌管刑庭、并监管公共游戏等事务。阿格里庇娜后又任命小塞尼加为尼禄的老师；尼禄在公元54年继位后，他又成为皇帝的顾问。但是，后来尼禄的性子越来越残暴，对小塞尼加也不再如以前那般信重。小塞尼加最后告老，只关注哲学和写作。公元65年因为据称卷入针对皇帝的阴谋而被迫自尽。

多葛派哲学家，尼禄皇帝的导师）创作的九部悲剧文学性强于戏剧性，同时受到早期罗马诗歌和希腊悲剧的影响。这几部作品最突出的特点就是着力渲染暴力，这在后世也影响了欧洲文艺复兴时期的戏剧，这一点从莎士比亚、马洛、本·琼生的作品中即可看出。

现存的拉丁语喜剧有普劳图斯（约前250—前184）的二十部作品和泰伦斯（生于前193/183—前159）的六部作品。这些作品都是对希腊新喜剧的改编，并且为了迎合罗马观众的口味加入插科打诨使场面更热闹。和它们的希腊前辈一样，这些剧目也含有一些固定的人物形象、埋藏的宝藏、身份的误会以及有情人终成眷属的情节。普劳图斯的作品在文艺复兴期间极负盛名，莎士比亚的《错误的喜剧》——关于一对自出生起就分离的双胞胎的故事——就是对其《墨奈赫穆斯兄弟》的改编。

即便在戏剧创作告别其古代的辉煌之后，它仍然是希腊罗马时期一种重要的公共艺术形式。就如同当代不断上演莎士比亚的作品一样，大量的节日也让雅典的悲剧作家充满激情。罗马帝国时期的演员都加入强大的公会，将戏剧传播到帝国的各个角落甚至别的国家。因此，雅典悲剧就成为宣扬希腊价值观的使节。

散文小说

　　散文叙事文学直到公元 1 世纪才出现。现存于世的有九部希腊长篇小说，另外还有两部小说的简介和大量残本，足以展现这种文学体裁的特点。那时的作品更准确地说应该叫做"传奇（小说）"，因为它们并不具备长篇小说的现实主义特点。换言之，这些作品并没有对普通的社会状况和心理活动进行具体描写。希腊的这些小说以爱情、历险、异域风情为主题，有时还会夹杂幻想。一般的故事情节如下：一对面目姣好的少男少女坠入爱河，却因故分离，在历尽千辛万苦（如牢狱之灾或遭遇海难）之后最终得以重逢。作品对情欲的关注让人联想到讽刺短诗和戏剧等其他的体裁。这个时期的作品修辞精当，一般已出现完整的对话、对艺术作品的描绘和对其他文学作品的引用，体现出丰富的地理知识。

　　朗努斯（公元 2 世纪）的《达夫尼斯和克洛伊》是这个时期的佼佼者。该书结合了希腊传奇和忒奥克里特斯的田园风光，自 16 世纪以来已经有五百多个译本。故事讲述了两个弃儿，达夫尼斯和克洛伊，被牧羊人抚养长大并倾心相爱。但是，他们的爱情却因情敌、海盗、附近的大城市和城里的诱惑而横生枝节，波折不断。最后，虽然他们发现自己实为贵族后裔却还是毅然返回乡间过着牧羊的生活。朗努斯不吝笔墨地描述了男女主人公的性觉醒和乡间生活的魅力。熟悉莎士比亚喜剧（如《皆大欢喜》）的读者都会看出朗努斯小说的影响。

罗马的散文小说有两部幸存：阿普列乌斯（125—约170）的《金驴记》和佩特罗尼乌斯（公元1世纪）的《萨蒂利孔》（或译为《登徒子》）的部分。《金驴记》讲述了一位青年因为魔力低下误服魔药而变成毛驴的传奇经历。除了这条主线外还有几条副线，其中最为人熟知的是丘比特和普绪克的故事。这个时期出现了一个重大的突破——旁白变成了作者本人。

小说发展更重要的一只推手是佩特罗尼乌斯《萨蒂利孔》中更早期的一篇，也叫作"特里马乔的晚餐"。这个故事是一对同性情侣，恩科尔皮乌斯和基多的历险。恩科尔皮乌斯得罪了爱欲与淫乐之神普里阿普斯，被他施法变成性无能后不得不与多位情敌斗争捍卫他和基多的感情。这似乎是在恶搞希腊传奇小说的典型情节。

特里马乔是个白手起家的百万富翁，以前曾是奴隶。"特里马乔的晚餐"就是他在自己奢华俗丽的豪宅中举办的一场宴会。在小说中出现了散文体叙事等罗马体裁的特点：复杂的情节、几条副线并行、为满足情欲而施展的小伎俩、对希腊浪漫小说和柏拉图的《对话录·会饮篇》等哲学著作的恶搞，以及最重要的——讽刺。事实上，《萨蒂利孔》对社会现实的如实记录以及对超越希腊传奇固有形象的特里马乔这一角色的塑造，说明它已经具备了现实主义小说的雏形。佩特罗尼乌斯对暴发户的无情嘲讽和对道德沦丧的严厉挞伐不时让人联想到《了不起的盖茨比》和巴尔扎克或狄更斯的作品。

文学批评

诗歌在古代的公共生活中无处不在，因此批判性、系统性的思考诗歌的技巧和宗旨也就成为一项重要的学术活动。柏拉图（约前429—前347）在其作品中最早使用的"模仿"（即诗歌是在模仿具体的形势和情感）一词，直到今天也是个经常使用的批评概念。柏拉图对模仿不以为然。他认为对某种感情的描绘会让读者或观众产生这种情绪反应，从而在潜移默化中更容易接受之。所以，在柏拉图看来，艺术具有道德操纵力，因为通过模仿对象，它既能塑造好人，也能创造坏人。

亚里士多德（前384—前322）的《诗学》确立了关于文学，特别是后世对文艺复兴产生巨大影响的戏剧相关的几个概念。我们已经提过，他认为悲剧能唤起观众的"同情和恐惧"，从而实现情感净化。所以，与柏拉图正好相反，他并不认为描绘情感就会产生情感所以不赞同这种模仿，而是认为观众心中的情感被唤醒，而且代替文学中的人物宣泄掉是个疗伤过程。《诗学》中其他的重要概念还包括"性格弱点"，即一个基本算得上好人的人因为悲剧性的缺点或错误而招致命运的大逆转。亚里士多德也提出诗歌比历史更具有哲学性，因为前者论述的是可能性而不仅仅是现实，因而更有普适性。

还有一篇希腊论说文的影响也异常深远，那就是朗吉努斯（约公元1世纪）的《论崇高》。朗吉努斯超越了以往仅从技术的正确性上追求"崇高"的想法，以及在面对天才时读者由衷产生的愉悦和敬畏。他通过对几篇希腊诗歌和散文的分析，充分揭示了文学之美。17世纪朗吉努斯作品的法译本（尼古拉斯·布瓦洛译）出版后，"崇高"就成为文学鉴赏和哲学的重要概念。

　　或许最具影响力的古代文学批评著作应属贺拉斯的《诗艺》。这首书信体诗歌是写给皮索两兄弟的。诗歌开篇即以充满睿智的语言说明优秀诗歌的规则：必须是个统一的整体，风格应与主题相匹配，等等。这些规则对后世诗人，如蒲柏，造成了很大影响。今天我们使用的一些说法就源自《诗艺》，如"文表华艳"指文章中毫无必要的花团锦簇；"直入中段"，即故事不该突兀开头，而要先铺垫后由中间展开；"荷马也有打瞌睡的时候"则是说大师有时都会犯错；最重要的理念则是文学应当"寓教于乐"，即带给人美学享受的同时还具有哲学或道德寓意。

　　不幸的是，仅有小部分古代灿烂文学的学术著作保存至今。我们只能想象已经遗失在漫长历史中那些作品的价值，如亚里士多德关于喜剧的论文，厄拉托希尼的同命题作品或伊壁鸠鲁派哲学教师斐洛德摩的《论诗》，等等。我们必须记住，有很多学者与文法家作出了自己的贡献：他们竭力确定正确的文本，编纂书目辞典，对作者进行点评，并为解释作品的原则做出规定。[1]可惜这些作品不是遗失就是仅剩残本。不过，流传至今的古代文学批评和学术著作足以表明对文学和语言的研究在古代是个复杂尖端的学科，它为后世研究西方文学创造了条件。

---

〔1〕这种古代手迹中的评论，阐释和批评意见被称作"旁注"，这些学者被人们称为训诂学者。

演讲与修辞

正式的公开演讲是古代政治、艺术、宗教生活的重要组成部分。如前文所述，诗歌尤其是种公众表演形式。

政治活动经常涉及在议会和集会时面对所有的城民公开演说，而庭审大部分都是控辩双方在数百位陪审员面前的唇枪舌剑。财力富余的人会雇佣专人撰写演讲稿。因此以雄辩的口才说服他人的能力也就成了担任公职的必要条件，而专门研究演讲技能和技巧的修辞学也就成为人们争相学习的对象。

现存的多篇演讲词让我们得以了解古代的政治、外交和社会生活。[1] 其中有一系列希腊演讲词（其中三篇题为《讨菲利普书》）为狄摩西尼斯（前384—前322）所作，他试图召集希腊各城邦对抗实力和野心不断膨胀的菲利普二世（马其顿国王，亚历山大大帝的父亲）。这些演讲后来被自由卫士引用向民众示警，提防暴君的阴谋，因为暴君往往因为民众的自负和腐败而执掌大权。

与政治演说相比，庭辩不那么为人所知，但提供的关于古希腊民生的信息——包括继承、财产、公民权利与义务、婚姻、

---

〔1〕其他的希腊重要演说家还包括伊塞优斯（约前420—前340）、艾索克拉底（前436—前338）、埃斯基涅斯（约前397—前322），和希波里德斯（前389—前322）。

通奸和同性恋——同样很有价值。如狄摩西尼斯一篇名为《驳奈阿依拉》的演讲提到了一个假装成平民家眷的妓女。我们从这篇演讲中可以获悉大量关于女性身为公民和妻子的地位以及她们的价值观和行为模式。同样，里西亚斯（约前458—约前380）的《论厄拉托西尼的被害》为一名杀死妻子情夫的男子辩护，为我们打开了一扇了解古代雅典家庭生活和家庭内行为方式的窗。

今人对罗马演讲的了解都是来自于西塞罗（前106—前43）。他有五十八篇演讲存世，向我们呈现了公元前1世纪罗马的历史、政治和社会道德。这些演讲有些是为庭辩而作，如著名的系列演说，有的呼吁处决暴虐的西西里总督菲雷斯，也有的为塞里乌斯（加塔拉斯情妇克洛蒂娅的情夫，加塔拉斯指控塞里乌斯企图毒死她）辩护。由这些演说我们得以了解罗马社会历史和各行省政府的结构。

同样，西塞罗的政治演说也提供了大量关于罗马共和国终结的史实；在此事上，西塞罗既是演说家又是政治家，贡献良多。我们烂熟于心的一句名言"人心不古，世风日下"就出自西塞罗暴露加蒂蓝（前63—前62）阴谋的四篇演讲。他还以《讨菲利普书》（得名于狄摩西尼斯的同名演说）对安东尼大肆批判，并为此献出了生命，但这篇檄文却给我们留下了捍卫自由反抗独裁的典范。西塞罗的作品对后世欧洲文化及政治演讲产生了重要影响。

鉴于演说的作用，研究修辞就成为一门飞速发展的学科。亚里士多德的《修辞学》是现存希腊修辞研究中最具影响力的著作。该书涉及修辞论据和哲学论据的区别、听众心理和操纵听众情绪的技巧，以及风格和修辞手段的使用。亚里士多德认为，演说分为五个准备阶段，这种分类在接下来的数个世纪一直为西方世界所沿用:"取材"——选择适合主题的语言;"谋篇"——分解主题,组织结构;"措辞"——包括风格,修辞等;"呈现"——包括姿态和发音;"记诵"——背诵演说稿的技巧,因为演说时鲜少会照本宣科。

罗马一流演说家西塞罗也创作了几篇修辞方面的论文并保存至今,其中有一些关注的是取材等技术性较强的方面。不过,更重要的几篇《论雄辩家》、《布鲁图斯》和《雄辩家》则向我们展示了怎样才算理想的演说家:仅仅掌握些修辞技巧远远不够,同时还必须"文理皆通",要熟读文学、哲学,了解文化。这些观点直接影响了文艺复兴关于人文教育和人文属性的看法。[1]

西塞罗之后昆体良(公元35—公元1世纪90年代)的巨著《雄辩术原理》是最重要的作品。昆体良开篇即明言演说家就像孩童,是以触及了教育学的问题,如恰当的课程安排和优秀教师应当具备的素质。文中他引用了大量希腊罗马书面例证并辅以自己对其价值的评价。

---

〔1〕作者不详的《赫拉纽姆修辞学》(约前86—前82)按照风格(恢弘、混合以及简朴)分成各部分。

书 信

古代流传至今的书信除之前提过的书信体诗歌以外还有几种形式，其中包括在埃及沙漠中幸存下来的私人信件和官方信函、城市和君主之间的通信、名人信札、致群众书，还有一些名人创作的书信体小说。

当然这些作品几乎都没能留存下来，其中尤以亚里士多德的信件（由亚提蒙出版）之遗失最令人扼腕。至于致多人的信件，我们有柏拉图的十三份作品，其中详述了他在西那库斯君主狄翁和迪奥尼修斯处的经历。第七首事实上不一定为柏拉图所作，但其中关于他生活的信息很有可能是准确的。书信体最受那些希望将信息传达给大众的哲学家青睐。伊壁鸠鲁最重要的作品就是以书信形式创作的。而以大规模民众为对象的书信最著名的例子当然是圣保罗写给希腊和亚洲各教会的信，这些信收录在《新约》中。

罗马文化中最重要的书信集是西塞罗写给亲友——特别是阿提库斯和布鲁图斯（恺撒的刺杀者）——的信。

这些信件中既有官方公函，也有致公众的通告，另外还有些不太正式的信件，不仅可以让读者了解西塞罗的个人生活，还能一窥古罗马的社会与家庭生活。西塞罗的政治信函日期都在公元前50至40年代，因此提供了罗马历史中这一关键时期的重要资料，因为这段历史见证了恺撒辉煌之后的陨落和屋大维的崛起，以及共和国在内战后的终结，西塞罗最终也因此而死去。

小普林尼（约61—约113）的十卷书信集也极具历史价值，他本人也很清楚自己书信的文学特质和作为编年史的意义。第十卷记录了普林尼任俾提尼亚—本都省（在今土耳其境内）总督任内发生的事，对历史学家而言最为宝贵。这些信件不仅向我们展示了行省政府的运作，同时也是《新约》之外对基督教传教的记载，并且还提供了迫害处死基督教徒的理论基础。和希腊一样，罗马的哲学家也将信件作为宣传思想的平台。小塞尼加就在自己的《道德书简》中宣扬斯多葛哲学。这些信件更接近我们所说的散文，涉及友情、幸福、自杀、至善的要素和对死亡的恐惧。这些信件还包括塞尼加和其所属时代的信息，所以兼具历史和哲学价值。例如，我们能通过其中的某些信件大致了解当时人们对奴隶制——其时仍是普遍现象——的态度发生了转变。塞尼加曾写道："你们称他们为奴隶，但他们与你们同一个种，沐浴着同样的阳光，像你们一样呼吸、生活、死亡。"这都暗示公元1世纪时奴隶制的道德基础已经受到了质疑。这种以书信方式进行哲学讨论的传统——后因圣保罗在《新约》中的信件而发扬光大——在基督教作者中尤其盛行。

传　记

　　古代关于名人生平的故事有不同的形式，既有相对准确的历史，也有近似于杜撰的颂辞，还有对名人的诋毁。诗人和哲学家因为曝光率高，所以是"名人生平"——即通过个案说明不同类型的影响和发展——最受欢迎的灵感来源。只可惜这些作品到如今大部分只剩下残本或对它们的引述。其中的代表作是狄奥奇尼斯·利尔提乌斯（公元前3世纪）的《贤哲传》。这本书可能是利尔提乌斯把此前的传记作者和编纂者的作品综合后的结果，其中收录了从最早的"圣哲"到伊壁鸠鲁的所有主要流派和代表人物。尽管利尔提乌斯主要依靠前人的资料，而这些资料通常又几经换手，导致可靠性时而受到质疑，但他的作品保存了关于哲学家的轶闻和对他们作品（多数已经遗失）的大量引用，因而无比珍贵。

　　色诺芬（约前354）的作品中有不同风格的传记。《回忆苏格拉底》记录了苏格拉底就各种话题的发言，从朋友、家庭到教育、美德不一而足。同时，该书又讲述了苏格拉底的很多轶闻趣事和他同别人的交往。《居鲁士的教育》以类似史书的风格描述了波斯帝国的缔造者居鲁士大帝。色诺芬一方面提供了波斯帝国的有用信息，一方面又以小说笔法叙述了居鲁士一步步登上帝位的过程。书中还包括很大篇幅的旁白和对话，都是关于领袖素质的。另外色诺芬的《阿格西劳斯》直白地歌颂了这位公元前4世纪的斯巴达国王，他曾与波斯人和希腊人战斗过。

对色诺芬而言，他就是好人和伟人德行的化身。

古代最有影响力的传记作者是普卢塔克（约 50—120）。他的《对传》比较了十九位希腊罗马名人，除了四个人以外，其余人物都有类似的生涯。和色诺芬等早期希腊传记作家一样，普卢塔克也注重展示善恶在生活中的发展和影响，以及伟人的特质。因此，他认为传记的目的不仅是提供一段人生的真相，而是从中汲取道德伦理的经验教训。他的工作使我们掌握了丰富的信息和大量典故，以及古代的大事件（虽然他的可信性有时也值得怀疑）。文艺复兴之后普鲁卢克对欧洲文化的影响非常大，这一点从莎士比亚的诗歌中可以看出——莎士比亚曾经阅读过托马斯·诺思爵士的译本。

罗马传记流传至今的同样很少，不过从这些稀有的典籍中，人们获得了珍贵的罗马历史资料。名人或其友人通过作传为其事业辩护或使其事业正义化，比如西塞罗对共和国烈士加图的盛赞（现已失传），恺撒以《驳加图》（也已失传）作为回应。这种体裁的一个重要例证是罗马帝国的创始人奥古斯都（前 63—14）的《奥古斯都行述》，在文中奥古斯都为自己享有的权力、地位和人民给他的支持是否合乎宪法进行了辩护。撇开明显的自私目的不谈，此文提供了与这段关键历史时期相关的重要历史细节。

尼波斯（约前 110—前 24）是第一个超越了仅仅为传记对象辩护的罗马传记作者。他的《名人录》收录了四百个名人的生平。这本传记和大加图以及西塞罗之友阿提库斯的传记比国外著名领袖的传记更有生命力。尼波斯的书大部分内容都是赞美传记人物，从他们的生平中吸取经验教训。

为名人及其行止辩护正名是古代传记的一贯主题。历史学家塔西佗（约 56—约 118）就曾经为自己的岳父阿格里科拉（公元 77/78—84 年曾任不列颠总督）作传。在这部传记中塔西佗在批判暴君——特别是图密善皇帝——的背景下称颂了阿格里科拉的生平。苏维托尼乌斯（约 70—约 130）则以更为犀利辛辣的笔触揭露了罗马的诸位皇帝，引人入胜。不过，他的叙述有时并不很可靠。苏维托尼乌斯还曾为诗人、演说家、哲人等名人作传，但保存较完整的则是以修辞学家和语法学家为对象的作品。他的《罗马十二帝王传》从恺撒写到图密善，共记录了十二个罗马皇帝，极大地影响了我们对早期罗马皇帝的态度。苏维托尼乌斯的传记都围绕对象的性格和成就，叙述中常常加入这些名人的轶闻趣事，因此他把笔下的人物实则放在了一个公平的平台上，以罗马人民对统治者的普遍期望为标杆对他们进行衡量。苏维托尼乌斯的传记之所以出名还因为他毫不避讳，甚至不吝笔墨地记录名人的不伦恋情及其他恶行。其后，六名无名氏创作的系列皇家传记——《罗马皇帝传》，时间跨度从公元 117 年到 284 年，就是以他的作品为模板。[1]

　　传记是一种非常重要的历史体裁，因为古人相信是伟人的作为造就了历史，而这些作为反过来又反映了一个人的品格。且不论其真实性和准确性，古希腊罗马传记中对民生细节的记述确实为我们描绘了一幅古代世界和君主的画卷。比如，今天对埃及艳后的普遍认知大都来自莎士比亚对普卢塔克的恺撒和安东尼传记的重新演绎。

---

〔1〕另一部自古代传下来的传记是斐罗斯特拉图创作的《泰安那的阿波罗尼俄斯》（公元 3 世纪）。阿波罗尼俄斯是个圣贤，也是个创造奇迹的人，斐罗斯特拉图的作品为我们了解异教徒的宗教信仰提供了珍贵的资料。斐罗斯特拉图还创作了《诡辩家生平》，这部作品是对演说家公开发表演说的简单描述。

历 史

在古希腊人之前，历史（其希腊语词源意为"问询"）不过是编年体，即逐条记录下伟人——如法老或国王——身边发生的大事。希腊人最早有意识地记录大事件和信息，目的是在不涉及怪力乱神的前提下理性地探索这些事件的意义及发生的原因，并对其进行评价。希腊最早一批史学家出现在公元前6世纪晚期，他们被称为"记录官"或散文作者。赫卡塔埃乌斯（约前500）是其中的佼佼者。他的作品涉及家系、神话和地理，但是只有一些片段得以保存。

希罗多德（约前490—约前425）之所以被称为"历史之父"，是因为在他之前的作品早已遗失。他的《历史》开篇即对公元前490年和公元前480至479年希腊人和波斯人的战争进行记录和说明。在此过程中，希罗多德同样也描绘了希腊的邻国（特别是埃及）的风俗、历史、宗教和地理。尽管他的批评不乏错误，但他没有简单地记录事件而是理性地审视证据，试图找出事件背后的深意，这一点相当值得尊敬。他将希腊人最终取得胜利部分归因于其独特的文化价值观，尤其是对政治自由的热爱。

希罗多德之后的一位重要希腊历史学家，也是人类历史上最伟大的史学家之一，就是修昔底德（约前460至455—约前399）。他的《伯罗奔尼撒战争史》关注的是公元前5世纪后半叶发生在雅典人和斯巴达人之间的这场战役。这是史上对于城邦（国家）之间冲突最为透彻的分析。修昔底德对于准确性的执着、对人类本性和政治心理的洞察、对不伦情感的悲剧本质的宽容、对超自然力量的不屑一顾和贯穿始终的公平感（虽然读者仍然可以看出他对某个人物的喜恶）都成为后世著史的标准。他的后辈都无比诚恳、不遗余力地直击真相，他们的作品——借用修昔底德对自己作品的评价——可以"永垂不朽"。

《伯罗奔尼撒战争史》在距离战争终结还有几年的地方戛然而止，所幸色诺芬的《希腊史》（一直写到公元前 362 年）补足了最后的这几年。虽然作为史学家完全不能与修昔底德相提并论，但色诺芬的作品还是提供了斯巴达人统治时期（直到公元前 371 年在留克特拉大败于底比斯）的珍贵史料。色诺芬的另一部重要作品《远征记》记录了一万希腊雇佣兵（包括色诺芬本人）为觊觎波斯王位的居鲁士冲锋陷阵的这段历史。居鲁士败亡后，这些佣兵不得不深入波斯境内以便到达黑海之滨从那里返回故乡。这段令人热血沸腾的冒险故事同时也体现了希腊人的文化价值观在面临巨大压力时是何等坚定。

另一位值得一提的希腊史学家是波利比奥斯（约前 200—前 118），他在亚该亚（为抵抗罗马人而建立的城邦联盟）战败后被放逐到罗马，在那里他与后来战胜迦太基的罗马将军西比奥建立了友谊。因此，波利比奥斯得以亲眼见证罗马在两次迦太基战争中击溃迦太基，势力遍及地中海地区。波利比奥斯用四十卷书记录了罗马征服整个地中海的不世成就。但是如今仅存其中五卷，其余三十五卷只余简介或摘录。波利比奥斯作为史学家一贯致力于准确地呈现历史，这就要求他做大量的调查研究。而且，波利比奥斯还习惯于解释事件的起因，特别是人们在综合各种因素后所做的决定。他对罗马"混合宪政"（贵族政体、寡头政体和君主政体的结合）的探讨，对后世——尤其是美国国父——的政治理念影响巨大。

接下来的这位史学家是以希腊语写作的犹太贵族约瑟法斯（生于约 37—约 100）。他亲历耶路撒冷的沦陷，记录了犹太战争和犹太人民，对犹太地被征服后罗马举行的凯旋庆典都进行了描述。约瑟法斯始终捍卫自己的同胞和他们的历史，他为公元 1 世纪这一关键历史时期提供了重要的史料。[1]

罗马史学家比希腊史学家更注重通过史书规范世人的行为与价值观，因此在他们笔下历史总是以能够加强教化的方式呈现。例如塞勒斯特（前 86—前 35）的作品。塞勒斯特记录了加蒂连的阴谋，以及罗马与北非国王朱古达之间的战役。在对这两个事件的叙述过程中，揭露了贵族阶级的腐朽和道德沦丧以及因此而导致的政治社会动荡。

罗马史学家中有很多人本身就是行动派，曾经参与甚至左右过该时代的大事件，其中最突出的就是恺撒大帝（前 100—前 44）。他曾评论过自己对高卢（今天的法国）和对庞培的战争。前者对他有时不合宪的行为做出了解释，这些解释非常微妙，但的确提供了不少宝贵资料，让今天的读者可以了解罗马的战争策略、将领素质以及居住在高卢和不列颠的凯尔特人的风俗、地理和宗教。

---

〔1〕以下希腊史学家的作品也得以保存至今：狄奥多罗斯·西库路斯（活跃于约前 60—前 30），哈利卡纳苏斯的狄奥尼修斯（约前 30），阿庇安（约 160），卡修斯·狄奥（约 150—235）以及阿里安（生于 85—90），以上都曾写过亚历山大大帝。还有一些史学家的作品仅剩残本，如创作了希腊及小亚细亚地区各城邦历史的埃弗鲁斯（前 4 世纪），以及和色诺芬一样继续修昔底德事业的提奥庞普斯（约前 376—约前 323），他记述的对象是马其顿的菲利普。

历史著作的教育功能在李维（前59—17）的著作中最为鲜明。他写道："研读历史是医治灵魂的良方。"因为史书记载了大量高尚的行止和优秀的作为，世人可以向其学习以摒弃恶行。他的《罗马史》共一百四十二卷，追溯了罗马从台伯河畔的小村庄发展为世界霸主的过程，现存大约二十五卷和其余一百多卷的简介或概要。这二十五卷记录了罗马历史中的重要篇章：如迦太基的汉尼拔挺进阿尔卑斯以及他对罗马的压倒性胜利（罗马险些因此而毁灭）。李维希望通过这些记载阐明造就罗马辉煌的道德根源，后来正是因为这些道德基础的朽毁才会导致社会动荡和残酷的内战。罗马历史中的很多记载后来被西方文学及艺术一再演绎，例如罗马城的缔造者罗慕路斯和雷穆斯两兄弟的故事、贞妇瑠克利希娅以及罗马勇士霍雷修斯保卫战略大桥的故事，李维的书中都有记载。

最后一位伟大的罗马史学家是《历史》和《编年史》的作者塔西佗（约56—120）。《历史》总计十四卷，记录了公元69至96年的历史，不过现在仅存四卷。《编年史》和恩尼阿斯的史诗一样也从每年大事记的传统中获得灵感，由公元14至68年记载了提比略、卡利古拉、克劳狄乌斯和尼禄几朝的大事件。共计十六卷的《编年史》约有三分之一得以留存至今。塔西佗的优势在于他洞悉人性——他和大部分古人一样认为人性是历史的推手，而且对于君主的软弱或腐败给罗马造成的后果也十分清楚。和李维一样，塔西佗也认为史学家就该贬恶褒善："我认为历史最重要的使命就是不任由高尚事迹默默无闻，并且能够让人因为担心遗臭万年而不敢出恶言行恶举。"他的帝国历史由阿米亚努斯·马尔切利努斯（330—395）续写。马尔切利努斯虽是希腊人，但以拉丁语写作，他的三十一卷书有十七卷保留下来。[1]

古希腊罗马的历史著作标志着人类通过审视过去而理解自身及所处时代的最早尝试。过去并非由神力造就，而是人类自己的行为、价值观和性格的结果。也因此，古代史、古代诗歌或哲学一样是人文学科，它关注的永远是"人类"（修昔底德语）。

---

[1] 其他有作品存世的罗马史学家还包括马西穆斯（公元 1 世纪早期），他编纂了《名人言行录》；库修斯（公元 1 世纪），曾书写过亚历山大的历史；以及十卷本罗马历史调查的作者尤特罗庇乌斯（公元 4 世纪）。

古典文学的宝贵遗产

上文提及的所有著作都只是古代文学灿烂成就最为菁华的部分。流传至今的很多作品或许不如它们家喻户晓，但都包含着珍贵的信息，让今天的读者可以了解古代的生活和文化，因此也是古典文学研究的重点。有很多古代学者为其他作者的作品撰写概要，即"梗概"，就是对较长著作的总结和删节版。时至今日，很多古代文人的作品也仅剩这种梗概。另外一种保存古代作品的形式就是丛书。《希腊诗文选》收录了从公元前7世纪到公元6世纪之间的四千首诗。如果这部作品遗失，我们对古希腊诗歌的理解就会留下巨大的空白。同样，还有很多悲剧和喜剧的片段，以及其他文学作品保存在斯托比亚斯（公元5世纪早期）的"精选"和"文丛"中，斯托比亚斯按不同主题将这些作品分门别类。

另外，有些现存作品无法归入任何一个标准的门类，但其中都载有对某些失传作品的引用和轶闻趣事。阿特纳乌斯（约200）的《宴饮丛谈》共十五卷（现存十二卷）就含有大量珍贵的引用、摘录和轶闻。奥卢斯·盖里乌斯（约130—180）的《阁楼夜话》共二十卷，收录了话题广泛的散文。这些都是作者本人阅读过的希腊罗马文学，其中包含大量珍贵的信息和引用。最后，普卢塔克的《道德论集》则广泛收集道德哲学论说文。这部合集涉及的话题之多令人惊叹，包括《给已婚夫妻的建议》、

《佞友与真友》等。除了展现古代的价值观和道德观,《道德论集》也影响了培根、蒙田等散文家,从而奠定了现代散文的基础。这些著作今天读起来或许诘屈聱牙,但对于学者而言却不啻为宝藏,蕴含着无可估价的轶事、引用、信息和古代思维方式的例证。

希腊罗马文学之趣味、精深、丰富,显然不是这本小小的导读可以道尽的,古代作者对其经历的叙述、对人性的分析和描绘都为我们提供了自我表达、解释自己和自身经历的范本。研究古希腊罗马的语言、文学和文化不仅是为了掌握本学科,更是为了了解我们的历史、现状以及未来。

延伸阅读

古典文学专业的现状、希腊罗马文明对西方文化的关键意义可以参见 E. 克里斯蒂安·科普夫的《人人都懂拉丁语：为什么美国需要古典文学传统？》（ISI 出版社，1999）；特雷茜·西蒙斯的《诗山有路：再向希腊语和拉丁语致歉》（ISI 出版社，2002）；维克多·汉森和约翰·希斯的《谁杀了荷马？古典文学教育之死与希腊智慧的回归》（尹康特出版社，2001）；维克多·汉森、约翰·希斯和布鲁斯·桑顿的《人文篝火：在文荒年代拯救古典文学》（ISI 出版社，2001）；布鲁斯·桑顿的《希腊之道：希腊创造西方文明》（尹康特出版社，2000）；伯纳德·诺克斯的《欧洲男性文人历史溯源》（诺顿，1993）。有两部作品讨论希腊罗马文学对后世西方文明的影响：吉尔伯特·海伊特的《古典文学传统：希腊罗马对西方文学的影响》（牛津大学出版社，1949）；以及库修斯的《欧洲文学和拉丁中世纪》（维拉德·特拉斯克译；普林斯顿大学出版社，1953）。

如果同学们想概览希腊罗马历史、文化和文学，可以从约翰·博德曼、贾斯伯·格里芬与奥斯文·穆瑞合编的《牛津古典世界历史》（牛津大学出版社，1983）开始。如果只是对古典文学感兴趣，可以阅读《剑桥古典文学历史》（剑桥大学出版社，1982—1985）收录的论文。对于本书没有收录的希腊罗马作者，想欣赏他们作品译文的读者可以选择哈佛大学出版社出版的罗勃古典文学图书馆系列。

希腊文学。荷马作品最好的直译者为里奇蒙德·拉蒂摩尔，两部史诗仍然在版：《伊利亚特》（芝加哥大学出版社，1962）、《奥德赛》（哈珀与罗，1967）。罗伯特·费格斯则创作了最佳的意译版：《伊利亚特》（维京，1990），《奥德赛》（维京，1996）。他的译文中同时收录了伯纳德·诺克斯所作的介绍论文，这是目前最好的荷马介绍。另外，塞思·谢恩的《凡人英雄：〈伊利亚特〉介绍》（加利福尼亚大学出版社，1984）也是不错的选择。赫西俄德的作品和《荷马式赞美诗》已经由阿波斯托罗斯·阿塔纳萨基斯翻译，约翰霍普金斯大学出版社 1976 年出版。

喜欢悲剧的学生可以阅读里奇蒙德·拉蒂摩尔和大卫·葛林合编的《希腊悲剧全集》（芝加哥大学出版社，1992）。也可以选择《英雄气质：索福克勒斯悲剧研究》（1964；加利福尼亚大学出版社再版，1983）和《言与行：古代戏剧论文集》（约翰霍普金斯大学出版社，1979），这两部书收录了伯纳德·诺克斯关于希腊悲剧的论文。至于希腊诗歌则可以参看五卷本《希腊抒情诗》，该书由大卫·坎贝尔编辑，属于罗勃古典文学图书馆系列（哈佛大学出版社，1982—1993），也可以选择《希腊文丛和其他古代讽刺短诗》（彼得·杰译；企鹅，1981）。大卫·马尔罗伊翻译的《希腊早期抒情诗》（密歇根大学出版社，1999）也很有参考价值。

对阿里斯托芬的喜剧有兴趣的同学可以考虑同属罗勃古典文学图书馆系列的杰弗里·汉德森译本。唐纳德·麦克道威尔的《阿里斯托芬与雅典》（牛津大学出版社，1995），以及多佛的《阿里斯托芬的喜剧》（加利福尼亚大学出版社，1972）都是优秀的介绍性作品。至于《阿耳戈英雄纪》，可以参看彼得·格林所译的《阿耳戈英雄纪：伊阿宋和寻找金羊毛的故事》（加利福尼亚大学出版社，1997）。忒奥克里特斯的最佳翻译是沙金特，参看《忒奥克里特斯抒情诗》（诺顿，1982），也可以选择托马斯·罗森梅尔的研究著作《绿橱柜：忒奥克里特斯和欧洲田园抒情诗》（加利福尼亚大学出版社，1969）。

至于历史学家，可以选阅大卫·葛林翻译的希罗多德的《历史》（芝加哥大学出版社，1987）和罗伯特·斯特拉斯勒编辑的《修西底德地标：〈伯罗奔尼撒战争史〉导读》（自由出版社，1996）；另外，企鹅文丛还出版了色诺芬作品的两个译本（均由雷克斯·华纳翻译)：《我的当代史》（纽约，1978）和《波斯远征军》（巴尔的摩，1961，1967，1972）。波里比乌斯的作品，可以参看伊安·斯科特—吉尔维特翻译的《罗马帝国的崛起》（企鹅，1979）。

英国诗人约翰·德莱顿翻译的《普卢塔克生平》收录在现代图书馆系列中，依然在版。如果对希腊演说兴趣浓厚，可以选择罗伯特·康纳翻译的《希腊演说：公元前四世纪》（1966；威夫兰出版社再版，1987）。

罗马文学。加塔拉斯的作品目前有好几个版本，笔者推荐G.H.希森的《加塔拉斯诗集》（维京，1966）。最近，大卫·马尔罗伊也出版了一部优秀的翻译作品《加塔拉斯诗歌全集》（威斯康辛大学出版社，2002）。对加塔拉斯的优秀介绍文字还包括肯尼思·奎因的《加塔拉斯阐释》（纽约，1973）和T.P.威斯曼的《再评加塔拉斯和他的世界》（剑桥大学出版社，1977）。

卢克莱修的《物性论》的最好译者是弗兰克·科普雷，诺顿1977年出版。

维吉尔的《牧歌》，可以参见北卡罗莱纳大学出版社1977

年出版的芭芭拉·福勒译本。《农事诗》则可以阅读企鹅于 1982 年出版的 L.P. 威尔金森译本，或是他的研究专著《维吉尔的农事诗》（剑桥大学出版社，1969）。至于《埃涅阿斯纪》，则可以参见艾伦·曼德尔鲍姆的译本（矮脚鸡，1971）。另外，S.J. 哈里森编辑的《牛津维吉尔〈埃涅阿斯纪〉解读》中也收录了该作品的现代研究论文，由牛津大学出版社 1990 年出版。凯瑟琳·金的《阿喀疏斯：从荷马到中世纪的战争英雄范式》（加利福尼亚大学出版社，1987）将维吉尔的作品与荷马式的英雄主义理想完美融合，提供了全新的阅读体验。

狄巴拉斯的诗歌可以参看康斯坦斯·卡里尔的译作《诗集》（印第安纳大学出版社，1968）。狄巴拉斯诗歌的介绍则可以阅读 F. 卡恩斯的《狄巴拉斯：希腊诗人在罗马》（剑桥大学出版社，1979）。

普洛柏修斯的作品有加利福尼亚大学出版社 1972 年出版，J.P. 麦克卡洛翻译的《普洛柏休斯诗集》，以及剑桥大学出版社 1976 年出版的 J.P. 沙利文的《普洛柏修斯：批判性介绍》。

芝加哥大学出版社出版了两卷版贺拉斯作品，分别是史密斯·博伟翻译的《贺拉斯讽刺诗歌和书札集》（1956），以及约瑟夫·克兰西翻译的《贺拉斯颂歌和抒情诗》（1960）。另外，耶鲁大学出版社于 1989 年出版了大卫·阿姆斯特朗所作的简介——《贺拉斯》。

奥维德的作品可以选择盖伊·李翻译的《奥维德的爱经》（维京，1968）、因尼斯翻译的《变形记》（企鹅，1955）、彼得·格林翻译的《情色诗集》（企鹅，1982；格林的简介也很值得一读），以及贝蒂·纳格尔翻译的《日历：罗马节日》（印第安纳大学出版社，1995）。除此以外，1988 年耶鲁大学出版社还出版了莎拉·麦克的概述性作品《奥维德》。

鲍布斯—梅里尔1968年出版的《讽刺短诗精选》收录了马休尔的拉尔夫·马切里诺译本。朱文诺尔作品有1958年印第安纳大学出版社出版的《讽刺诗集》，由罗尔夫·亨弗雷翻译。密歇根大学则在1959年出版了由威廉·埃罗史密斯翻译的佩特罗尼乌斯的《萨帝利孔》。

至于拉丁语散文，罗勃古典文学图书馆系列中西塞罗的多卷作品是最容易理解的。他的作品还可以参看企鹅出版社在1960年出版、由迈克尔·格兰特翻译的《西塞罗作品精选》。有关西塞罗的另两部重要作品是格兰特的《论美好生活》（企鹅，1971），以及乔治·萨宾和斯坦利·史密斯翻译的《论公民社会》（鲍布斯—梅里尔，1929）。企鹅分别于1967年和1951年出版了简·加德纳翻译的恺撒评论集：两卷本《内战》，以及S.A.韩德福翻译的《高卢》。现存李维的历史作品有企鹅出版的《罗马早期历史》、《与汉尼拔的战争》、《罗马和意大利》，以及《罗马和地中海》。塔西佗的作品有摩西·哈达斯编辑、阿尔弗雷德·彻奇与威廉·布罗德里布合译的《塔西佗全集》（现代图书馆，1942）。至于塞勒斯特的历史著作，可以阅读企鹅于1963年出版的《朱古达之役与加蒂连的阴谋》（韩德福译）。

A STUDENT'S GUIDE TO
LITERATURE

INTRODUCTORY NOTE:
THE PARADOX OF LITERATURE

Literature is paradoxical both in its nature and in its effect upon readers. Although letters inscribed upon a page or the words of a spoken utterance are the media of a literary work, the work itself is neither the ink and paper nor the oral performance. A successful poem or story compels our attention and seizes us with a sense of its reality, even while we know that it is essentially (even when based upon historical fact) something made up—a fiction. The most memorable works of literature are charged with significance and cry out for understanding, reflection, interpretation; but this meaning carries most conviction insofar as it is *not* explicit—not paraded with banners flying and trumpets blaring. "We hate poetry that has a palpable design upon us," says John Keats. The role of literature in society is similarly equivocal. It can be explained simply as entertainment or recreation; men and women have always told stories and sung songs to amuse themselves, to pass the time, to lighten the burdens of "real life." At the same time, literature has assumed a central place in education and the transmission of culture throughout the history of Western civilization, contributing a sense of communal identity and shaping both individual and social understanding of human experience. The intimate part played by literature in cultural tradition has been a source of alarm to moralists and reformers from Plato to the media critics and multiculturalists of our own day.

Literature, then, must be approached both with caution and abandon. A primary purpose of the study of literature is to learn to read critically, to maintain reserve and distance in the face of an engaging, even beguiling, object. And yet, like any work of art—a symphony, for example, or a painting—a novel or an epic yields up its secrets only to a reader who yields himself to its power. It is for this reason that literary study is a humane or humanistic discipline, not an exact or empirical science. The ideal researcher in the physical sciences, insofar as he sticks rigorously to science, will be absolutely objective in the sense that his humanity will exert no influence on his methods or conclusions. Even a medical researcher will be interested in the human body only as a biological mechanism, not as the outward manifestation of a person with a soul. The literary scholar must of course be objective in the sense that he is disinterested; he must not have an individual or personal stake in the interpretation. And yet, although the critic's fate is not the fate of King Lear, the critic's human sympathy with the plight of that tragic protagonist is part of his critical response to the play as literature. The human compassion of the cancer researcher for the victims of the dis ease, while it may be an important motive, is not part of his research, not an element in his science as such. The natural sciences, therefore, provide a very poor model for scholar ship in the humanities. To be sure, there are factual, "scientific" elements of great importance to inquiry in all the arts: a knowledge of Elizabethan stagecraft and printshop practices can furnish a good deal of useful information about how *Hamlet* was seen by contemporaries and how the text was preserved, but such facts will never explain why the play is still moving and important. Works of literature are not natural phenomena or specimens; they are rather part of the cultural fabric of the world that we all inhabit. A poet, says William Wordsworth, "is a man speaking to men." We cannot approach poets and poems as an entomologist approaches ants and ant hills.

Literature is vast and complex; a "guide" of this length can only be a modest sketch of the subject. My purpose is to provide a brief description of the nature and purpose of literature and some sense of how it may be best approached. I shall say something about the concept of literary kinds or genres, and something about how literature has developed along with the development of Western civilization. I shall not discuss the literature of other civilizations, principally because I lack the competence, but also because I suspect that *literature* in the sense that I use the term, although no longer unique to the West, is a uniquely Western idea. Finally, I shall list some of the indispensable works of our tradition, of which every educated person should have some knowledge, as well as lesser works that are also very fine or very influential and well worth perusal. The list will not be comprehensive: this essay is intended not only for undergraduate literature majors, but for students of any age who wish to have a knowledge of literature commensurate with a baccalaureate degree. Nothing that I can say will take the place of simply reading these works, but I hope that this *Guide* will enable students to plan their own literary education, or fill in the gaps of such awareness as they possess, with confidence and prudence.

A STUDENT'S GUIDE TO LITERATURE

The first problem one encounters in attempting to define the nature and purpose of literature is the ambiguity of the key terms. The word "literature" itself comprises a wide variety of sometimes incompatible meanings. Its etymological origin, the Latin word *littera*, means, like the English word "letter," both a graphic mark representing a sound or a missive or written communication. *Litteratura* in Latin, like "literature" in English and the corresponding cognate words in the various European ver nacular tongues, had as its most important sense those writings which constitute the elements of liberal learning. Hence a *litteratus* was a man notable for knowledge and cultivation. This notion is the basis for the English phrase "a man of letters." "Literature" as a term for written works of art—what Wellek and Warren call "the literary work of art" —is, however, a nineteenth-century development. The older generic term was "poetry," but today this word is applied almost exclusively to works written in verse rather than prose; that is, poetry deploys language measured off in metrical "feet," or at least divided into free verse lines. Hence, for much of this century, English departments have offered introductory courses and patronized introductory anthologies to "Literature," divided into units on "Poetry," "Fiction," and "Drama."

Although it was generally rejected as a substantial distinction by ancient and Renaissance criticism, the force of the prose/verse distinction has strengthened over the past two to three centuries because of the rise of prose fiction, which has taken over the business of telling stories and confined verse almost exclusively to lyrical and satirical modes. Narrative verse is rarely written now, and contemporary verse drama tends to have an air of artificiality. So far as I know, no one has written scientific exposition in verse since Erasmus Darwin (grandfather of the more famous Charles) published *The Botanic Garden* in heroic couplets late in the eighteenth century. Hence it makes sense in the twentieth century to regard short to moderate length lyrical, reflective, or satirical *poetry* as a particular kind of literature as distinguished from fiction and *drama*, which tell stories through narration and theatrical representation.[1] My own practice will be to alternate the terms "poetry" and "literature"; the latter is the more common usage today, while the former will serve as a reminder that it is *imaginative* literature that is under discussion.

The account of literature given here will rest upon the

---

[1] There are, to be sure, twentieth-century poems that are quite long, but no one, I think, has ever found a coherent story in Ezra Pound's *Cantos* or David Jones's *Anathémata*.

ancient assumption of Plato and Aristotle that the essence of literature, or poetry, is **mimesis**; that is, the **imitation** or **representation** of reality or the human experience of reality. Whether this fundamental element of literature is cause for the disapproval of Socrates in Plato's *Republic* or for Aristotle's approval in the *Poetics*, the mimetic function of literature is generally taken for granted by classical thinkers. This basic fact is difficult to demonstrate precisely because it is the self-evident intuition of all mankind: when a friend has just read a new novel or seen a new movie, our first question is, "What is it about?" We expect, above all, a description of the characters as they act and relate to one another. We wish to know what this particular work shows us about how life is lived. As a representation of reality, a work of literature is an object *made* by an author. Our word "poet" comes from the Greek verb *poieo*, "to make." Our word "fiction" is similarly derived from the Latin *Ingo*, "to fashion," "to feign," or "to form." All of these terms suggest

---

Homer, it is now generally agreed in accordance with ancient tradition, composed the *Iliad* and the *Odyssey* around 700 B.C., drawing upon an oral tradition of poetic material handed down by memory. Probably a native of Chios or Smyrna, he may well have been blind (heroic oral poetry would be an obvious choice of career for a blind man in a warrior society), and some contemporary may well have written the poems down in the letters that the Greeks were just been in the process of adopting from the Phoenicians.

that at the center of literature or poetry is a verbal creation, made or formed to imitate or feign some aspect of the human experience of life.

To a remarkable extent, the categories devised by Aristotle in the *Poetics* to analyze tragedy are applicable, *mutatis mutandis*, to all the genres of literature. The **plot** *(mythos)* or story or arrangement of incidents is the primary element, because, he maintains, while character makes

---

Virgil (Publius Vergilius Maro, 70–19 B.C.), was born into the landed gentry near Mantua, and, after receiving the standard rhetorical education of the day, he declined to become a pleader in the courts of law and pursued philosophical studies under the Epicurean Siro at Naples. His father's land was expropriated for distribution to veterans of Octavian's army in the aftermath of the Civil Wars, and tradition holds, somewhat implausibly, that *Eclogues* I celebrates the restoration of these lands by the man who would be Virgil's imperial patron as a result of the intercession of the poet's friends. There is no doubt that Virgil enjoyed the friendship, as well as the patronage, of the Emperor's advisor and confidant, Maecenas, who brought him to the attention of his master. Although Virgil was thus a court poet, the grim account of the human cost of Aeneas's quest to lay the foundation of the Roman Empire and the pervasive melancholy of the *Aeneid* suggest that the poem is hardly an uncritical celebration of imperialism. According to Boswell, Dr. Johnson "often used to quote, with great pathos," lines from Virgil's *Georgics* (III.66–68), which sadly recount how wretched man's best days slip through his fingers, and he is undone by sickness, age, labor, and ruthless death. Virgil is propagandist for no political platform.

men what they are, it is action that determines happiness and unhappiness. The second, closely related element is **characterization** (*ethos*), which determines how individuals will act. **Diction** *(lexis)* or language or, best, **style** is the next element; it is closely related to **thought** *(dianoia)* or **themes** or ideas that emerge in the discourse. The final two elements, **spectacle** *(opsis)* and **music** *(melopoiia)* or **song** are, in the strict sense, specific features of ancient Greek tragedy, but even here we can find parallels in other genres. The "special effects" and the "sound track" are obvious corollaries from modern films, but even purely literary genres can provide similarities: the careful evocation of the setting of Thomas Hardy's Wessex novels is indispensable to their effect and import, and "music" emerges both in the style and structure of Henry James's prose fiction and Tennyson's verse.

Because careful attention to these comparatively minor elements—precise, vivid diction, evocative representation of scenes, and compelling speech rhythms—is the key to literary impact, works of nonfiction that are distinguished for beautiful or lively style are often counted as literature and thus survive after their more pragmatic original function has ceased to interest. Lucretius's *De rerum natura* would be at most a footnote in the history of philosophy if it were merely an exposition of Epicureanism; however, its powerful imagery and the spell cast by the melody of its hexameter verse have assured its enduring significance as a poem.

Similarly, many of Emerson's essays furnish a compelling, literary experience of the life of the mind even for readers who regard him as singularly defective as a moralist, and one need not be a highchurch Anglican to be enthralled by the prose of Donne's sermons. There are also works that seem to be on the border of literature and some other discipline from the outset. Plato's dialogues are the indispensable foundation of Western philosophy, but some of the dialogues— the *Symposium*, for instance, and the *Phaedrus* seem to work as effectively as dramatic literature. The interpretation of Saint

---

Horace (Quintus Horatius Flaccus, 65–8 B.C.), son of a freed slave who prospered, came from more modest origins than his friend Virgil. Nonetheless, his father had him well educated at Rome and then Athens, where he was induced to join the army of Brutus, whose defeat and suicide at Philippi are so dramatically rendered by Shakespeare in *Julius Caesar*. With his father's property mostly confiscated upon his return, Horace secured a place in the Roman civil service. His poetry came to the attention of Maecenas, who soon won for him the patronage of the forgiving Emperor Augustus. Horace's disposition is the opposite of his melancholy comrade Virgil. Throughout his poetry—whether in the wry wit of his *Satires* and *Epistles* or the lyrical beauty of his Odes—Horace evinces a tolerant, detached skepticism and good humor. He was pleased to accept the benefactions of Augustus and Maecenas, but he resisted their efforts to involve him in politics or government. Preferring the leisure of the Sabine farm that his poetry made famous, Horace's most important bequest to European poetry is the theme of the superiority of rural retirement to the ambitious life of court or city.

Thomas More's *Utopia* hinges, to a large extent, on whether it is treated as a treatise in political philosophy or a work of literature. This does not mean that the distinction between fiction and nonfiction, between a poem and a treatise, is negligible; it simply means that there is a broad grey area at the border. We know the difference between day and night, but a long period of dusk makes it difficult to say when one ends and the other begins.

At the center of imaginative literature or poetry, then, is *mimesis* or *imitation:* the representation of human life—or more precisely, the representation of human experience. We are naturally curious creatures, but not merely in the manner of cats and monkeys; our specifically *human* curiosity is inspired by our consciousness—our awareness of the world around us and of our selves as situated within it. This self-consciousness necessarily entails a recognition of other selves, other souls. The poet is important because, by expressing himself, he opens up to us the mind and heart of another, and the knowledge of our likeness and difference from others is essential for our self-realization. The individual can only be defined—indeed, can only exist—in relation to other individuals. Thus while literature is the self-expression of the author, it is also the representation of the reader. A uniquely personal vision representing nothing save the bard's own genius would fail to be intelligible as literature; by the same token, a purely subjective reading, which ignores the structural and generic features of a work, which pays no heed to the intention inscribed in its intrinsic verbal substance, would fail to be an interpretation of the work itself. Literature—like the language from which it emerges—presupposes a communal culture, which in turn rests upon a common human nature.

The knowledge of human nature and the human condition that literature yields is the basis of its educational role. A poet or a novelist contributes to the moral and so cial formation of his readers less by providing moral precepts or lessons in citizenship than by shaping the moral imagination. Literature, then, is less concerned to assert what is right and wrong than to evoke the experience of good and evil. Shakespeare does not tell us that Edmund, in *King Lear*, is evil. Instead, he unfolds the layers of his villain's arrogance and self-pity, of his ambition and envy; and he allows him to make claims upon both our sympathy and fascination. Such is the peril of literature: one may choose to ignore the import of the drama as a whole and accept Edmund's claim to be a victim. A character on a grander scale of wickedness—the Satan of Milton's *Paradise Lost*—is notorious for having attracted the favor of romantically inclined readers from Blake and Shelley to William Empson. But if poetry is more dangerous than precept, it is also more powerful and engaging. The reader or theatrical spectator who has felt the full impact of *King Lear* has a knowledge more profound and moving than the simple proposition that deceit, betrayal, and murder are never justified; he will gain an emotional and imaginative revulsion at evil dressed up in bland excuse and political pretext. He will have an inner resistance to collaboration with the Edmunds he meets in the world, or to complicity with the Edmund who lurks within each of us.

"Poets aim either to teach or delight," is Horace's famous dictum in *The Art of Poetry*, and Sir Philip Sidney

———————————

Ovid (Publius Ovidius Naso, 43 B.C.–A.D. 17), lacked the discretion (or the connections or the luck) of Virgil and Horace, who could maintain both their independence and the favor of the emperor. Ovid's early erotic poetry, its sensuality salted by witty self-mockery, seems designed to provoke respectable opinion. About the time Virgil's posthumous *Aeneid*, with its sombre portrayal of patriotic self-sacrifice, is appearing to universal acclaim, Ovid is suggesting that the seducer of another man's wife, when he breaks down her door, outwits rivals, and engages in a "night attack," is also a soldier in love's war (*Amores I.ix*). This classical version of "Make love, not war!" was bound to infuriate Augustus, whose imperial program demanded a restoration of the patriotism and chastity of the ancient Republic; when Ovid was involved in a scandal at court—possibly involving the Emperor's notoriously promiscuous granddaughter—Augustus banished him for life to the howling wilderness of Pontus, on the Black Sea at the edge of the Empire. Ovid's grand, quasiepic retelling of Greek myth in the *Metamorphoses* and his celebration of Roman religious holidays in the *Fasti* were of no avail. His final poems, the Ex Ponte and the *Tristia*, are versified pleas for clemency that met with stony silence from Augustus and his successor, Tiberius. Rome's gayest and most charming poet died in miserable exile.

refines the saying by suggesting that teaching and delighting are bound up with one another: "But it is that fayning notable images of vertues, vices, or what els, with that delightfull teaching, which must be the right describing note to know a Poet by...." Neither Horace nor Sidney is altogether free of the "sugar-coated-pill" theory of literary teaching; but, as the quotation from the latter suggests, their best instincts tell them that the morality in poetry is built into the poetic essence as such: "the fayning notable images of vertues, vices, or what els" *is* the poetry. As Sidney stresses, the power of literature to teach is bound up with its power to represent the human experience of life, but life as it has meaning for us. "Right Poets," he says, are like "the more excellent" painters, "who, hauing no law but wit, bestow that in cullours vpon you which is fittest for the eye to see: as the constant though lamenting looke of *Lucrecia*, when she punished in her selfe an others fault; wherein he painteth not *Lucrecia* whom he neuer sawe, but painteth the outwarde beauty of such a vertue." Literature moves us by uniting goodness and beauty in our imagination; it seeks truth by means of fiction.

In assessing the representational element in literature, it is important always to bear in mind that, excepting drama, it is all done with words. Imaginative literature puts enormous pressure on language, with the salutary result of expanding, enriching, and refining the resources of that most characteristic yet remarkable of human traits. It is difficult to conceive of men and women without speech; hence we must think of language less as a human achievement than as a necessary condition of humanity. Speech, however, can develop or degenerate: among numerous other factors, the splendor of Shakespearean drama is in part the result of a tremendous growth in the power and subtlety of the En glish language in the course of the fifteenth and sixteenth centuries. But the writing and reading of poetry are a cause of linguistic burgeoning as well as an effect. Poetry is speech at its most intense: it requires all the resources of meaning and expression that a language can provide, but it also contributes to the creation of those resources. It would thus be difficult to determine whether the decline of Latin literature in late antiquity and the early Middle Ages resulted from a loss

---

Dante Alighieri (1265–1321), was born in Florence, but exiled in 1301 as the result of a political vendetta while he was serving on an embassy to the pope in Rome. An idealist in politics as well as love, Dante steadfastly refused to make the admissions or concessions that would win him a reprieve, and so he never set foot in his native city again. *The Divine Comedy* is the work of an exile who knew the bitter taste of another man's bread and the wearying steepness of his stairs (*Paradiso* XVII.58–60). Dante was thus supremely fitted to recognize that life on this earth is exile, our true home in heaven. In Florence's storied Santa Croce Church, which holds the remains of luminaries such as Michelangelo, Machiavelli, Galileo, and Rossini, there is an empty tomb and monument for Dante, who lies buried, still an exile, in Ravenna.

of complexity and refinement in the Latin language, or the language deteriorated because the poetry that was being written became cruder and less imaginative. What can be said with certainty is that the study of literature requires the study of language, and that a knowledge of any language finally depends upon an acquaintance with the literature in which a language finds its most thoughtful and vital articulation. To be able to read critically, reflectively, and confidently requires wide reading in the great literature that has formed the linguistic culture of a society; and eloquent writing requires *a fortiori* a command of the most powerful resources of a language, which are only available, again, in its most important literature.

The interrelationships among literatures of different languages, cultures, and ages define the critical relationship between history and literature. Although a poet is inevitably affected by the social and political setting in which he writes, the crucial context of his work is the history of literature itself. Whatever the personal motives or public pressures that act upon a writer, the definitive goal of his efforts is, recognizably, a work of literature. Swift never actually admits that *A Modest Proposal* is a satire and not an actual scheme for using Irish infants as a foodstuff, and he never confesses that Lemuel Gulliver is a made-up character whose *Travels* were spun out of Swift's own fertile fantasy. Likewise, Thomas More appears to guarantee the authenticity of Raphael Hythlodaeus's account of a distant, perfectly ordered state by introducing himself as an uncomfortable auditor into the text of *Utopia*. Only the most naïve reader, however, would doubt for a moment that these works are fictions, created by their authors to respond to and take their place among the poems and stories of other authors. The relationship of literature to actual history—including an author's own biography—is always important, but always oblique. For this reason, the place of literature in education is unique. It involves a good deal of historical knowledge of persons, places, facts, dates, and the like; but these matters are, finally, ancillary to the study of literature perse, which dwells in the realm of the human spirit. Even as a particular poem is a structure of tension between author and reader, between a unique verbal form and the literary and linguistic

---

Geoffrey Chaucer (C.A. 1340–1400), was born into a family of prosperous wine merchants, but by virtue of good education and innate gifts, he came to be on familiar terms with nobles and kings. As a young man he was a courtly lover and a soldier, taken prisoner by the French and subsequently ransomed in the Hundred Years' War. In his later years, he worked as a diplomat and a civil servant and enjoyed the patronage of John of Gaunt as well as both Richard II and Henry IV. His masterpiece, *The Canterbury Tales*, is the fruit of a lifetime rich in experience and observation of humanity. The surface tone of the work is a detached, tolerant, and good-humored skepticism, yet there is nothing cynical in Chaucer, whose work bespeaks not only wisdom but an abiding sympathy for his fellow man born of a profound charity.

conventions that constitute its matrix, just so is literature itself (like all creations of the mind) an institution within but not wholly of the flux of human history.

The history of literature is thus best pursued in terms of the emergence, development, and transformation of **genres** or literary "kinds." The difficulty of this approach is that "genre," like "literature" itself, is an ambiguous term. There is more than one principle for dividing up literary works into categories, and the generally recognized genres that have emerged in the course of literary history are not always logically compatible. Most works draw on a variety of generic conventions, and practically no memorable work fits comfortably into the definitions offered by scholars—one of the marks of literary greatness is a testing of the conventional boundaries of the recognized genres. The conventions are not, therefore, irrelevant or unimportant. Even in "realistic" novels, we unconsciously accept impossibly knowledgeable and coherent narrative perspectives because the conventions of prose fiction are part of our literary culture. And it is those innovative authors who challenge or subvert the conventions that most depend upon them. Any reasonably literate person can work out the conventions of the Victorian novel in the course of reading, but it requires a high degree of critical sophistication—a conscious awareness that the usual means of story-telling have been discarded—to respond to the stream-of-consciousness narration of To *the Lighthouse* or the lack of a conventional plot in *Waiting for Godot*.

In the course of Western literary history, genres have developed in terms both of formal features and aspects of tone and content, and the same term can be used to specify either a closely defined literary form or a general theme or subject. Pure examples of specific genres are the exception rather than the rule. For example, much of the poetry of Robert Frost may reasonably be described as "pastoral," but he did not write formal pastorals on the model of Theocritus's *Idylls* or Virgil's *Eclogues* or strict Renaissance imitations like Petrarch's *Bucolicum carmen*. Indeed, many of the greatest literary achievements grow out of an author's reimagining both the generic form and the spiritual vision of his great predecessors: for example, an "epic" novel—a prose narrative on a grand scale, like *Moby-Dick* or *War and Peace*—can be seen as a modernized version of the quest and con.ict motifs of ancient epic as founded by Homer and Virgil. Genre, then, is an indispensable literary concept as it applies both to the form of individual works and to the historical unfolding of literary tradition; however, it would be foolish to bind particular poems, plays, and stories to generic models, as if they were so many beds of Procrustes. One way of regarding a work of literature is to see it as a result of a poet coming to terms with the conventions of his art and the limits of nature, while at the same time, in Sidney's grand phrase, "freely ranging onely within the Zodiack of his owne wit." Or as T S. Eliot says, literature represents a confrontation and convergence of "Tradition and the Individual Talent."

At the fountainhead of Western literature is the **epic**—the story of a hero struggling against the constraints of the human condition. Western literature—and in some measure Western culture and education—begins with the *Iliad* and the *Odyssey*, traditionally ascribed to the blind bard Homer, who probably put the poems in roughly their present form about seven centuries before the birth of Christ. Beginning in Athens and the other Greek city-states at least as early as the fifth century B. C., the epics of Homer have spread throughout the Western world and been a continuous

———————

Miguel de Cervantes (1547–1616), lived a life plagued with misfortune. Heroic service in the Battle of Lepanto (1571), which turned the tide in Christendom's struggle against a growing Turkish threat, cost him his left eye and the use of his left arm. In 1575 he was captured by Barbary pirates and languished five long years in an Algerian prison before being ransomed. He spent the rest of his life eking out a meager living as a writer and minor government functionary. He was more than fifty when he attained his first success with the first part of Don Quixote (1605), and even this work and its glorious second part (1615) brought him little prosperity to match his fame. Cervantes, unlike Virgil and Horace, endured extremely ill fortune in patrons—the noblemen to whom he dedicated the first and second parts of his masterpiece, and who would otherwise be forgotten, were insensible to his genius and ignored him. The most influential work of Western fiction brought its author lasting fame, but no worldly success.

in.uence upon culture, education, and literature even to the present day. Of course the same argument could be made about the opening books of the Bible, especially Genesis and Exodus, attributed to Moses. These books go back more than 1200 years before the birth of Christ, and they are certainly epic in their theme and scope and in the grandeur of their style. The account of the Hebrews' escape from slavery in Egypt and their conquest of the Promised Land, for instance, is an undeniably epic tale. The books of the Bible, however, have been preserved not as poetry, but rather as sacred history and revealed truth. Indeed, the survival of classical literature, with its idolatrous and often unedifying mythology, was possible in a severely Christian world largely because the attitude of the ancient Greeks and Romans toward their gods and the stories about them never involved the rigorous claims of truth that Christians and Jews attach to their Scriptures. Although the influence of the Bible on Western culture is thus as great as that of Homer and all of Greek and Roman literature combined, it is an in.uence of a different order. Until the last two or three centuries, almost no one would have thought of Exodus as "poetry" in the same way as the *Iliad*.

It is the *Iliad*, the tale of the wrath of Achilles in the tenth and final year of the Greek siege of Troy, and its companion piece, the *Odyssey*, which recounts the ten-year quest of the hero Odysseus to return to his homeland, that define the characteristics of the epic for the Western literary tradition. These characteristics will be familiar to most students who have read a few fragments of the *Odyssey* or the *Divine Comedy* or *Paradise Lost* in a literature anthology. *An epic is a poem about a great quest or conflict that involves the des tiny of nations. Its characters are of imposing stature— gods and heroes—its style is grand and dignified, its setting encompasses heaven and earth, and it deploys specific epic devices like the extended Homeric simile and the catalogue of warriors.* And so on. This standard description is certainly unexceptionable as far as it goes, but it leaves out the speed of the narration, the clean simplicity of the style ("grand" must not be allowed to suggest "heavy" or "stodgy"), the vivid humanity of the "heroic" characters, and above all the tight focus of the plot not on the fate of peoples, but on the passionate struggles of individual men and women. The *Iliad* picks up in the tenth year of the war and begins with tawdry quarrels over captive concubines. It ends not with the wooden horse and the sack of Troy, but with the brutal and tragic slaying of Hector and the sure knowledge that his conqueror Achilles will soon follow him to an early grave. The Odyssey likewise begins in medias res in the final year of the hero's quest, and its focus is on his very personal story: a man trying to come home after a war to be reunited with his wife and son. Homer has endured because he has told with surpassing beauty, but also with unflinching moral realism, stories that still resonate in our minds and hearts.

The Western world has produced three other epics that

are essential to a liberal education. Virgil's *Aeneid*, Dante's *Divine Comedy*, and Milton's *Paradise Lost*. Although

William Shakespeare (1564–1616), undoubtedly wrote the plays attributed to him, and no more improbable substitute has been suggested than the current favorite, the feckless seventeenth Earl of Oxford, Edward de Vere. Most great writers are very intelligent, but they are usually not intellectuals, infrequently scholars, and very rarely aristocrats—Lord Byron and Count Tolstoy are in a decided minority. Shakespeare had all the education and experience he needed because he was, in Henry James's phrase, a man "on whom nothing was lost." He was almost certainly reared Catholic at a time of increasing persecution of the old faith on the part of Queen Elizabeth's government. A growing body of evidence suggests that he worked as a school master and journeyman actor in Catholic households in the North of England during the "lost years" of the later 1580s, and this lends some probability to the report (or accusation) by a late seventeenth-century Anglican clergyman that the playwright "died a papist." Shakespeare's plays and poems, especially his mysterious Sonnets (1609), may be safely assumed to grow out of his own experiences, interests, and longings; their actual relationship to his life, however, cannot be determined with any certainty. More than any other poet, Shakespeare created a secondary world of remarkable depth and richness in a theatre fittingly called the Globe. His works, analogous to the great work of creation itself, tell us unerringly that there is a creator behind them, but they reveal almost nothing of his inner being. It is difficult to ascertain how or why the world came into being, yet impossible to imagine it not being, it is difficult to understand how anyone could have created Shakespeare's dramatic world, yet impossible to imagine it not being there.

Homer was the first epic poet, there can be no doubt that Virgil exerted a greater direct influence on the development of the literary tradition. After the gradual disintegration of the Roman Empire, Western Europe was generally ignorant of Greek, and Homer's works were known largely by report. Virgil, however, was read throughout the Middle Ages and exercised an incalculable influence on an enormous variety of writers over the next 2,000 years down to our own day. In contrast to the *Iliad* and the *Odyssey*, the *Aeneid* is a reflective poem about a hero of self-renunciation. A reluctant warrior, "pius Aeneas" always pays reverence to the gods and to his destiny; he always does his duty. But while Virgil celebrates the triumphant origins of the grandeur that will be Rome, he also ruefully acknowledges the bitter anguish that bloody triumph costs. Virgil is so intensely aware of human limitations, so profoundly concerned with the spiritual trials of his hero, that it is no wonder that he was long regarded as half-Christian. That the central epic of the Western literary tradition is full of ambiguity and doubt about conquest and warfare suggests that European culture is less an unthinking exercise in triumphalist hegemony than many surmise.

The place of Virgil in Western literature and civilization is indicated by the next indispensable epic of that tradition: in the *Divine Comedy*, Dante takes the character "Virgil" as his mentor and guide through hell and purgatory during the first two-thirds of the poem. His understanding of literary style and his aspiration are shaped by the poet Virgil, and it is Dante's explicit intention to join Virgil and his classical predecessors in the exclusive circle of culture-defining poets and philosophers. As Homer is taken to be an expression of the Greek heroic age and Virgil of the Roman Empire, so Dante is often read and taught as the embodiment of the medieval worldview, and especially of the Thomistic theological synthesis. Naturally, there is an element of truth in these propositions, but they are still superficial clichés. Dante's *Comedy* is certainly a vivid depiction of many aspects of his world—political, religious, social—and it brings to the fore both the philosophical out look he derived from the thinkers of his era (including Saint Thomas Aquinas) and his bitter personal experience. But the poem is above

---

John Donne (1572–1631), son of Saint Thomas More's great niece and with two Jesuit uncles, was reared as a Catholic recusant ("refuser") in a time of increasing persecution. His bold and witty early love poems, as well as his satires, were a provocation to Protestant respectability in Elizabethan England in the same fashion that Ovid affronted respectable society in Augustan Rome. Donne, whose personae in his love poems often assume the pose of a cynical seducer, threw away all his worldly prospects to elope with the seventeen-year-old daughter of a wealthy country gentleman. After ten years of poverty on the margins of Jacobean society, Donne found a way to reconcile his conscience with membership in the Church of England. He became a clergyman and eventually Dean of St. Paul's Cathedral. His spiritual struggles produced some of the most powerful devotional poetry in English, and his sermons and *Devotions upon Emergent Occasions* are among the glories of English prose.

all a dramatization of a man's self-discovery and quest for salvation—the restoration of that self. His journey involves the confrontation with sin, the experience of penitence, and the glory of reconciliation with God. The terms of the poem are irreducibly Christian, and it is otherwise unintelligible; however, the Christian account of the human situation is sufficiently resonant to adherents of other religions or of no religion at all for Dante's poem to engage their intellects and touch their hearts. In the course of creating in the Tuscan vernacular a style to challenge Virgil's Latin, Dante, with his younger contemporary Petrarch, laid the groundwork of the modern Italian lan guage. In this feat is manifest the intimate and essential relationship between language and literature, which was so significant to Renaissance humanism: by the act of literary creation a language and thus a culture achieves a kind of permanence and ideal realization. As it becomes the Esperanto of the global marketplace, English is showing the same wear and tear and debasement that Latin suffered in the later imperial era. Yet as long as the works of Shakespeare and other great English writers are available, the genius of the language—its responsiveness to the powers of imagination—will remain.

One of the writers who expanded the capacities of the English language is John Milton, author of the last great Western epic. In Milton, as in Dante, the infiuence of Virgil is prominent, and the closest a reader of English can get to the verbal "feel" of the epic hexameters of the *Aeneid* without reading it in Latin is to read the blank verse of *Paradise Lost*. There is no poem in English that better exemplifies the heroic dignity of the grand style, and it is one of the paradoxes of literature that one language can be served so well by bending it to the imperatives of another. It is the measure of Milton's insight and taste that he so unerringly knows exactly how far he can craft English verse to the turns of Latinate diction and syntax in the pursuit of "Things

---

John Milton (1608–74), was a truly learned poet in academic terms, who also traveled widely and was directly involved in the most important political and religious affairs of his day. His major works are, predictably, learned and overtly engaged with the leading issues of his society. The case of Milton shows us the kind of works that the "unlearned" Shakespeare would have produced had he enjoyed the extensive formal education and worldly advantages that disdainers of "the man from Stratford" think he should have had in order to write his plays and sonnets—which in fact are rather popular and earthy in tone and style in contrast to Milton's highly intellectual and scholarly poetry. Milton in fact displays all the perversity of a radical intellectual. His Christmas poem, "On the Morning of Christ's Nativity," virtually ignores the tenderness and affectivity of the manger scene and compares the Baby Jesus to the serpent-strangling infant Hercules in what has been called an "epic Christmas carol." In *Comus* Milton uses the masque—a genre notorious as a pretext for song, dance, sumptuous costumes, and elaborate stage sets—as a vehicle for the exposition of an austere Christian Neoplatonism. Although he was the most important poet of the seventeenth century, Milton devoted his prime middle years to

unattempted yet in Prose or Rhime" (I.16). What Milton does with the thematic substance of epic is another paradox. *Paradise Lost* is, indisputably, a great epic poem of classical style and heroic scale, and yet it not only is the last epic; it may also be said to have finished off the epic. The epic catalogues are mostly lists of fallen angels; the character who is most consistently heroic in word and action and attitude is Satan. Most telling, the only epic battle in the entire poem—the War in Heaven in Book VI—is inconsequential and borders at times on the comic, since none of the angels are able to suffer serious injury, much less death, because of their ethereal substance. Whether Milton is shaping a new vision of the heroic military virtues in terms of inner, spiritual strength or simply rejecting them is a question that scholars

---

political and religious controversy in prose. He won the admiration of Puritans by attacking the liturgy and episcopal hierarchy of the Church of England and lost it by supporting the legalization of divorce (Milton's first marriage, to a seventeen-year-old royalist, was not a happy one). His vigorous defense of the execution of Charles I favorably impressed Cromwell, and the poet served for a number of years in the Lord Protector's Interregnum government. It was only after the Restoration of Charles II and the bishops of the Church of England, when Milton had lost his political hopes, his standing in society, and even his eyesight that he wrote those works on biblical themes in classical form that established him among the world's greatest poets: *Paradise Lost, Paradise Regained*, and *Samson Agonistes*.

continue to debate. In any case, no one in the Western world has been able to write a genuine or unqualified epic since.

Of course there have been numerous important poems that make us think of epics: mock epics, like Dryden's *Mac Flecknoe* and *Absalom and Achitophel* and Pope's *Rape of the Lock* and *Dunciad*, apply epic conventions to the trivial or ridiculous with satiric intent. Romantic epics, like Wordsworth's *Prelude*, Byron's *Childe Harold's Pilgrimage* and *Don Juan*, and Whitman's *Song of Myself* (indeed, the entirety of *Leaves of Grass*) treat the subjective experience of their equivocal heroes in quasiepic terms.

Among the many other ancient long poems that are worth whatever time a student can find for them, mention has been made already of Lucretius's *On the Nature of Things*, but the one indispensable poem among them all is Ovid's *Metamorphoses*, an elaborate retelling of a vast array of Greek myths involving change of form. The most important source

---

John Bunyan (1628–88), was the son of a tinsmith who learned to read and write at a village school. A veteran of the Parliamentary Army during the Civil War, Bunyan joined a Non-conformist church in the 1650s and became a powerful Calvinist preacher. With the restoration of the monarchy and established church in 1660, unlicensed preaching became a crime, and Bunyan was jailed twice, the first time for more than twelve years. The fruit of the second of his imprisonments was *The Pilgrim's Progress*, an allegory of sin and redemption that has appealed to Christians of every persuasion.

of ancient mythology for medieval and Renaissance writers, the *Metamorphoses* is also a unique work of both sparkling sophistication and deep feeling. From the Middle Ages, the essential long work of poetry besides Dante's *Comedy* is

---

Alexander Pope (1688–1744), was born a Roman Catholic in the year of the "Glorious Revolution" that expelled James II, put William III on the throne of England, secured the real sovereignty for Parliament, and ended any hope of a Catholic restoration. Although he consorted with skeptical rationalists and could have enjoyed numerous benefits (e.g., government sinecures) by nominally conforming to the established church, Pope remained true to his faith until his death. He suffered physical as well as religious disabilities: tuberculosis of the spine contracted as a child turned him into a hunchback who never grew much over four feet tall. His chronic ill health produced his famous phrase, "This long disease, my life" (*Epistle to Dr. Arbuthnot*, 132). Pope compensated by becoming the first English author to earn a substantial living by publishing his work. The great success of his translation of the *Iliad* into heroic couplets won him financial independence and retire ment at a modest rural estate. Pope's heroic couplets are often regarded as the poetic expression of Enlightenment rationalism, but, as William Wimsatt decisively demonstrates, rhyme is inherently antirationalist in its juxtapositioning of words on the basis of sound alone. Pope's work has more in common with the poetry of wit of the sixteenth and seventeenth centuries than with the cool skepticism of a Voltaire or Diderot. It is not surprising, therefore, that Pope eschewed the symmetrical formalism of French gardens at his Twickenham estate in favor of the "natural" garden that foreshadowed Romanticism.

Geoffrey Chaucer's *Canterbury Tales*, a collection of comic tales in rhyming couplets. Another remarkable collection of comic tales from the Middle Ages is Giovanni Boccaccio's prose *Decameron*, while Francois Rabelais's *Gargantua and Pantagruel* is an unclassifiable narrative, also in prose, which reflects the mischievous, satirical side of humanist learning also seen in Desiderius Erasmus's *Praise of Folly* and Thomas More's *Utopia*.

Drama is the most social or communal art, because the individual dramatist is altogether dependent upon a host of collaborators to see his work realized, and periods of great drama are understandably rare. There is no dispute about the origin of Western drama in festivals of Dionysius in Athens during the fifth century before the birth of Christ. The plays that have survived from that century—the tragedies of Aeschylus, Sophocles, and Euripides and the comedies of Aristophanes—are the first dramatic works of our tradition and they are arguably the best. Two millennia will pass before anything comparable emerges. It is late in the Renaissance, in the sixteenth and seventeenth centuries, that we come upon the next great wave of theatrical genius in England, France, and Spain. The greatest of these dramatists, certainly the greatest dramatist of all time and possibly the greatest writer, is William Shakespeare. Ideally, every English-speaking student should read all of his plays and poems, but a bare minimum would include the second *Henriad (Richard II, 1 and 2 Henry IV, and Henry V)*, a selection of his mature romantic comedies *(The Merchant of Venice, As You Like It, Twelfth Night)*, his late romance, *The Tempest*, and the greatest of the tragedies: *Romeo and Juliet, Hamlet, Othello, King Lear, Macbeth*, and *Antony and Cleopatra*. Among Shakespeare's English contemporaries, Christopher Marlowe's Dr. *Faustus* and at least a few of Ben Jonson's comedies—for example, *Volpone* and *The Alchemist*—should not be missed. Seventeenth-century France boasts its great triumvirate: the tragedians Corneille and Racine and the comedian Moliere. For Corneille, *Le Cid* is the obvious choice; for Racine, *Andromache* or *Phaedra*; for Moliere, *The Misanthrope* or *Tartuffe*. Spanish Golden-Age drama—the theatre of Cervantes' contemporaries—is an undiscovered treasure for most Americans. Lope de Vega is notable for his prodigious fecundity rather than for any one outstanding play. His younger contemporary, Calderon de la Barca, was also remarkably productive, but his *Life Is a Dream* stands out as perhaps the most powerful and representative baroque drama, while *The Prodigious Magician* is a fascinating version of the Faust legend. Tirso de Molina is known for one extremely powerful and influential play, *The Joker of Seville and the Dinner Guest of Stone*, the earliest theatrical treatment of the Don Juan legend.

Claims may be made for Congreve during the period of the Restoration and for Sheridan, Beaumarchais, and Schiller during the eighteenth century, but the one indis putable dramatic masterpiece since the Renaissance is Goethe's *Faust*. Perhaps more of a dramatic epic than a conventional stage play, *Faust* is probably the greatest single work of Romanticism and of German literature. Its place at the summit of world literature results from its unique blend of stylistic power, dramatic characterization, and philosophical depth and sophistication. Norway's Henrik Ibsen is probably the indispensable dramatist at the beginning of the modern period, but claims could be made for George Bernard Shaw, Bertolt Brecht, Samuel Beckett, Eugene

---

Samuel Johnson (1709–84), was the son of a bookseller whose death in 1731 left his family in poverty before his son could finish his degree at Oxford. Sickly as a child and suffering ill health all his life after years of deprivation and failure, by dint of perseverance and intellectual effort Johnson made himself into the most important English man of letters of the later eighteenth century. He is famous not for a particular great work of literature, but for his overall achievement. He compiled the first dictionary of the English language (1755), was important in the development of the essay and periodical literature, wrote a number of fine poems and an engaging philosophical romance (Rasselas, 1759), collaborated with James Boswell on an important work of travel literature, produced an edition of Shakespeare (1765) that is a landmark in textual editing and interpretive commentary, and laid the foundation for literary biography in The Lives of the Poets (1779–81). Johnson is himself the subject of the greatest biography in English, Boswell's Life of Johnson (1791), which records his wit, wisdom, and deep compassion, often concealed by a gruff exterior.

Ionesco, and Luigi Pirandello.

The dominant literary form of the twentieth century is prose fiction, especially the novel. Although it is by no means the earliest piece of extended prose fiction, the novel may be said to begin with Miguel de Cervantes's *Don Quixote,* written in the early seventeenth century, which defines itself pre cisely as a narrative of naturally explicable events among recognizable characters of everyday life, as opposed to the fantastic exploits and magical escapades of chivalric romance. The central character's generally futile efforts to dwell in the enchanted realm of unfettered fancy are thus instrumental in laying down the *realistic* boundaries of the workaday world in which this *new* form, the novel, typically takes place. The **realism** associated with the novel (and the short story) refers principally to the accurate and convincing evocation of the concrete features of an ordinary world inhabited by recognizable human beings. Even a science fiction novel (as opposed to a work of fantasy) attempts to create a plausibly factual world of the future by extrapolating from current scientific fact and theory. Works of fantasy—from *Beowulf* to *The Faerie Queene* to *The Lord of the Rings*—although they include purely imaginary features (enchanted lakes, dragons, elves) may, nonetheless, be works of powerful *moral* and *spiritual realism.* "Realism" in this latter sense is not, however, a strictly literary term denoting a generic character- istic. The genius of *Don Quixote* lies in its dwelling in the territory of rigorous realism while glancing continuously and longingly at the ideal kingdom of chivalric imagination, thus merging "realism" in its literary and moral senses.

Cervantes's most effective early disciples in the development of the novel as a realist genre were eighteenth century Englishmen, and among their novels the most important are probably Daniel Defoe's *Robinson Crusoe*, Henry Fielding's *Tom Jones*, and Laurence Sterne's *Tristram Shandy*. The great age of the novel is the nineteenth century, and England again boasts a remarkable galaxy of fiction whriters. At the turn of the century Jane Austen created six exquisitely crafted comedies of manners that combine sparkling style, keen irony, and profound moral insight. *Pride and Prejudice* may have been displaced as the most important by *Emma* as the result of a flurry of excellent cinematic

---

Jane Austen (1775–1817), was the daughter of a clergyman of the Church of England. She never married and lived with her family throughout her apparently uneventful life, thus giving the lie to the notion that powerful writers must have wide experience of the world, extensive education, and deal with great events (she never mentions the French Revolution or Napoleon). Writing about the domestic affairs of the rural gentry and village shopkeepers and the marital aspirations of their daughters—"the little bit (two inches wide) of ivory on which I work with so fine a brush as produces little effect after much labor" is her own description of her literary métier Jane Austen captures a vision of ordinary life in society that is unsentimental, ironic, and morally acute. She is, as C. S. Lewis opines, less the mother of Henry James than the niece of Dr. Johnson—a classical mind in the age of Romanticism.

adaptations. *Among* the great victorian novels, Dickens's *David Copperfield, Bleak House,* and *Great Expectations*; Thackeray's *Vanity Fair*; George Eliot's *Middlemarch* and *Mill on the Floss*; and Trollope's *Barchester Towers* and *The Way We Live Now* would seem to be indispensable. In America, Melville's very long *Moby-Dick* and very short *Billy Budd* and Mark Twain's wonderful *Huckleberry Finn* are contemporaneous achievements. Whether Mary Shelley's *Frankenstein* and Nathaniel Hawthorne's *Scarlet Letter* should be classified as novels or gothic romances, they are both books that should not be missed. In France the three great nineteenth-century novelists are Victor Hugo, espe cially for *Les Miserables*, Honore de Balzac, especially for *Pere Goriot*, and Gustave Flaubert, especially for *Madame Bovarie*. But it may be Russia that has the strongest claim to have produced the greatest novels of all time in Leo Tolstoy's *Anna Karenina* and *War and Peace*, Fyodor Dostoyevsky's *Crime and Punishment* and *Brothers Karamazov*, and Ivan Turgenev's *Fathers and Sons*.

In England *Heart of Darkness* and other works by the transplanted Pole, Joseph Conrad, and the late novels of the transplanted American, Henry James, mark the beginning of the twentieth century. The three great names of "high modernist" fiction in the first half of the twentieth century are the Irishman James Joyce, the Frenchman Marcel Proust, and the German Thomas Mann, whose characteristic works, *Ulysses, Remembrance of Things Past,* and *The Magic Moun tain,* respectively, are marked by a preoccupation with alienated subjective consciousness and innovative technical virtuosity that renders their work very difficult—if not inaccessible—to most readers. Joyce's greatest disciple, and one of the greatest novelists of the twentieth century, is William Faulkner in works like *The Sound and the Fury* and *As I Lay Dying*. Yet the most enduring novelist of the early twentieth century, although she lacks academic cachet at the present, may be Sigrid Undset for her multivolume historical works, *Kristin Lavransdatter* and *The Master of Hestviken*. Perhaps no one comes closer to the

---

Samuel Taylor Coleridge (1772–1834), who as a young man was a romantic visionary like his friend Wordsworth, was inspired by the French Revolution and the prospect of the imminent reform of the world. By the time their joint production, *Lyrical Ballads*, appeared in 1798, both men were growing disillusioned by the excesses of the Revolution and both would become increasingly conservative as they grew older. Coleridge's chief contribution to *Lyrical Ballads*, "The Rime of the Ancient Mariner," is among the most remarkable poems in English, but by 1802 he was lamenting the loss of his poetic powers in "Dejection: An Ode," a paradoxically splendid poem on the inability to write poetry. Coleridge's muse was in fact departing, as he slid into despondency over his unhappy marriage to Sarah Fricker and his futile love for Wordsworth's sister-in-law. His life was also bedeviled for many years by addiction to opium, which he began taking for medicinal purposes. He compensated for his failing powers as a poet by becoming the greatest English literary critic since Johnson. *Biographia Literaria* (1817) is his principal theoretical work.

great nineteenth-century Russians in achieving the esssential task of the novelist: to shape a complex, compelling narrative, peopled with convincing characters, and transfigured by profound spiritual significance.

It remains to mention the various genres of shorter po ems: pastorals, satires, epigrams, and the lyric. While the extended narrative works—epic poetry and the novel—involve telling a story about various characters by means of a third-person narration, and drama by means of firstperson dialogue among the characters, the typical shorter poem seems to be the utterance of the poet himself, speaking or singing his own thoughts or feelings. Certainly part of the power of both lyrical and satirical poetry is a sense of intimacy with the poet, of gazing through a window into a creative mind. This preoccupation with the actual, historical poet is, however, an illusion and a distraction from the poetry itself, which is always a fiction, always a representation. Once a poet has set about to *compose* a *poem* (something made), the sense of sincerity and spontaneity are part of the fiction. The poet is playing a role, assuming a voice, creating a persona, even if the poem has been inspired directly by his own *personal* experience. **Persona**, in Latin the mask worn by actors in Roman drama, is the literary term of art for precisely the "mask" or "countenance" the poet puts on and hides behind in order to provide a vehicle for the emotion and insight that must be detached from his own private experience in order to become part of ours. Hence even if someone discovers indisputable evidence of the identity of "Mr. W. H." or proves that there really was a "Dark Lady" in Shakespeare's actual life, these facts about the poet will not settle the interpretation of the poetry of the *Sonnets*.

Since the shorter poetic forms are even more dependent than drama and narrative on nuances of style, it is very difficult to get any sense of the power and beauty of translated lyrics, epigrams, or satires. A few poets are so critical to understanding the development of Western culture, not to say literature, that they must be known, even if only in translation. Among these I would include the surviving lyrics of Sappho, at least a few of the lyrics of Catullus, Ovid's *Amores*, and, above all, Petrarch's sonnets to Laura, which are crucial to our complex and equivocal ideas of sexual love even to this day. Equally important are the *Odes (Carmina)* of Horace, which are one of the principal sources of the idea of the virtuous, modest, but independent country life—a perennial theme in Anglo-American literature; his satires, which supply both the classic image of the inescapable bore and the earliest version of the Country Mouse/City Mouse story; and the satires of Juvenal, which provide an in. uential condemnation of corrupt urban life, the idea of the "Vanity of Human Wishes" (in Dr. Johnson's English adaptation), and the telling satirist's phrase, "savage indignation."

There are many beautiful medieval lyrics, but the great tradition of the English lyric begins with Wyatt and Surrey early in the sixteenth century. Sidney's *Astrophil and Stella*,

Spenser's *Amoretti* (along with his *Epithalamion*—the finest wedding song in any language), and Shakespeare's *Sonnets* are the best English sonnet sequences. The seventeenth century is a treasure trove of lyrical poetry. John Donne's *Songs and Sonets*, his *Satyres, Holy Sonnets*, and *Hymns* are at the top of the list along with the "minor poems" of John Milton. Ben Jonson, Robert Herrick, and Andrew Marvell wrote exquisite lyrics and poems of re. ection; George Herbert's *The Temple* is the finest collection of religious lyrics in English, but Crashaw's *Carmen Deo Nostro* and Henry Vaughan's *Silex Scintillans* are worthy successors. John Dryden, already mentioned as an author of mock epic, pro-

---

Sigrid Undset (1882–1949), was the daughter of a Norwegian archaeologist—a lineage which may in part account for the scrupulous historical accuracy of her treatment of medieval Norway in her historical fiction. Her life was marked by great sorrows, including divorce from her artist husband and the death of one of her sons in battle against the Nazis in the early stages of World War II; her novels give a generally grim view of human sinfulness and the struggle against passion. Undset's depictions of modern life are especially bleak, but her reputation rests on two massive fictional treatments of medieval Norway: the trilogy Kristin Lavransdatter (1920-22), and the tetralogy The Master of Hestviken (1925-27). It was after publication of the former that she was received into the Catholic Church in 1924. Undset was awarded the Nobel Prize (1928) largely on the basis of her historical novels, but her novels in modern settings are also fine works, and she was an excellent essayist on historical, social, and religious themes.

duced two of the best works of religiopolitical satire in *Religio Laici* and the very much underrated *The Hind and the Panther*. Dryden lays the foundation for the tremendous achievement in satire and mock epic of Alexander Pope, who dominates the eighteenth century.

The next great burst of lyrical poetry comes with the Romantic movement: Blake's *Songs of Innocence* and *Songs of Experience*, Coleridge's *Rime of the Ancient Mariner*, and the great odes of Shelley and Keats are among the most memorable of English poems. Wordsworth and Byron, mentioned for their variations on epic, also wrote many fine lyrics. The Victorian successors to the Romantics (most notably Tennyson, Browning, and Matthew Arnold) all produced poems— "Ulysses," "My Last Duchess," and "Dover Beach" immediately spring to mind—that everyone should know. Gerard Manley Hopkins, whose work remained unpublished for almost thirty years after his death, was the greatest English devotional poet since Herbert. The first great American poets come late in the nineteenth century: the reclusive spinster Emily Dickinson and the bumptious, self-educated and self-promoting Walt Whitman. William Butler Yeats may well be the greatest poet to write in English in the twentieth century, and I would add Robert Frost, T S. Eliot, and Wallace Stevens.

All the authors and works that I have mentioned are worth reading, and every educated man and woman will wish to have at least a passing acquaintance with almost all of them; but of course these are works that require (and repay!) close attention and repeated readings. Still, much of one's reading should be for pleasure, and everyone will have a personal interest in certain books and authors because of sympathy with their religious or ethnic attachments or

---

T. S. Eliot (1888–1965), was born in St. Louis of a prominent family descended of early New England settlers, and he could trace his lineage back to the Tudor humanist, Sir Thomas Elyot. He went to England and France to complete work on a Harvard Ph.D. dissertation in philosophy, but eventually abandoned philosophy for poetry and never took his degree, settling permanently in England in 1915. The publica tion of *The Waste Land* in 1922 was one of the seminal events of twentieth-century literature, comparable in its effect to the first performance of Stravinsky's *Rite of Spring* or Picasso's cubist paintings. With this single poem, deploying numerous literary allusions and a dense, difficult stream-of-consciousness technique, Eliot's fame and notoriety were established. He seemed to be mounting a radical attack on the impersonal industrial society from which modern man feels a deep sense of alienation; hence it was a great shock to the intellectual world when, in 1928, having just become a British citizen, Eliot proclaimed himself a classicist in literature, a royalist in politics, and an Anglo-Catholic in religion. Over the succeeding decades he would establish himself as the most important modern literary critic of the English-speaking world and an important conservative commentator on religious and cultural affairs. His efforts to reestablish verse drama in plays like *Murder in the Cathedral* and *The Cocktail Party* have attained, at best, mixed success; however, in works like *Ash Wednesday* and *Four Quartets*, he has offered the finest devotional poetry of our century.

their philosophical or political views. Such interests ought to be pursued, but all one's reading will be enhanced by a sense of the overall contours of Western literature and by an acquaintance with its greatest monuments. Readers, like authors, need to know where they stand in relation to the past in order to live fully in the present; they need to recognize the genius of others in order to realize their own.

BIBLIOGRAPHICAL APPENDIX

This appendix consists of four parts. The first, and most important, is a list in alphabetical order by author that comprises all the important primary works of literature recommended in the text of the essay with a few additional items not mentioned there. The second part discusses some of the most important works that established the Western tradition of literary criticism and scholarship along with some of their most valuable twentieth-century successors. The third part calls attention to some of the more egregious offenders against literature in the post-modern era, and the fourth indicates books that have challenged the postmodernists' current hegemony in academic literary study.

PRIMARY WORKS OF LITERATURE

Penguin Classics and Oxford World's Classics are the most prolific publishers of great works of literature in inexpensive paperback editions, and they usually provide good introductions and notes with reliable translations. Although Penguin and World's Classics are especially good in the area of ancient classical authors, for anyone with even a smattering of Greek and Latin, the Loeb Library editions, published in the United States by Harvard Press, which furnish the original text and a translation on facing pages, are the obvious choice. Norton Critical Editions have for many years published great books in editions featuring reliable texts and translations, along with a useful selection of background materials, both primary and secondary. Recent editions have tended more and more to include secondary essays on the basis of political correctness rather than scholarly or interpretive value (see the Cervantes entry below). Many very fine older Norton editions are, happily, still available.

Aeschylus (525/456 B.C.), *Oresteia* (*Agamemnon; Liba-tion Bearers; Eumenides*). There are numerous fine trans lations of this trilogy, but Paul Roche's is especially commendable.

Aristophanes (CA. 445–ca. 385 B.C.), *Clouds; Frogs; Lysistrata.* Benjamin Bickley Rogers is widely regarded as the translator who sets the standard.

Matthew Arnold (1822–88). A handful of poems, especially "Dover Beach," "The Buried Life," "Empedocles on Etna," and "Thyrsis," are indispensable.

Jane Austen (1775–1817), *Pride and Prejudice; Emma; persuasion.*

Honors de Balzac (1799–1850), *Pere Goriot; Eugenie Grandet.*

Pierre Augustin de Beaumarchais (1732–99), *The Barber of Seville; The Marriage of Figaro.*

Samuel Beckett (1906–89), *Waiting for Godot; Endgame.*

William Blake (1757–1827), *Songs of Innocence; Songs of Experience.* His "prophetical" works are best left to enthusiasts.

Giovanni Boccaccio (1313–75), *Decameron.*

Bertolt Brecht (1898–1956), *Mother Courage and Her Children; The Caucasian Chalk Circle.*

Robert Browning (1812–89), *Men and Women; Dramatis Personae; The Ring and the Book.*

John Bunyan (1628–88), *The Pilgrim's Progress.*

George Gordon, Lord Byron (1788–1824), *Childe Harold's Pilgrimage, Don Juan.*

Calderon de la Barca (1600–81), *Life Is a Dream.*

Catullus (CA. 84–54 B.C.), *Poems.* A superb bilingual edition by Guy Lee is available from World's Classics.

Miguel de Cervantes (1547–1616), *Don Quixote.* Samuel Putnam's translation and notes are still the best. The latest Norton Critical Edition offers a flat and sometimes inaccurate translation by Burton Raffel and a selection of essays emphasizing "gender" and peculiar notions of sexuality.

Geoffrey Chaucer (1340–1400). *The Canterbury Tales* should be read in Middle English. There are numerous good editions that provide adequate help for a diligent student.

Samuel Taylor Coleridge (1772–1834). "The Rime

of the Ancient Mariner," "Christabel," "Kubla Khan," the "conversation" poems, and "Dejection: An Ode" are essential.

William Congreve (1670–1729), *The Way of the World.*

Joseph Conrad (1857–1924), *Lord Jim; Heart of Darkness; Nostromo; Victory.*

Pierre Corneille (1606–84), *Le Cid.*

Richard Crashaw (1612/13–1649). Crashaw is notorious for the extravagant conceits of "The Weeper," but the poems to Saint Teresa and the hymns on the Nativity, the Epiphany, and the Holy Name are among the glories of English devotional verse. George Walton Williams's *Complete Poetry of Richard Crashaw* is a model of fine editing.

Dante Alighieri (1265–1321), *The Divine Comedy.* Allen Mandelbaum's bilingual edition in three inexpensive pa perback volumes with good introduction and notes is a remarkable bargain. Charles Singleton's massive three-volume edition is a monument of learning and critical sophistication. Dorothy Sayers's translation is highly esteemed for its commentary.

Daniel Defoe (1660–1731), *Robinson Crusoe; Moll Flanders.*

Charles Dickens (1812–70), *Bleak House, David Copper. eld, Great Expectations.*

Emily Dickinson (1830–86). Thomas Johnson's edition of the poems is the standard.

John Donne (1572–1631). The old-spelling editions of the poems by C. A. Patrides and John Shawcross both have their virtues. A. J. Smith's modernized edition (Penguin) has especially good notes. The Norton Critical Edition by A. L. Clements is extremely useful. Oxford publishes Anthony Raspa's fine edition of the *Devotions upon Emergent Occasions* in paper, and there is a paper back selection of the sermons by Evelyn Simpson, editor of the ten-volume standard edition.

Fyodor Dostoyevsky (1821–81), *Notes from Underground, Crime and Punishment, The Brothers Karamazov.*

John Dryden (1631–1700), *Absalom and Achitophel; Mac Flecknoe; Religio Laici; The Hind and the Panther.*

George Eliot (Mary Ann Evans, 1819–80), *The Mill on the Floss; Middlemarch.*

T. S. Eliot (1888–1965). *Selected Poems,* in paperback, contains "The Love Song of J.Alfred Prufrock," "Gerontion," "The Hollow Men," *Ash Wednesday, The Waste Land,* and most of the important poems except *Four Quartets,* which is also available in paper, as is *Murder in the Ca thedral,* the most important verse drama.

Ralph Waldo Emerson (1803–1882). *Essays,* first and second series, contain the most important work.

Desiderius Erasmus (1466–1536). The best translation of *Praise of Folly* is by Clarence Miller, but it lacks the useful background material of Robert M. Adams's fine Norton Critical Edition.

Euripides (CA. 485–CA. 406 B.C.), *Alcestis; Bacchae; Hippolytus; Medea.*

William Faulkner (1897–1962), *The Sound and the Fury; As I Lay Dying; Absalom, Absalom!; Light in August.*

Henry Fielding (1707–54), *Joseph Andrews; Tom Jones.*

Gustave Flaubert (1821–80), *Madame Bovary.*

Robert Frost (1874–1963). There are too many fine, characteristically American poems to list. His work is easily accessible and available. His biographers should be ignored.

Johann Wolfgang von Goethe (1749–1832), *Faust*, trans. Louis MacNeice.

Thomas Hardy (1840–1928), *Far from the Madding Crowd, The Return of the Native, Jude the Obscure.*

Nathaniel Hawthorne (1804–1864), *The Scarlet Letter.*

George Herbert (1593–1633), *The Temple.* The most use ful edition for students is by Louis L. Martz, paired with the poems of Henry Vaughan in the Oxford Authors series.

Robert Herrick (1591–1674). *Hesperides* and *Noble Numbers* are charming secular and sacred poems published together in a fine paperback edition by J. Max Patrick.

Homer (FL. CA. 700 B. C.). There are superb modern translations of the *Iliad* and the *Odyssey* by Robert Fagles, Robert Fitzgerald, and Richmond Lattimore, but the Elizabe than translation of the *Iliad* by George Chapman and the eighteenth-century translation by Alexander Pope are both currently available in paperback from Princeton and Penguin, respectively, and are well worth perusal.

Gerard Manley Hopkins (1844–89). The Oxford Authors edition by Catherine Phillips and the Penguin edition by W. H. Gardner are both recommended.

Horace (65–8 B.C.). James Michie's translation of the *Odes* is exceptional, and Palmer Bovie's *Satires and Epistles* is satisfactory. David Ferry's translation of the *Odes* has been met with acclaim.

Victor Hugo (1802–85), *NotreDame of Paris; Les Miserables.*

Henrik Ibsen (1828–1906), *A Doll's House; An Enemy of the People; Hedda Gabler; Peer Gynt.*

Eugene Ionesco (1912–44), *The Bald Soprano; Rhinoceros.*

Henry James (1843–1916), *The Portrait of a Lady; The Wings of the Dove; The Ambassadors; The Golden Bowl.*

Ben Jonson (1572–1637), *Volpone; The Alchemist; The Silent Woman.*

James Joyce (1882–1941), *Dubliners; A Portrait of the Artist as a Young Man; Ulysses.*

John Keats (1795–1821). There are numerous adequate editions. The indispensable poems are the great odes "To a Nightingale," "On a Grecian Urn," and "To Autumn"; the short narrative "The Eve of St. Agnes"; and some of the sonnets, especially "On First Looking into Chapman's Homer."

Lucretius (CA. 94–CA. 55 B.C.), *De rerum natura.*

Thomas Mann (1875–1955), *Tonio Kroger; Death in Venice; The Magic Mountain.*

Christopher Marlowe (1564–1593), *The Jew of Malta; Edward II; Dr. Faustus.*

Andrew Marvell (1621–78). There are excellent paper

back editions of the poems by George deF. Lord and Elizabeth Story Donno. The former is more generous in attributing disputed poems to Marvell.

Herman Melville (1819–91), *Moby-Dick; Bartleby the Scrivener; Billy Budd.*

John Milton (1608–74). The Merritt Hughes one-volume edition of the *Complete Poems and Major Prose* is a tremendous bargain. The Longman edition of the poetry by John Carey and Alistair Fowler offers a remarkably thorough commentary.

Moliere (Jean Baptiste Poquelin, 1622–73). Richard Wilbur's translations of *Tartuffe* and *The Misanthrope* are simply superb.

Saint Thomas More (1478–1535). The most useful edition of *Utopia* for students is the Norton Critical Edition edited and translated by Robert M. Adams. The Penguin edition by Paul Turner attempts injudicious modernization and is nearly unreadable. *A Dialogue of Comfort against Tribulation* is available in paperback from Yale by the editors of the standard Yale edition.

Flannery O'Connor (1925–64), *A Good Man Is Hard to Find; Wise Blood.*

Ovid (43 B.C.–A.D. 17). Rolfe Humphries and Horace Gregory have produced excellent verse translations of the *Metamorphoses,* and Guy Lee's bilingual edition of the *Amores* is fine. Peter Green's translation of the *Erotic Poems* (*Amores, Art of Love,* etc.) is especially valuable for its introduction and commen-tary.

Francis Petrarch (1304–74). Robert M. Durling's *Petrarch's Lyric Poems,* available in paperback from Harvard, provides the original text, lucid prose translations, and a thorough and learned commen-tary. It is the only choice.

Luigi Pirandello (1867–1936), *Six Characters in Search of an Author.*

Alexander Pope (1688–1744). *An Essay on Criticism, The Rape of the Lock, The Dunciad,* and the verse epistles are most important. The one-volume Twickenham Edition, edited by John Butt, is probably the best choice, but there are fine selected volumes edited by scholars like William K. Wimsatt Jr. and Aubrey Williams.

Marcel Proust (1871–1922), *Remembrance of Things Past.*

Francois Rabelais (1494?–1553), *Gargantua and Pantagruel.*

Jean Racine (1639–99), *Phaedra; Andromache.*

Sappho of Lesbos (B. CA. 612 B.C.). The surviving fragments constitute one of the main sources of the love lyric of the Western world.

Friedrich von Schiller (1759–1805). Schiller is most famous for his "Ode to Joy," brilliantly set to music in the final movement of Beethoven's Symphony no. 9. *Wallenstein, Maria Stuart, The Maid of Orleans,* and *Wilhelm Tell* (which inspired Rossi-ni's opera) are important dramas.

William Shakespeare (1564–1616). The best complete one-volume edition is the Riverside, general editor G. B.

Evans. The Norton Shakespeare combines the problematic Oxford text with a wearisome new his toricist commentary. The Arden edition of the plays and poems in individual volumes is rightly regarded as the standard, but the Signet editions are much cheaper and quite satisfactory. The Arden edition of the *Sonnets* by Katherine Duncan-Jones and the Penguin edition by John Kerrigan both feature modernized texts and impressive commentaries. Perhaps the best choice remains Stephen Booth's Yale edition with the editor's modernized version and the 1609 quarto version on facing pages plus an extraordinarily full commentary.

George Bernard Shaw (1856–1950), *Saint Joan; Arms and the Man; Man and Superman; Pygmalion.*

Mary Wollstonecraft Shelley (1797–1851), *Frankenstein.*

Percy Bysshe Shelley (1792–1822), *Prometheus Unbound;* "Ode to the West Wind"; "To a Sky-Lark"; "Adonais."

Richard Sheridan (1751–1816), *The Rivals; The School for Scandal.*

Sir Philip Sidney (1554–86), *Astrophil and Stella; The Countess of Pembroke's Arcadia.*

Edmund Spenser (1552–99). The complete *Faerie Queene* is available in a well-annotated paperback edition edited by Thomas Roche. Among the minor poems, the *Shepheardes Calender* is the most important set of pas toral eclogues of the English Renaissance, and the *Amoretti* and *Epithalamion* the finest celebration of courtship and marriage.

Laurence Sterne (1713–68), *Tristram Shandy.*

Wallace Stevens (1879–1955). *Collected Poems* is available in paperback as well as a generous selection of poetry and prose in *The Palm at the End of the Mind.* The Library of America volume of *Collected Poetry and Prose* is most useful.

Jonathan Swift (1667–745), *A Modest Proposal; Gulliver's Travels; A Tale of a Tub.*

Alfred, Lord Tennyson (1809–92), *In Memoriam;* "Ulysses"; "Tithonus"; "Mariana."

William Makepeace Thackeray (1811–63), *Vanity Fair; Henry Esmond; The Luck of Barry Lyndon.*

Theocritus (CA. 300–CA. 260 B.C.), *Idylls.*

Tirso de Molina (1580–1648), *The Joker of Seville.*

J. R. R. Tolkien (1892–1973), *The Hobbit; The Lord of the Rings.*

Leo Tolstoy (1828–1910), *Anna Karenina; War and Peace.*

Anthony Trollope (1815–82), *Barchester Towers; The Prime Minister; The Way We Live Now.*

Ivan Turgenev (1818–83), *Fathers and Sons.*

Mark Twain (Samuel Clemens, 1835–1910), *Huckleberry Finn.*

Sigrid Undset (1882–1949), *Kristin Lavransdatter; The Master of Hestviken.*

Henry Vaughan (1622–95), *Silex Scintillans.*

Lope de Vega (1562–1635), *The Sheep Well; The Foolish Lady.*

Virgil (70–19 B.C.). Excellent verse translations of

the *Aeneid* by Robert Fitzgerald and Allen Mandelbaum are available in inexpensive paperback editions. Guy Lee's bilingual edition of the *Eclogues* (World's Classics) is perhaps the finest of his superb translations of Latin poets. L. P. Wilkinson has produced a very good trans lation of the *Georgics* with an excellent introduction and commentary (Penguin).

Walt Whitman (1819–92), *Leaves of Grass.*

Virginia Woolf (1882–1941), *Mrs. Dalloway; To the Light house.*

William Wordsworth (1770–1850), *The Prelude;* "Lines Composed a Few Miles above Tintern Abbey"; "Ode: Intimations of Immortality"; "Lucy" poems.

William Butler Yeats (1865–1939), "The Wild Swans at Coole"; "The Second Coming"; "Leda and the Swan"; "Among School Children"; "Sailing to Byzantium"; "Byzantium"; "Under Ben Bulben."

THE CRITICAL AND SCHOLARLY TRADITION

Literary criticism begins with **Plato** (CA. 429– 347 B.C.), whose critique of poetry in the *Ion* and the *Republic* first raises philosophical questions about the form and the ethical and intellectual content of literature. The Symposium and the *Phaedrus* are also especially important for the literary tradition for their discussion of love in its various manifes tations (a perennial theme of poets), and the *Phaedrus* and the *Gorgias* for their critique of rhetoric. **Aristotle's** *Poetics* is the first systematic treatise in literary theory, and it provides a rejoinder to Plato by defending the formal integrity and social utility of poetry. The terms and concepts that Aristotle introduces in the *Poetics* remain at the heart of literary discussion to this day. **Horace's** *Art of Poetry* (actu ally *Epistles* 11.3, "Ad Pisones") is both a fine poem and a wide-ranging discussion of poetic issues. *On the Sublime* by "Longinus" is probably not by Cassius **Longinus**, the third-century A.D. rhetorician, but is more safely dated to the end of the first century A.D.

The great tradition of literary criticism in English begins with **Sir Philip Sidney's** *Apology for Poetry* (or *Defence of*

Poesie), which is an intelligent and original rethinking of the Aristotelian/Platonic tradition as it is filtered through the Italian humanist critics of the six-teenth century. **Ben Jonson's** dramatic prefaces and his *Timber, or Discoveries* (an elaborate commonplace book) makes an important contribution, and **John Dryden** initiates the tradition of the critic as man of letters writing to a polite, sophisticated general audience. In addition to the prefaces to his own works, his *Of Dramatic Poesy: An Essay* is especially important. This style of addressing the educated general reader is continued by **Joseph Addison** (1672–1719) and **Richard Steele** (1672–1729) writing in early examples of the cultivated periodical, the *Tatler* and the *Spectator*. **Alexander Pope's** *Essay on Criticism,* like Horace's *Art of Poetry* on which it is modeled, is both a brilliant poem and a thoughtful discussion of critical issues in literature. **Dr. Samuel Johnson** (1709–84) was the first English lexicographer, a fine poet and essayist, and certainly the greatest critic to write in English. In addition to essays in the *Rambler* and the *Idler*, his best criticism is contained in his great edition of the works of Shakespeare and his *Lives of the Poets*.

The "Preface" composed by **William Wordsworth** for the 1800 edition of *Lyrical Ballads,* a collection of poetry by Wordsworth and Samuel Taylor Coleridge, is the first great English statement of the principles of Romanticism. The greatest Romantic critic, and one of the greatest of all English critics, is **Coleridge** himself. The most important work is *Biographia Literaria,* but there is also very important critical theory scattered through Coleridge's comments on Shakespeare and seventeenth-century poetry. **Shelley's** *Defence of Poetry* is a piece of grand critical rhetoric, and the letters of **John Keats** contain a great deal of provocative literary criticism. Although much maligned by the contemporary postmodernist establishment, **Matthew Arnold,** the dominant man of letters of the Victorian era, remains a literary and cultural critic of great insight and judgment. The literary criticism of **G. K. Chesterton** (1874–1936) is unique for its good humor as well as its good sense.

The twentieth century has seen the ascendancy of academic literary criticism written by professors in universities and colleges as opposed to the criticism of poets and men of letters. Of course, many poets and men of letters have found a haven in universities during our time, and for much of the century the great tradition of English literary criticism was maintained in the academic world. I wish to call attention to a few modern critics whom I believe to be particularly useful for students seeking guidance or models in the interpretation and evaluation of literature. There is no pretense of mentioning every important, influential, or valuable critic here, and the selection is largely determined by my own interests and experience.

Despite the academic bias of the past few generations, **T. S. Eliot,** who is in some ways the most important poet of this century, is certainly its most important critic. *Selected Essays* makes a good sample of his literary thought available, including his single most important essay, "Tradition and the Individual Talent." Eliot's poetry and criticism were a principal in.uence on the American New Criticism, which begins in the Southern Agrarian movement of the 1930s. The poet/critics **John Crowe Ransom** (1888–1974), whose most important work is *The World's Body,* and **Allen Tate** (1899–1979), whose *Essays of Four Decades* has recently been reprinted by ISI (1999), are its most important representatives. A student of Ransom, **Cleanth Brooks** (1906 –93), exerted tremendous influence on the teaching of literature by means of introductory anthologies, like *Understanding Poetry* (with **Robert Penn Warren**, 1905– 89), as well as on literary scholarship in such works as *The Well Wrought Urn.* At Yale, Brooks was joined by a number of kindred spirits including **René Wellek** (1903–95) and *William K. Wimsatt* (1907–75). Wimsatt collaborated with Brooks on *Literary Criticism: A Short History,* which is a remarkably readable and thorough account of its subject in a reasonably compact format. Wimsatt's collections of essays, *The Verbal Icon, Hateful Contraries,* and *The Day of the Leopards* provide the most sophisticated expositions and defenses of the moral and aesthetic principles of the New Criticism available. Wellek's collaboration with **Austin Warren,** *Theory of Literature,* is a brilliant epitome of serious thought about the nature and purpose of literature through the middle of the twentieth century.

Among critics who take various theoretical perspectives while providing illuminating commentary both on the nature of literature in general and on the interpretation of specific works, I would especially recommend **M. H. Abrams** (b. 1912: *The Mirror and the Lamp; Natural Supernatural ism*); **Erich Auerbach** (1892–1975: *Mimesis*); **Wayne Booth** (1921–2005: *The Rhetoric of Irony; The Rhetoric of Fiction*); **C. S. Lewis** (1898–1963: *The Allegory of Love; The Discard-ed Image*); **Maynard Mack** (1920–2001: *Everybody's Shakespeare*); Louis Martz (1915–2002: *The Poetry of Meditation*); and **Lionel Trilling** (*1905–75: The Liberal Imagination; The Opposing Self*) .

THE POSTMODERNIST ASSAULT

The critics mentioned in the preceding section, for all their differences, accept the essential integrity of the literary work of art as a meaningful representation of the reality of moral significance. Since its emergence in the 1960s, a broad movement of reductivism, culminating in the postmodernism of the 1990s, has sought to diminish literature to the status of a mere cultural phenomenon—a product of ideology reducible in theory to its material causes. Although the emergence of postmodernism could be traced back through the entire tortuous history of modern philosophy, with its inception in epistemological doubt, and be hind that into medieval nominalism, the immediate philo sophical impetus comes from the work of the German philosophers **Friedrich Nietzsche** (1844–1900) and **Martin Heidegger** (1889–1976). Nietzsche, who began his career as a brilliantly original classical philologist, is a forerunner of existentialism, and his later work, as he drifted into madness brought on by syphilis, became increasingly nihilist. Heidegger was a brilliant disciple of the phenomenologist Edmund Husserl, but Heidegger came to regard the entire Western tradition, beginning with Plato, as radically flawed and sought to reconstruct it from the ground up after attempting to obliterate the work of all his predecessors. He was also a Nazi until Hitler's defeat and seems to have remained unrepentant until his death—an embarrassing fact that his adherents have difficulty explaining.

The rather dubious heritage of these German philosophers has become a major factor in literature departments in American universities and colleges largely through the efforts of three Frenchmen: **Jacques Derrida** (1930–2004), **Michel Foucault** (1926–84), and **Jacques Lacan** (1901–81). Sometimes **Roland Barthes** (1915–80) is included in this group, but he has not generally been considered as intellectually profound or influential—probably because his writing is usually free of deliberate obscurity and is not without a certain puckish humor. It is important to note that Derrida's academic training was in philosophy, Foucault's in philosophy and psychology, and Lacan's in psychiatry and psychoanalysis; that is, not one of them is a literary scholar, and yet their in. uence among English departments in America and Great Britain is immense. The style of these men is dif.cult by design, and a great deal of the mystique is generated by deploying arcane, coterie jargon, improbable syntax, and acrobatic leaps in logic. With that in mind, the most accessible work by Derrida is *Speech and Phenomena,* which also includes (in the American translation by David Allison) a translation of the important essay, "Writing and Difference." Another important and relatively intelligible essay is "Plato's Pharmacy," which is reprinted in *Dissemination.* Foucault's single most important work is the essay, "What is an Author," reprinted in *The Foucault Reader.* Some sense of what has happened to academic literary study may be perceived by observing that no books are more influential in English departments than Foucault's *History of Sexuality,* his *Discipline and Punish: The Birth of the Prison,* and his *Madness and Civilization.* This preoccupation with sociological his tory suggests that literary scholars have lost their confidence in literature as a valid field of study in itself. Finally, Lacan has presented a radical revision of Freudian psychoanalysis derived from linguistics, and it is in fact the prominence of language, which is thought to determine mind and mental activity (rather than the other way around), that unites the work of these three men, who seemed to have regarded one another with jealousy and suspicion. Lacan's writing is uniformly impenetrable, but the general idea can be gathered from a selection edited by Juliet Mitchell and Jacqueline Rose, *Feminine Sexuality: Jacques Lacan and the école Freudienne.*

Derrida is the father of **deconstruction**, and his preemi nent publicist in this country was **Paul de Man** (1919–83), whose most important work is a heterogeneous collection of essays, *Blindness and Insight.* After his death, de Man was found to have written anti-Semitic articles for a collabora tionist newspaper in Nazi-occupied Belgium when he was a young man (is there a pattern here?). De Man was helped out by **Geoffrey Hartman** (b. 1929) and **J. Hillis Miller** (b. 1928); the fourth member of the Yale "Gang of Four" (how things changed at Yale in barely a decade!) was **Harold Bloom** (b. 1930), who offered a robust, Emersonian version of Freud in works like *The Anxiety of In.uence: A Theory of Poetry and Agon: Towards a Theory of Literary Revisionism.* In recent years he has become what passes for a conservative in contemporary academe by defending Shakespeare and the West ern canon. Lacan is most influential among radical feminists like **Julia Kristeva** (b. 1941) and **Jane Gallop**, who maintain that human nature and "gender roles" are "socially constructed" and have no basis in human nature. The greatest influence by far is now Foucault, whose work is the principal intellectual foundation for **cultural materialism** in Great Britain and the new historicism in America, as well as various offshoots, such as queer theory. New historicism and its various permutations are so pervasive that it is hardly worth attempting to compile a list of the usual suspects—their names are legion. Whenever phrases like "the gendered body as a site of contestation" or "transgressive revisions of the constructed other" appear, it is a sure thing that someone is seeking tenure and promotion. There are also a number of self-designated Marxists still around, like **Terry Eagleton** (b. 1943) in En gland and **Fredric Jameson** (b. 1934) in America. The latter, an unrepentant defender of Mao Zedong and Stalin, is one of the most widely quoted critics in America. Finally, special mention must be made of **Stanley Fish** (b. 1938), who is rather hard to characterize because his positions keep changing. He glories in the accusation of sophistry, and the only constant in his work is a persistent intellectual and moral relativism, which he calls "anti-foundationalism." His only solid commitment is to the power and prestige of the professoriate, which he seems to regard as an end in itself. In fairness, it must be noted that Fish is unusual among contemporary literary critics for the lucidity and liveliness of his style, but the substance of his work is sadly summed up in a recent title: *There's No Such Thing as Free Speech and It's a Good Thing, Too.*

RESPONSES TO POSTMODERNISM

The hegemony (to appropriate a favorite postmodern-ist term) of postmodernism and political correctness in

American higher education in general, and especially in departments of English and foreign languages, is far more total and repressive than is usually acknowledged in the news media or recognized among the general public. Nevertheless, there have been rejoinders. I mention only a few important works that take up the matter from a speciflcally literary perspective: John M. Ellis, *Against Deconstruction* and *Literature Lost: Social Agendas and the Corruption of the Humanities;* David M. Hirsch, *The Deconstruction of Literature: Criti cism After Auschwitz;* David Lehman, *Signs of the Times: Deconstruction and the Fall of Paul de Man;* Stanley Stewart, *Renaissance Talk: Ordinary Language and the Mystique of Critical Problems;* René Wellek, *The Attack on Literature and Other Essays;* and R. V. Young, *At War with the Word: Literary Theory and Liberal Education* (published by ISI).

A STUDENT'S GUIDE TO CLASSICS

INTRODUCTION

Politics, philosophy, *history, epic, poetry, comedy, trag-edy, rhetoric, democracy, aesthetics, science, liberty, senate, republic, judiciary, president, legislature*—the terms included in this brief but impressive list have two things in common: first, their referents constitute much of the political, intellectual, and cultural infrastructure of Western civilization; second, they all derive from ancient Greek and Latin.

Classics is the discipline that studies the language, literature, history, and civilizations of ancient Greece and Rome, two cultures that bequeathed to the West the greater part of its intellectual, political, and artistic heritage. For centuries Western education comprised the study of Greek and Latin and their surviving literary monuments. A familiarity with classics provided an understanding of the roots of Western culture, the key ideals, ideas, characters, stories, images, categories, and concepts that in turn made up a liberal education, or the training of the mind to exercise the independent, critical awareness necessary for a free citizen in a free republic.

Times of course have changed, and the study of Greek and Latin no longer occupies the central place it once held in the curriculum. Classics today is a small, shrinking university discipline kept alive, where it can be afforded, more because of prestige and tradition than because of a recognition of its central role in liberal education and in teaching the foundations of Western civilization. Yet at a time when Western civilization and its values are under assault, the need for classics is as urgent today as it was in the past. And people are still interested in antiquity: translations of classical texts continue to sell well, and popular films, *Gladiator* for instance, testify to an enduring fascination with the ancient Greeks and Romans. I hope that this brief introduction to classics will encourage students to study in more depth what Thomas Jefferson called a "sublime luxury," the ancient Greek and Latin languages and literatures.

WHAT IS CLASSICS?

The discipline of classics actually is made up of several different areas of study, all linked by a grounding in the Greek and Latin languages, the study of which is called "philology." The first skill a classics student must learn is to read Greek and Latin, which means mastering their vocabulary, grammar, syntax, and morphology. [1] The study of these languages, moreover, usually proceeds through sentences adapted or taken whole from Greek and Roman authors.

Right from the start, then, classics students are learning about the great writers and works of antiquity, rather than learning how to ask for directions to the train station or the museum. Thus, even the technical study of Greek and Latin vocabulary and grammar exposes the student to some of the greatest literature, writers, and ideas in history. Here is an important difference between classics and other disciplines in the humanities: to a much greater degree classics teaches languages in a way that also introduces students

---

[1] Latin and Greek are inflected languages, which means that nouns, pronouns, and adjectives change their form to show their grammatical function in a sentence. The term *morphology* refers to the study of these forms.

to the culture, history, philosophy, and literature of Greece and Rome. But the first step remains learning the languages themselves, so that students eventually can read Greek and Latin masterpieces in their original languages.

After learning basic grammar, students begin to read ancient authors and decide in which specific area of classics they wish to concentrate. But no matter where students eventually focus, most will have first read a wide range of ancient texts in literature, history, and philosophy. This is another advantage of classics: since it is grounded in languages, students are compelled to become broadly educated in the whole culture of ancient Greece or Rome rather than just in some narrow subspecialty. Moreover, the habits of analysis and close reading required to understand the ancient languages often carry over into other areas, lessening (but not alas eliminating) the chance that students will be attracted to, or will themselves put forth, subjective or ideologically slanted interpretations. For in the end, no matter what ideological axe you want to grind, the Greek and Latin have to be accurately read and correctly translated, and this empirical, concrete procedure makes it difficult to get away with fuzzy or interested readings.

The possible areas of concentration in classics include the whole gamut of the humanities and social sciences: history (including religious, social, and intellectual history), philosophy, art (including vases, mosaics, and sculpture), architecture, literary criticism (including metrics and poetics), grammar, rhetoric, archaeology, geography, political science, and the histories of science, medicine, engineering, war, mathematics, and geometry. Moreover, classics is a fundamental discipline for those interested in the history of Christianity, the formation and transmission of the text of the NewTestament, and the early Christian theologians and their doctrines (*patristics*).

In addition to these concentrations there are more technical foundational disciplines:

Epigraphy. This is the study of inscriptions engraved on stone, pottery, and sometimes wood (coins are the concern of *numismatics*). Thousands of inscriptions from the ancient world have survived, some intact, others badly mutilated. Once an inscription is discovered, the epigraphist must clean and decipher it. This process can be very difficult, not just because of the often-deteriorated condition of the stone but also because usually words are not separated and there are no small letters. Also, over time the style of some letters changes or letters pick up decorative flourishes. Inscriptions are valuable for historians of all sorts, whether social, political, religious, legal, or literary, since inscriptions cover a wide range of subject matter, from political decrees to expressions of affection for a dead spouse or child.

A fascinating example of epigraphical sleuthing involves the Colosseum in Rome. An inscription still visible today concerning repairs made in the fifth century A.D. is covered with holes in which were once anchored the metal letters of an earlier inscription. In 1995 Géza Alföldy of Heidelberg reconstructed the original inscription by analyzing the hole patterns. The reconstructed inscription dated to the time of the emperor Vespasian and specifically to the completion of a phase of construction of the Colosseum around A.D. 79. What we learn from this inscription is that the Colosseum was built "from the spoils" of a war; the only war that could have provided the necessary riches was the Jewish Revolt of A.D. 66–70, which ended with the destruction of the Temple and the removal of all its treasures. In other words, the plundered treasures of the Temple in Jerusalem financed the building of the Colosseum.

Papyrology. Ancient writing was predominantly recorded on papyrus, a kind of paper made from a reed that grows mainly in Egypt. Papyrus deteriorates in damp climates, but the arid climes of Egypt and the Middle East, where many Greeks and then Romans lived for centuries, have allowed many papyrus documents to survive. Papyrology is the study of writing on papyrus and also fragments of pottery (*ostraca*) and wooden tablets, if discovered at the same site. Up to now about thirty thousand papyrus texts have been published, and many more remain in collections around the world. A papyrologist must decipher various styles of handwriting and then transcribe the writing, accounting for errors, misspellings, etc. A papyrus document is frequently damaged, with holes or torn-off sections, and so the text must be filled in with conjectures or simply left incomplete. Many great works of ancient Greek literature have survived only on papyrus. These include portions of several comedies by Menander, significant extracts from prose narratives, and philosophical works like the fourth-century B.C. *Constitution of Athens*—a discussion of Athenian government—along with numerous social documents such as letters, edicts, petitions, contracts, and receipts. Like epigraphists, papyrologists provide original sources for historians of literature, philosophy, politics, law, religion, and daily life.

A subdiscipline of papyrology is *paleography*, the study of how words and letters are written on papyrus. Paleography concerns the reading of ancient scripts and the history of their development and changes, which helps in dating documents, as well as the study of materials used in writing such as papyrus and inks.

Textual Criticism. Textual critics try to establish as correct a version of an ancient text as possible based on all surviving versions, including manuscripts, quotations in other authors, and fragments found on papyrus or ostraca. Most versions of ancient texts are the result of copies of copies over generations, and so errors by scribes frequently creep in. The modern textual critic must weigh all the surviving versions, determine which version is more reliable, reconstruct omissions, identify and correct scribal errors, and detect inconsistencies of authorial style, meter, or genre, all in an attempt to provide a text as close to the original as possible. The typical Greek or Latin text published today will provide at the bottom of each page a "critical apparatus," a list of all the variants and corrections ("emendations").

Knowledge of textual variants frequently is necessary when interpreting ancient literature. For example, a poem by the Roman poet Catullus (who is discussed below) is addressed to his friend Caelius and concerns a woman called Lesbia, with whom Catullus had a passionate affair but who now is seeing Caelius. In one variant of the text, he calls her "*our* Lesbia," which suggests that Caelius and Catullus are both seeing Lesbia. In the other variant, he calls her "*your* Lesbia," which implies that Catullus is through with her. One's interpretation of this poem and the speaker's attitude to Lesbia will necessarily be influenced by which variant is followed.

It should be obvious that all these technical disciplines overlap somewhat and interconnect very closely. Most classicists have a basic knowledge of all these skills and will call on all or many of them when working with specific ancient texts or areas of research. Someone interested in the Colosseum, for example, will need to be knowledgeable about architecture, engineering, and epigraphy, but also will have to be familiar with the texts and manuscript traditions of works such as Martial's description of the opening games held in the Colosseum, or Suetonius's *Lives of the Caesars.*

More importantly, however, the scholars doing this technical work provide the foundational material—especially the
texts—upon which every classical scholar depends whether
he or she is studying history, art, literary criticism, philosophy, or social history.

The primary experience of most people with the field
of classics, however, will come with texts, the great surviving masterpieces that have influenced Western civilization
for roughly twenty-five hundred years. And that experience
in turn will most likely be with translations. Thus, the rest
of this guide will focus on written texts, organized by genre.
This approach means that whole important areas of ancient
culture, particularly art and architecture, must regretfully be
omitted. For more on ancient philosophy, the reader should
consult Ralph M. McInerny's volume in this series.

A few other points should be kept in mind. First, while
today we experience literature mostly by reading books silently by ourselves, in the ancient world literature was much
more an oral and public experience. Thus, literature was
necessarily social and political, rather than just a private taste
or pastime. In other words, literature was taken much more
seriously, its moral, political, and social implications more
clearly accepted and recognized.

Second, we possess only a fraction of all the ancient
Greek and Latin literature that once existed, and much of
what we do have exists only in fragmentary form. To see
how much has been lost, consider tragedy. We have thirty-

three complete Greek plays from three playwrights. But in roughly a century of tragic performances (about 500–400 B.C.) there were probably a thousand plays produced, written by scores of poets. They exist now only as names and snippets of text, sometimes a mere few words long. Our generalizations about ancient literature, then, must always recognize that they apply in the main only to those works that have survived.

EPIC

The earliest surviving literature of the West can be found in the two epics attributed to Homer (c. 750 B.C.) the *Iliad* and the *Odyssey*. A continuing scholarly question (the "Homeric question") centers on whether an actual person named Homer ever existed and composed the poems, or whether Homer is a fiction, the poems actually being a compilation from the oral epic tradition put together by several editors. Today most scholars attribute the poems to one or perhaps two authors.

The *Iliad* and the *Odyssey* are written in dactylic hexameters, a metrical pattern consisting of six feet of dactyls (a long syllable followed by two short ones) or spondees (two

---

Homer (c. 750 B.C.) lived in the eighth century B.C., but we have very little reliable information about him. References in his poems suggest that he had knowledge of the eastern Aegean, and ancient testimony puts his home in Ionia, the Greek islands and cities on the coast of modern Turkey. The island of Chios or the city of Smyrna are his likeliest birthplaces. Everything else repeated about Homer—for example, that he was blind—is fanciful conjecture.

long syllables), with the fifth foot always a dactyl, and the sixth foot consisting of two syllables, the last either long or short. Originally epic was performed by a bard who had memorized thousands of traditional "formulae," whole lines or set phrases such as "long-haired Achaians（Greeks）" or "rosy-fingered dawn," which he then combined into a coherent story as he was performing. How old the oral epic tradition was by the time Homer composed his poems, whether Homer himself knew how to write or dictated to a scribe, and how much of his epics is traditional and how much invented by Homer himself are all fascinating but impossible-to-answer questions.

The subject matter of epic comprises the adventures, values, and experiences of aristocratic warriors who live in a world frequented by the gods, with whom they interact. Homer's epics are concerned with the period of the Trojan War and its aftermath (the hero's return home or *nostos*), i.e., the twelfth century B.C. In the modern era, archaeological discoveries have indeed confirmed that there once existed a civilization, called Mycenaean (after its most important ruins, discovered at Mycenae in central Greece) that resembled in many respects, particularly in its material culture, the world described by Homer. Yet thematically, Homer's epics reflect the period of the ninth to eighth century B.C., when the power of aristocratic clans was being challenged by the rise of the city-states and consensual governments.

The *Iliad*, the longer and probably the earlier of the two Homeric epics, covers a few weeks in the tenth year of the fighting at Troy. It focuses on the character of Achilles, the "best of the Achaians," who becomes enraged after a quarrel with Agamemnon, the leader of the Greek expedition and the brother of Menelaus, whose wife Helen ran off with the Trojan Paris and started the war. Homer traces the effects of Achilles' wrath, which include the death of his best friend Patroclus and the Trojan champion Hector, whose death at Achilles' hands signals the fall of Troy.

In the course of telling this story Homer brilliantly reveals the destructive effects of the aristocratic hero's code of honor and vengeance, which in the end sacrifices the community to the hero's personal quest for glory. Homer shows us that a political community cannot exist when ideals are based on personal honor achieved through violence, that our humanity depends on the "ties that bind," or our obligations to other humans, obligations that the hero, by contrast, will sacrifice to achieve glory.

The *Odyssey* tells of the hero Odysseus's adventures on his return home after the fall of Troy. It is a more accessible story than the *Iliad*, filled with fabulous locales, seductive temptresses, and fearsome monsters. But the *Odyssey* also movingly details the effects on the home front of a warrior's prolonged absence. Odysseus is a much more attractive character than the brooding, egocentric idealist Achilles. For one thing Odysseus is older, with a wife and son, and he displays a practical realism and an acceptance of those tragic limitations of life against which Achilles chafes.

Besides the wily Odysseus, the *Odyssey* contains several remarkable female characters, particularly Odysseus's wife Penelope, whose tricky ways are the equal of her husband's. The marriage of Penelope and Odysseus, based on similarities of character, virtues, and values, demonstrates the central role social institutions play in making human identity and a stable social order possible. The natural world is a harsh and dangerous place, but humans can flourish because they have minds like Odysseus's that can think up various contrivances that allow life to be successfully navigated, and also because they live in communities whose shared values, institutions, and codes lessen the destructive effects of nature's forces and our own equally destructive appetites and passions.

In both epics Homer describes an impressive depth and range of human behavior and motivation. He also recognizes the contradictions and complexities of the soul and the tragic limitations of human existence. Finally, Homer is a fabulous storyteller whose diction, similes, imagery, precise and vivid description of action, and economy of narrative are still fresh and entertaining after twenty-seven hundred years.

After Homer other epics were composed on various subjects, including the Trojan War and its origins, the wars fought over the city of Thebes by Oedipus's sons, and the return home of various Greek heroes. The collection of these stories is called the "Epic Cycle," and it has survived only in fragments and later summaries. In the third century A.D. **Quintus of Smyrna** (years of birth and death unknown) picked up where Homer left off in the *Iliad* to tell the story of Achilles' death, the Trojan horse, and the sack of Troy, among other adventures. Another important collection of hexameter poetry once attributed to Homer and written in the epic style comprises the "Homeric Hymns," which date from the eighth to the sixth centuries B.C. These are thirty-three poems of various lengths describing the adventures and attributes of the gods. The most interesting are the second, which tells the story of Demeter and her daughter Persephone, who is kidnapped by Hades, king of the underworld, and the fifth, which describes Aphrodite's liaison with the mortal Anchises.

Among the Greeks, Homer's literary and cultural authority was similar to that of Shakespeare among the English-speaking peoples—he was a master impossible to imitate. Yet in the early third century B.C. **Apollonius of Rhodes** (years of birth and death also unknown) published amidst much controversy the *Argonautica* (c. 270–45 B.C.), a hexameter poem about the voyage of Jason and the Argonauts in search of the Golden Fleece. The *Argonautica* is on one level a reworking of Homer, repeating many of epic's conventions and stylistic elements, such as the "extended simile," a detailed comparison that goes on for several lines. Yet at the same time the *Argonautica* reflects more contemporary (for Apollonius) concerns, such as the psychology of sexual passion, magic and fantasy, science and geography, and a learned interest in the origins of cult and ritual. Apollonius's self-consciousness about his poem's relationship to a venerated literary tradition is part of the work's appeal and interest.

The *Argonautica* was very popular among the Romans, and its influence can be seen in the *Aeneid* of **Virgil** (70–19 B.C.). Before Virgil, the *Annales* (c. 169 B.C.) of **Ennius** (239–169 B.C.) had used Latin hexameters to portray Roman history as a Homeric epic, but only fragments of the

---

Virgil (Publius Vergilius Maro, 70–19 B.C.) came from a village near Mantua and was educated in Milan, which suggests that his family was fairly wealthy. He lived for a while in Naples as a follower of the Greek philosopher Epicurus, who counseled retreat from the world into a community of like-minded friends. A long tradition has Virgil's father's land confiscated by Octavian and Marc Antony as part of a general proscription of land to pay off their legions in 40 B.C. But this biographical detail, along with the restoration of the land by Octavian, most likely derives from a crude biographical reading of the poet's first and ninth *Eclogues*, which mention the confiscations. Sometime after the *Eclogues* Virgil entered the circle of Maecenas, Octavian's friend who doled out largesse to poets. He quickly became one of the most celebrated (and richest) of Roman poets and was mentioned several times by other poets, including Horace, who praised his "tenderness and charm," and Propertius. Virgil was on his way to Greece when he caught a fever and died in Brundisium; his masterwork, the *Aeneid*, was nearly complete at the time (there is no evidence to support the story that he wanted his friends to burn the manuscript). He was buried in Naples.

Annales have survived (Ennius also was inspired by the traditional Roman practice of making a yearly public record of events, which was called the *annales maximi*). Virgil's *Aeneid*, however, was for centuries arguably the most influential work of classical literature in the West (Homer's epics were lost to Europe for centuries). The *Aeneid* tells the story of "pious Aeneas," the Trojan who flees the fall of Troy to found the city of Rome, experiencing along the way Odyssean adventures and then having to fight Iliadic battles with the Latins once he reaches Italy. But the *Aeneid* is much more than just a Romanization of Homer.

Combining the Ennean tradition of epic history with a complex literary conversation with Homer, Apollonius of Rhodes, and Greek tragedians like Euripides, Virgil created a masterpiece that examines the possibilities of order on the divine, natural, psychological, artistic, ethical, and political levels. No mere propagandist for the emperor Augustus and no mere imitator of Homer, as he is often mischaracterized, Virgil recognizes the necessity of order, including the political, yet at the same time he acknowledges the terrible price that often must be paid to achieve that order. He sees a cosmos riven from top to bottom by the intimate interplay of order and chaos, a vast conflict in which struggling mortals have a role to play and a burden to bear, often at great personal cost. This combination of optimism and pessimism, hope and despair, idealism and grim realism gives the *Aeneid* its distinct character. At the same time, the *Aeneid* is a virtuoso performance of poetic skill and craft at every level, from its memorable characters and vivid descriptions to its chiseled lines that for a thousand years were the common cultural possessions of every educated person.

Another influential Latin work usually classified as an epic, since it is written in dactylic hexameters, is the *Metamorphoses* (c. A.D. 8) of **Ovid** (43 B.C.–A.D. 17). But the twelve books of Ovid's poem do not address the usual epic subjects of warrior heroism and battle. Instead, starting with the creation of the world and ending with Julius Caesar's transformation into a god, Ovid intricately interlocks scores of short tales whose common thread is change of bodily

---

Ovid (Publius Ovidius Naso, 43 B.C.–A.D. 17) came from the Abruzzi, or the "heel" of Italy. His father was descended from an old equestrian or "knightly" family. Ovid went to Rome for his education and toured Greece, as was usual for a young man of his social class. After some minor posts in the judiciary, he devoted his life to poetry. At the height of his fame Augustus banished him from Rome to the dreary Black Sea city of Tomis. Ovid mentions two "offenses" that led to his exile: a "poem" and a "mistake." The poem is his "Art of Love," a witty parody of advice manuals on how to carry on an adulterous affair, the sort of thing that countered Augustus's attempt to restore the old Roman morality. As for the mistake, it probably involved some scandal, inadvertently witnessed by Ovid, that concerned the royal house: the poet refers to the myth of Actaeon, a hunter who accidentally saw the virgin goddess Diana naked and was torn apart by his own dogs. Ovid died in Tomis, leaving behind a daughter and two grandchildren as well as his wife, who had stayed in Rome.

form. Well-known stories include that of the famous singer Orpheus and his bride Eurydice, whom the singer descends into Hell to rescue, and Arachne, who challenged the goddess Minerva to a weaving contest and ended up being turned into a spider. Along the way Ovid self-consciously engages a wide range of Greek and Roman writing and myth, telling his tales with a keen eye for narrative and visual detail that anticipates at times the realist novel. The *Metamorphoses* was an important influence on Renaissance literature, its tales providing the subjects for numerous paintings, sculptures, and literary works. Shakespeare knew it in Arthur Golding's translation.

After Virgil no epics survive that reach the level of poetic and philosophical sophistication of the *Aeneid*. **Statius's** (first century A.D.) *Thebaid*, about the war between Oedipus's sons for the rule of Thebes, was popular in the Middle Ages and the Renaissance, no doubt partly because of a tradition that Saint Paul had converted Statius to Christianity. Another influential epic was the *Bellum civile* or *Pharsalia* (*The Civil War*) of **Lucan** (A.D. 39–65), which detailed in epic style the destruction of the Roman Republic and the loss of freedom that followed the wars between Julius Caesar and Pompey in 48 B.C. In the eighteenth century Lucan was a favorite of champions of republicanism, particularly for his portrait of Cato of Utica (95–46 B.C.). Cato committed suicide rather than submit to Caesar, and so became the emblem of the principled republican who prefers freedom to tyranny.

POETRY

A rich variety of poetry has survived from ancient Greece and Rome, spanning over a thousand years and a wide range of genres and meters. One of the oldest kinds is **didactic** poetry, or poetry that teaches. **Hesiod** (c. 700 B.C.) is often categorized as an epic poet, since he writes in the hexameters and style of Homer. His subject matter, however, is very different.

Hesiod's *Theogony* describes the creation of the cosmos and the birth and genealogies of the gods; especially important is the story of Prometheus, who steals fire from heaven and saves the race of mortals from extinction. The *Works and Days*, also written in hexameters, is a hodgepodge of maxims, proverbs, fables, parables, and myths. A moral

---

Hesiod (c. 700 B.C.) was a near contemporary of Homer. His poems give us some biographical information: that his father gave up being a merchant and moved to Boeotia, the region northwest of Athens; that he once won a tripod in a singing contest; and that he was swindled by his brother Perses, with the collusion of local aristocrats, out of part of his inheritance. His poems suggest that he held the values and worldview of the small farmer who distrusts equally the city and the nobility.

treatise on the importance of hard work and the dangers of idleness, the poem is addressed to the poet's brother Persis, who apparently cheated Hesiod out of some of his inheritance and then squandered it. In addition, the *Works and Days* contains much practical knowledge concerning farming and sailing, with an almanac of lucky and unlucky days. Particularly noteworthy are the myth of Pandora, the first woman (whose curiosity unleashes evil on mankind); another version of the Prometheus story; and the myth of the Five Ages, which starts with a paradisiacal Golden Age and then degenerates into the wicked present, the Iron Age of suffering, hard work, disease, and moral decay.

Moral and philosophical instruction remained an important topic of didactic poetry after Hesiod. Philosophers such as **Empedocles** (c. 492–432 B.C.) and **Parmenides** (c. 450 B.C.) set out their ideas in poems that addressed issues such as how the world works (physics), the nature of existence or being (ontology), and the means of gaining knowledge (epistemology). Later during the Hellenistic period (c. 300–100 B.C.) more specialized topics turn up in didactic poetry, such as **Nicander's** (c. 130 B.C.) work on snakes, spiders, and poisonous insects (*Theriaca*), his treatise on poisons (*Alexipharmaca*), and **Aratus's** (c. 315 B.C.–c. 240 B.C.) *Phaenomena*, which concerns the constellations. The *Phaenomena* was very popular in the ancient world and was translated into Arabic.

The **lyric** genre of poetry comprised poems that were

sung to the accompaniment of a lyre; this poetry is sometimes called *melic*, from the Greek word for "song." The solo
performance of lyric was called *monody*, in contrast to choral
songs performed by a group of singers who also danced
in costume. The earliest lyric poetry dates to the seventh
century B.C., and even in fragmentary form the influence
of Homer is evident in its imagery and phrasing. In subject
matter, however, lyric frequently focuses on the personal
experiences of the poet, illustrated with traditional myths
and covering themes such as love, politics, war, friendship,
drinking, and settling scores with enemies.

Many names of lyric poets survive but most of their
poems have done so only in fragments. Two important
monodic poets came from the island of Lesbos. **Alcaeus** (born
c. 625–620 B.C.) in his surviving fragments writes about

Sappho (born c. 650 B.C.) was born on Lesbos, an island near the
coast of modern-day northern Turkey, in the second half of the seventh
century B.C. Imaginary biographical details about Sappho began circu-
lating even in antiquity—that she was a lesbian, a prostitute, short and
ugly, ran a finishing school for aristocratic girls, and threw herself off
a cliff over unrequited love for a ferryman. It is more certain that as a
member of an aristocratic clan she was involved in the political struggles
on Lesbos, which led to exile for a while in Sicily. Based on the fragments
of her poetry (one complete poem out of nine papyrus-roll books
survive), she had a husband, a daughter named Cleis, and a brother who
apparently squandered money on a courtesan.

friendship, the political struggles on Lesbos against various tyrants, exile, shipwreck, and drinking, all developed with vigorous descriptions and mythic exemplars. It is in Alcaeus that we find the earliest use of the "ship of state" metaphor. More influential has been **Sappho** (born c. 650 B.C.), known in ancient times as the "tenth muse." Only two of her complete poems survive, along with numerous fragments, but in them we see a wide variety of subjects, including Sappho's brother and daughter, poetry, beauty, marriage, hymns to gods, myth, and political struggles on Lesbos. Sappho is most famous for her poems describing her powerful sexual attraction to girls, in which her emotions are vividly rendered with striking imagery, yet always poetically controlled. The musical beauty of her poetry was famous in antiquity.

Choral lyric poetry was usually part of a public ritual or celebration. Examples include hymns to gods, including the "paean" for Apollo and the "dithyramb" for Dionysus, the maiden-song (*partheneion*), sung by a chorus of girls, and the wedding-song (*hymenaios*), among others. By the sixth century B.C. secular subjects appear in choral lyric: "panegyrics" to rulers and aristocrats who were the poets' patrons, and "victory odes" (*epinicia*) commissioned by aristocratic victors in public games such as the Olympics. These choral songs, often performed at competitions, were composed in elaborate metrical patterns and linked the occasion or subject to more generalized human experience. A mythic narrative usually served as the centerpiece of the song.

Two choral poets particularly noteworthy are **Simonides** (born c. 556 B.C.) and **Pindar** (c. 518–430 B.C.). Simonides composed, among many other genres of poems, victory odes and dithyrambs, the latter winning some fifty-seven competitions. Unfortunately, none of these poems survive intact. With Pindar, however, we have forty-five victory odes commissioned by winners in the four Panhellenic athletic festivals celebrated at Olympia, Delphi (the Pythian Games), Nemea, and Corinth (the Isthmian Games); however, he composed poems in nearly every type of choral song. His victory odes are very elaborate, complex, highly stylized celebratory descriptions of the athlete's achievement, with flattering references to his aristocratic clan and a mythic narrative usually linked to the athlete's family or city. The athlete's experience is set in the context of a more general view of human life and moral instruction.

Another influential genre of poetry is called **elegiac**, after the meter of the same name. This metrical pattern consists of couplets that alternate a dactylic hexameter line with a second made up of a dactylic pentameter. Elegiac poetry covers a wide range of subjects and lengths; its use in funeral laments and epitaphs gives us our modern somber meaning of the word elegiac.

The Athenian politician **Solon** (died c. 560 B.C.), whose reforms of the Athenian constitution were important developments in creating Athenian democracy, wrote elegiac poems explaining and defending his political reforms.

Archilochus (active c. 650 B.C.) treated many of the same subjects as the lyric poets—friendship, love, politics, and war. One of his most famous poems describes how he threw away his shield during a battle and ran away. "I can buy another just as good," he shrugs. The largest collection of elegy comprises the fourteen hundred lines attributed to **Theognis** (active c. 550–540 B.C.). Theognis was an old aris-tocrat displeased at the new status and power of men who "once lived like deer" but now think that their wealth makes them as good as the aristocracy. Theognis's poems are also filled with moral, practical, or ethical advice for his young friend (or lover) Cyrnus. By the fifth century b.c. the elegy was a form of poetry particularly associated with "symposia" or drinking parties at which the guests would recite verse and hold philosophical discussions (as in Plato's dialogue, the *Symposium*). Thus, many elegies take as their subjects drinking and love.

The **epigram** is another important poetic genre, one that is sometimes confused with elegy because epigrams were also written in elegiac couplets. Originally epigrams were written as inscriptions on objects such as tombs, and many early epigrams are anonymous. An early writer associated with epigrams is Simonides, whom we've already met as an elegist. Although there is some doubt that he actually wrote them, his epigrams about the Persian Wars (490 and 480/ 79 B.C.) are the most famous, especially the one commending the three hundred Spartans massacred at Thermopylae: "Go tell the Spartans, stranger, that we lie here dead, obedient to their commands."

By the Hellenistic period—the term we use to describe Greek culture from the death of Alexander the Great (323 B.C.) to the dominance of Rome (30 B.C.)— epigrams were composed more often as literature rather than as inscriptions and covered a wide variety of topics, including fictitious dedications to everyday people like hunters or prostitutes, funeral laments for dead pets, and the usual topics of politics, family, friends, drinking, love, and sex. In this pe-riod the epigram becomes highly stylized and self-conscious while still retaining its emphasis on brevity and wit. Two Hellenistic writers of epigrams worth noting are **Asclepiades** (c. 300–279 B.C.), whose repertoire of imagery describing the effects of sexual passion has influenced all subsequent love poetry; and **Callimachus** (born c. 310 B.C.), who sup-posedly wrote more than eight hundred books in a wide variety of genres, including hymns to gods (which have survived). Sixty-four of his epigrams are extant, perhaps the most beautiful being his moving epigram about his dead friend Heraclitus.

Most Greek poets wrote in various genres, and in the Hellenistic period poets were conscious of several centuries of predecessors. They were not content to remain restricted by generic categories or strictures and so self-consciously experimented with various forms and subject matters, challenging the tradition at the same time they paid it homage. Callimachus's *Aetia (Origins)*, of whose four thousand lines only a handful and some fragments have survived, used the elegiac form to present a wide range of literary subjects, from long epigrams about tombs and statues to narratives on mythic tales, all knit together by an antiquarian interest in "origins." Another Hellenistic poet, **Theocritus** (active c. 270 B.C.), composed, in addition to twenty-four epigrams, *Idylls*, which in Greek means something like "vignettes." These are highly finished, poetically complex depictions of "slice-of-life" scenes ranging from shepherds in Sicily to middle-class housewives in Alexandria. His so-called bucolic idylls, those describing rural life in Sicily, initiate the long-lived pastoral tradition in Western literature, which uses the life of shepherds as a metaphor for exploring love and art, leisure and freedom, politics and nature. Finally, both Callimachus and Theocritus display a creative and innovative self-consciousness about the craft of poetry that was an important influence on Roman poets.

This brief survey discusses a mere fraction of the poetry and poets who wrote over several centuries of Greek history. Unfortunately, most have survived only in fragmentary form. But enough has come down to us intact to reveal a remarkable tradition of poetic craftsmanship in a wide variety of metrical patterns, subject matter, and genres, a tradition that shaped and enriched the literature of the West.

Roman poetry was the first beneficiary of this priceless heritage. Roman poets were intimately familiar with the several centuries of Greek poetry that had preceded them, as well as with the Greek scholarship on poetry produced in the Hellenistic period. Much of the work of the early Roman innovators of the late second and early first centuries B.C. is lost or has survived only in fragments. However, we do know that these poets embraced Hellenistic Greek literature as models, and by the early first century were known as *neoterics* or "new poets."

Two of the greatest works of Roman literature are **didactic** poems. *On the Nature of Things,* by **Lucretius** (c. 95–55 B.C.), is an explication of the philosophy of Epicurus (341–270 B.C.). Epicurus taught that all reality is material, mere atoms in random motion; that the soul dies with the body and that the gods are indifferent to human behavior; and that the greatest good is the pleasure of the soul freed from anxiety and pain. Lucretius expounds Epicurus's thoughts in hexameter lines filled with remarkable imagery and set pieces such as the description of the sacrifice of Iphigenia by Agamemnon, which Lucretius concludes with the line that would become one of the Enlightenment's rallying cries: "Such great evils Religion has made acceptable!"

An even greater poem, though one owing much to Lucretius, is Virgil's *Georgics* (c. 29 B.C.), a brilliant meditation on the possibilities of human order in a harsh natural world. Farming had been the subject of other didactic works, including the *Re Rustica* (37 B.C.) of **Varro** (116–27 B.C.), written in dialogue form, and the prose treatise *De Agri*

Cultura of **Cato the Elder** (234–149 B.C.). But Virgil uses agriculture as a controlling metaphor for discussing man's relationship to the natural world and the gods, and for exploring the connection between the values of political order and those of farming. The modulation between optimism about man's ability to create order and pessimism over the disorder caused by his passions and appetites is as effective here for Virgil as it would be later in the *Aeneid*. The *Georgics's* exploration of the links between farming and political order was an important precursor to eighteenthand nineteenth-century agrarianism, particularly the agrarian social philosophy embraced by a good many of the American founders.

After Virgil the best didactic poems in Latin are actually parodies, Ovid's *Art of Love* and *Remedies for Love*. The first of these gives somewhat tongue-in-cheek instruction in how to court a mistress and carry on an illicit affair, replete with illustrations from myth and vivid observations of the Roman social scene. In a similar style, the *Remedies* advises its readers how to get out of an affair. Another didactic work of Ovid is the *Fasti* or *Calendar*, which devotes one book to each month of the Roman calendar and its religious celebrations (only the first six books survive).

The early innovators of Latin lyric are lost or survive only in fragments. However, we do have 114 poems by **Catullus** (c. 84–54 B.C.) in a wide variety of meters and subject matters, including epigrams, hymns, a narrative miniepic, and elegies on his love affair with a married woman he calls Lesbia. In these latter poems we see an important advance beyond the usually light-hearted treatment of sexual desire found in the Hellenistic poets. Catullus delves into the complexities and contradictions of illicit desire, the way it can divide the soul between duty and passion, pleasure and shame. Yet like his poetic mentor Sappho, Catullus always maintains the most rigorous poetic control over his subject, even when meticulously documenting the hysterical hatred and lust aroused by the shameless Lesbia.

Indeed, in order to attain the scope necessary for such psychological analysis Catullus expanded the epigram into a new genre, sometimes called the "subjective-erotic elegy," so called because these poems are written in elegiac couplets and focus on the impact of sexual desire on the poet's consciousness. Poets in this genre whose works have survived include **Propertius** (c. 50–c. 2 B.C.), **Tibullus** (c. 55–19 B.C.), and Ovid. Propertius's love poems concern his affair with a woman whom he calls Cynthia. They elaborate, with numerous mythological examples and sometimes complex allusions, the experience of illicit love into a full-time career that displaces the traditional Roman "course of honors" in politics and the military. The last two books of the collection treat a wider variety of subject matter, including poems on "origins" in the manner of Callimachus. Like Propertius, Tibullus is a "soldier" of love and the "slave" of his mistress Delia, and he documents the mundane details and psychological impact of this erotic soldiering and slavery. Finally, in Ovid's *Amores* we see the motifs of love elegy hardening into highly polished, ironic, witty conventions that lack the contradictions, doubts, and anxiety over the way illicit love challenges traditional Roman family values, a tension that makes the earlier poets' work more dramatic.

Two more lyric poets tower over the corpus of Roman poetry—Virgil and Horace. Virgil's first poetic work is the *Eclogues* or "Selections." These poems, often called "pastorals," are written in dactylic hexameter and take as their theme the rural milieu of farmers and shepherds explored in Theocritus's *Idylls*. Theocritus's imagined rural world of flowers and trees and streams, however, seems timeless and removed from the power of politics and the state. In contrast, Virgil's *locus amoenus,* or "pleasant spot," exists in the shadow of Roman political power and amidst the pressure of historical change that challenges the autonomy, freedom, leisure, and creativity of pastoral life. This conflict is seen in the first lines of the first *Eclogue*, which describe the shepherd Tityrus "reclining in the shade" while Meliboeus, his land appropriated for a Roman soldier, must go off into exile. So influential were the *Eclogues*, especially the first, on subsequent Western literature that literary historian E. R. Curtius once asserted that "[a]nyone unfamiliar with that short poem lacks one key to the literary tradition of Europe."

Next to Virgil, the Roman poet who influenced European poetry the most is **Horace** (65–8 B.C.). A huge body of Horace's work in several different genres has survived, including four books of *Odes* that self-consciously imitate earlier Greek lyric models, especially Alcaeus. Horace's poems cover the whole gamut of themes treated in earlier lyric— love, drinking, friendship, politics—and include a famous poem celebrating the death of Cleopatra. But Horace's poems are developed in the complex and sophisticated style of Hellenistic poetry, and as such are filled with learned allusions to other poetry, geography, and myth. Many of the poems also express philosophical advice about how to live, containing memorable statements concerning the brevity of life and the importance of enjoying each day. For centuries phrases from Horace's poems were an essential part of every learned person's education. The praise of moderation Horace calls the "golden mean" (*apream*

Horace (Quintus Horatius Flaccus, 65–8 B.C.) was born in Apulia in southeastern Italy. He was the son of a freedman (that is, an exslave, though probably an Italian) who was a small farmer and auctioneer. Horace's father must have done well, for he sent Horace to Rome and then Athens, where he met Brutus, the assassin of Caesar. Horace fought on the side of Brutus in the war against Octavian and Antony. Though his family lost their land after the defeat of Brutus, Horace was allowed to return to Italy, where he became a salaried government official, began to write poetry, and met Virgil, who recommended him to Maecenas (38 B.C.). Maecenas gave Horace a farm in the Sabine country northeast of Rome, which provided the poet with the leisure and financial independence to write poetry.

mediocritam); the rightness of dying for one's country (*Dulce et decorum est pro patria mori*); and the need to enjoy life expressed in the dictum to "seize the day" (*carpe diem*) all come from Horace's *Odes*.

Horace represents the high point of Latin lyric. After him, some lyric poems appear in other kinds of writing, and fragments and names of lyric poets survive, but the genre will not become vital again until Christian poets take it up.

The earliest Latin **epigrams** were usually written for the tombs of famous persons, such as Ennius's second-century B.C. epigrams on the tomb of Scipio Africanus, the Roman who defeated Hannibal at the Battle of Zama in 202 B.C.

Catullus, Gaius Valerius (c. 84–c. 54 B.C.) was born into a prominent family near Verona but lived most of his life in Rome. If his poems can be trusted, he was on the staff of a provincial governor in Bithynia, in modern Turkey, in 57–56; it was probably on his journey there that he visited the grave of his brother near Troy. He seems to have been an opponent of Caesar, but then he later accepted Caesar's friendship. Evidence suggests that Catullus was part of a social and artistic movement that rejected the ideas of Roman culture for the values of Hellenistic Greek civilization, which focused on the individual and his sensibility and experiences rather than on his duty to the state. If his poetry is an accurate reflection of his life, then Catullus was involved in a passionate affair with a rich aristocratic woman, most likely Clodia Pulcher Metellus, the wife of a consul. He apparently died young. As with Sappho, many fanciful biographical details about Catullus's life have been extrapolated from his poetry.

Only a handful of epigrams not written as epitaphs survive from the period preceding Catullus, though numerous fragments and references in other authors suggest that the genre was popular. In Catullus we find epigrams on love, politics, friendship, the composition of poetry, revenge on enemies, and a particularly moving epigram about the poet's visit to the tomb of his brother. In Catullus's hands, epigrams arising from the poet's everyday experiences transcend the merely witty detailing of trivia sometimes found in Greek epigram to become highly finished, complex works of art.

After Catullus the most important surviving Roman writer of epigrams is **Martial** (c. A.D. 40–104), who was born in Spain but lived most of his life in Rome. Some of Martial's epigrams are typical of Greek models, including epitaphs and occasional poems on various events. But most of his epigrams follow the model of Catullus both in meter and in the literary sophistication brought to the genre's usual topics. In Martial's hands the mundane details of everyday life and the passing scene are presented with social and psychological realism and biting wit. So acute are Martial's powers of observation that even after twenty centuries we can recognize in his poems the perennial foibles, contradictions, and absurdities of human nature. Martial is perhaps most famous for his endings, which often surprise the reader with some unanticipated point or twist, as in the following epigram about a doctor turned undertaker: "What he does as an undertaker, he had done as a doctor"—that is, he continues to bury his customers.

Satire is a poetic genre the subject matter of which is similar to that of some epigrams. According to the Roman rhetorician **Quintilian** (c. A.D. 35–90.), satire is a Roman invention. Like the Latin word for a dish full of a variety of foods from which it derives, satire treats a wide variety of subjects in an equally diverse variety of styles and authorial roles. But the essential element of all satire is an attack on hypocrisy and pretension delivered with brutal wit and driven by the imperative "to tell the truth while laughing," as the great Roman satirist Horace put it.

Despite its Roman origins, satire does have precursors

Martial (Marcus Valerius Martialis, c. a.d. 40–c. 104) was one of an influential group of Spaniards, also including Seneca the Younger and Quintilian, who were active in Rome in the first century. In Rome, Martial sought patronage from the emperor Domitian and wrote panegyrics for other powerful patrons. His reputation led to his being given a commission to celebrate in verse the opening of the Colosseum in 80, and he was awarded the *ius trium liberorum*, an honor started by Augustus to recognize parents by giving them certain exemptions, such as from being a guardian, which could be expensive. Martial, a friend of many of the most influential people of his day, wrote imperial propaganda—although he complains that he didn't make much money doing so. He was the most popular writer of his time, read even in the provinces. After the death of Domitian, however, his star fell. He returned to Spain in 98, where he lived on a small farm given him by a wealthy widow. He died in Spain sometime between 101 and 104.

in Greek literature. The motif of the author abusing the corruption of his society or the vices of his enemies appears in a type of Greek poem called "iambics," after one of the meters in which these poems were composed. Horace's *Epodes* (c. 30 B.C.) used the meters of iambics for the first time in Roman poetry, but not all of these poems employ invective to attack social and moral corruption. Another influence on Roman satire was the "diatribe," which purported to be a transcript of a public lecture given by a philosopher who used jokes, everyday language, and even vulgarity to attack vice and make a moral point. The Cynic philosopher **Menippus** (active c. 300–250 B.C.) gave his name to a style of satire that mixed verse and prose. The *Satyricon* of Petronius (see below) incorporated Menippean satires in its exposure of the *nouveau riche* vulgarity of imperial Rome.

All of these Greek influences can be found in the satirists writing before Horace, but unfortunately only lines and fragments of these earlier satirists survive. Horace's eighteen *Satires* (c. 30 B.C.), which he called *Sermones* or "conversations" in reference to their colloquial style and fluid shifts from subject to subject, are the most substantial examples of the genre from the late Republic. In these conversations Horace uses his own life and experiences, as well as the vices of others, to exhort his readers to moral improvement. Compared to the fragments of his model **Lucilius** (born c. 180 B.C.), Horace is more restrained and cautious in his choice of targets, perhaps reflecting the political uncertainty of the dying Republic and then, later, the character of Augustus's rule. Thus Horace tends to focus his satire on types rather than real people. One famous *Satire* retells the fable of the city mouse and the country mouse in order to chastise the excessive luxury and sensuality of the Roman ruling class.

In the sixteen satires of **Juvenal** (c. A.D. 60–130) the angry chastisement of vice and folly returns, though his later satires are more restrained and detached. Moreover, Juvenal's poems prefer the grand style of epic and tragedy to the coarseness of Lucilius or the conversational urbanity of Horace. Juvenal's topics include everything that to him typified the corruption of Rome: the decadence of the ruling class and patrons, sycophantic clients, promiscuous homosexuals, greed, social climbers, foreigners, the emperor and his toadying courtiers, effeminate men, loose wives. Particularly famous are the third satire, describing the miseries of living in Rome, and the tenth, a meditation on the insignificance of human achievement in the face of devouring time. Samuel Johnson composed imitations of both these poems. Juvenal's tone of "savage indignation"—as W. B. Yeats described Jonathon Swift's satire—has had a long influence on Western satiric literature, and his poems have generated numerous famous quotations, including "A sound mind in a sound body" (*mens sana in corpore sano*) and "Who will guard the guardians?" (*Quis custodiet ipsos custodes?*)

One last poetic genre that should be mentioned is the verse letter or **epistle**. This seems to be a wholly Roman invention, apart from a few Hellenistic poems that make an invitation in the form of a letter. Some fragments of epistles by Lucilius have survived, and a few poems of Catullus are cast as letters. Horace's *Epistles* (c. 20 B.C.) are the earliest sustained example of the genre. His fictitious letters are written in hexameters and take as their subject the question of the right way to live. (The second book of letters is known as the *Ars poetica* or *Art of Poetry*; it will be discussed later.) Ovid also wrote verse letters: the *Tristia* (A.D. 9–12) or *Sorrows* was written after Augustus sent Ovid into exile for an offense unknown to us. In these verse letters Ovid details the misery of living in a bleak backwater on the Black Sea, defends his life and work, and lobbies for his return to Rome. From the same experience come his *Epistulae ex Ponto* (*Letters from the Black Sea*), which treat the same themes.

The surviving body of Latin poetry was the vehicle for the transmission of the Greek tradition to European literature, as knowledge of Greek and many Greek texts themselves were lost for centuries. But Latin poetry consisted of much more than the imitation of Greek models. In the hands of poets like Virgil, Horace, Catullus, and Ovid, Hellenistic influences were transformed into something distinctly Roman, just as Europe would take the Greco-Ro-man literary heritage and out of it create a wholly new literary tradition.

DRAMA

Perhaps the most influential art forms invented by the Greeks have been **tragedy** and **comedy**, which originated in Athens around the late sixth century B.C. In that city both were produced as events in civic religious festivals, tragedy at the City Dionysia in the spring, and comedy at the Lenaea in winter, though tragedies were produced at the latter festival as well. Eventually dramatic festivals inspired by the Athenian model were held all over ancient Greece.

As a civic-religious ritual, Athenian drama was literally "political," the business of the polis or city-state, which oversaw and managed the production of the plays performed in an open-air theater on the slope of the Acropolis before some fifteen thousand citizens, whose elected representatives chose the prizewinners. Hence, tragedy confronted issues important to the whole community. It raised questions about the fundamental conditions and limitations of human existence and the conflicted relationship of individuals and the state, the family and political power, passion and reason and law. It is important to note as well that the playwrights enjoyed a remarkable freedom of subject matter and theme, which resulted in drama being an important vehicle of political criticism and commentary.

As an art form **tragedy** combined the grandeur of epic's towering heroes and gods with the music, dance, and complex metrical patterns of choral lyric. Typically, each of the three playwrights chosen to compete would produce three tragedies and a "satyr" play, a sort of comic-obscene interlude centered on the adventures of satyrs—lusty woodland wildmen addicted to sex and wine—and their father Silenus. In the early fifth century the three tragedies themselves formed a trilogy tracing a single story. Later, the three plays told independent stories. After the production, a panel of ten citizens would award first, second, and third prizes. The communal importance of tragedy can also be seen in the chorus, which frequently functions as the audience's representative on stage, both in its reaction to and commentary on the action and in its interactions with the characters.

Reading a Greek tragedy silently in translation captures only part of what an ancient Athenian must have experienced as he sat in the open air and heard the singing of the choral odes, watched the intricate choreography of the dances, and admired the expensive costumes, the actors' masks, and the painted scenery. But even in translation, and even after twenty-five centuries, the power of tragic themes and characters can still move us. For the Greeks this experience would have been civic and political, a collective confrontation with the primal contradictions and problems of human existence that, in Aristotle's famous description, aroused the emotions of pity and fear in order to purge them ("catharsis") and keep them from festering within the body politic.

The earliest tragedian whose work survives intact is **Aeschylus** (c. 525–456 B.C.), who composed between seventy and ninety tragedies and won first prize thirteen times. Seven of his tragedies have survived, [1] along with fragments of others. In Aeschylus's plays, terrible suffering results from a human nature driven by its passions and appetites into arrogance and excess ("hubris"), which bring down the retributive justice of the gods. This is the tragic vision: we live in a world defined by absolute limits that we attempt to transcend only at our peril. Yet Aeschylus also sees hope in the community and its political values, which can create a more stable order and minimize the disorder

---

Aeschylus (525–456 B.C.) was an Athenian playwright who fought at the Battle of Marathon (490) and probably also at Salamis (480). His first tragedy was produced in 499, and the first of his thirteen victorious plays was produced in 484; his last production was the *Oresteia* in 458. He died in Sicily. His self-composed epitaph ignored his numerous plays, as many as ninety, and mentioned only that he had fought the Persians at Marathon. Both of his sons, as well as a nephew, went on to become playwrights themselves.

---

[1] In addition to the *Oresteia*, which comprises the *Agamemnon, Libation Bearers,* and *Eumenides,* these include the *Prometheus Bound* (c. 478 B.C.), *Seven against Thebes* (467 B.C.), the *Suppliants* (date unknown, but early in Aeschylus' s career), and the *Persians* (472 B.C.), about the sea battle of Salamis (480 B.C.).

created by the passions. In the *Oresteia* (458 B.C.), the only surviving complete trilogy from Greek tragedy, Aeschylus traces the development of Athenian democracy from the dark Mycenean world of domestic violence, betrayal, blood-guilt, and vengeance in the household of the king Agamemnon to the sunlit world of democratic Athens and its institutions. Here reason, language, and law settle conflict, and the snake-haired Furies of blood and guilt have been subordinated to Athena, goddess of wisdom and the city that bears her name.

The next tragic poet whose work has survived is **Sophocles** (c. 496–406 B.C.), who wrote more than 120 plays and won some twenty first prizes. We have seven of these plays, including perhaps the most famous of Greek tragedies, *Oedipus Turannos* or *Oedipus Rex* (date unknown), which Sigmund Freud misread spectacularly. Rather than a drama of the "family romance," as Freud thought, the

---

Sophocles (c. 496–406 B.C.) author of more than 120 plays, won his first victory in 468. He thus competed against both Aeschylus and Euripides, whose death in 406 Sophocles marked by dressing his chorus in mourning. He won twenty victories altogether. Like Aeschylus, Sophocles participated in the political and civic life of Athens: he was treasurer in 443–42 and a general with Pericles c. 441–40. After the disaster in Sicily in 413 he was appointed as one of the ten "advisors" to deal with the crisis. He was also a priest of the cult for the hero Halon, and after his death he was himself worshiped as the hero Dexion.

Oedipus is really about the limits of reason to acquire sure knowledge in a world made uncertain by our own passions and the vagaries of time and chance. This theme is related to a representative feature of Sophocles' drama that Aristotle called "recognition" (*anagnorisis*): that moment when the protagonist realizes he has misjudged and misunderstood reality and now must pay for his mistake in suffering. Yet Sophocles acknowledges that despite our limitations, the need to search out the truth of the human condition is the driving force of human life, one admirable even if it leads to disaster.

The last tragedian whose work has survived is **Euripides** (c. 480s–407/6 B.C.). He wrote about ninety plays, nine-teen of which have come down to us (though a few of these might not actually be by Euripides). [1] Substantial fragments of nine other plays have survived as well. Euripides won only four victories, but later he became the most popular of the fifth-century tragedians. Euripides is thought of today as more of a "realist" than Aeschylus or Sophocles; the way in which he explores the darker psychological complexities of characters buffeted by their passions and desires makes him,

[1] *Alcestis* (438 B.C.), *Medea* (431 B.C.), *Hippolytus* (428 B.C.), *Andromache* (c. 426 B.C.), *Hecuba* (c. 424 B.C.), *Trojan Women* (415 B.C.), *Phoenician Women* (date unknown), *Helen* (412 B.C.), *Orestes* (408 B.C.), *Bacchae and Iphigeneia in Aulis* (405 B.C.), *Rhesus* (date unknown), *Electra* (date unknown), *Children of Heracles* (date unknown), *Madness of Heracles* (date unknown), *Suppliant Women* (date unknown), *Ion* (date unknown), *Iphigeneia in Tauris* (date unknown) and *Cyclops* (date unknown), a satyr play.

and them, more accessible to us moderns. He is particularly interested, in characters like Phaedra from the *Hippolytus* or Medea from the play of that name, in the destructive effects of sexual passion on the psyche. His plays detailing the ravaging effects of war, such as the *Trojan Women* and the *Hecuba*, testify to the remarkable freedom dramatic artists enjoyed in Athens, as these plays were produced during the Peloponnesian War with Sparta and were intended as pointed commentaries on Athens's sometimes brutal behavior during that conflict.

In addition to these thirty-three tragedies, hundreds of fragments from many other playwrights have survived, offering a tantalizing glimpse into a dramatic world of which we know only a fraction. But even in the small remnant that has survived we are faced with a remarkable artistic achievement the influences of which are immeasurable.

With **comedy**, the accident of survival has left us

Euripides (c. 480s–407/6 B.C.) saw his first play produced in 455, one year after the death of Aeschylus. He won his first victory in 441, and his last play, the Bacchae, won a posthumous victory. He was not as popular as Aeschylus and Sophocles, winning only four times out of some ninety productions. He left Athens for Macedon, where he wrote a play about the ancestor of the king Archelaus and eventually died. There is no evidence that he left Athens out of bitterness at his lack of success in tragic competition. At any rate, Euripides was very popular outside of Athens—it is said that the Athenians who escaped the disaster at Syracuse were allowed to live if they could recite from the tragedies of Euripides.

even less than what we have from the tragedians: only eleven plays from one dramatist have survived, though numerous fragments of others are also extant. The plays of **Aristophanes** (c. 450–c. 386 B.C.) come at the end of what is known as "old comedy," a term used to distinguish the genre from its later evolution. [1] In Aristophanes' comedies the political dimension of ancient drama is most obvious, for the fantastic plots, gross humor, obscenity, parody, satire, and outsized characters are all written with the explicit intention of commenting on and criticizing the Athenian democracy and its politicians, leaders, and philosophers, who are named and pilloried on stage in full view of their fellow citizens.

In his comedies, Aristophanes shows how the passions and appetites of humans, particularly the sexual, can be powerful forces of social and political disorder, and so require greater supervision and control than that provided by radical democracy. Yet like Athenian democracy, his comedies are in some senses egalitarian, in that he presents all humans, regardless of their wealth or rank or prestige, as subject to the same limitations and weaknesses. At the same time, we can detect in his invective a grudging admiration for the vitality and variety of human nature and its instinct for freedom and self-assertion. The subversive nature of

---

[1] *Acharnians* (425 B.C.), *Knights* (424 B.C.), *Clouds* (423 B.C.), *Wasps* (422 B.C.), *Peace* (421 B.C.), *Birds* (414 B.C.), *Lysistrata* and *Women at the Thesmophoria* (411 B.C.), *Frogs* (405 B.C.), *Women at Assembly* (392 B.C.), and *Wealth* (388 B.C.), in addition to nearly one thousand fragments.

Aristophanes' comedy is perhaps most obvious in the *Lysistrata*, in which the Greek women go on a sex-strike to force their husbands to end the war between Athens and Sparta. By play's end, every Greek male prejudice about women—that they can't control their sexual appetites or act politically, for example—has been turned on its head, for the men, not the women, give in to sexual desire, the war ends, and the women's political plot triumphs.

The last two plays of Aristophanes, the *Wealth* and the *Women at Assembly*, are considered to be early examples of "middle comedy," a new style of comic drama that pre-dominated during the fourth century B.C. Since no other examples from some eight hundred plays have survived, it is difficult to pin down precisely what characterized middle comedy. Judging by Aristophanes' last two plays, it seems that the role of the chorus was lessened and songs written specifically for it were eliminated. Ancient evidence also suggests that political commentary was reduced as well, as was the obscene language. Later, these comedies treated everyday people and situations, including romantic intrigue and the machinations of various con men.

From the genre of "new comedy," which dominated the third century, we are fortunate to have one play, the *Dyskolos* or *Grumpy Old Man*, and substantial portions of several others by **Menander** (c. 344–292 B.C.), who wrote around one hundred comedies. In Menander's plays the political criticism, obscenity, and fantastic plots have disappeared, and the chorus performs only between the acts. His plots involve the adventures of various stock characters such as the boastful soldier, the parasite, the misanthrope, the clever slave, and the handsome but slow-witted young man in love. Most stories revolve around romance, mistaken identity, lost treasure, and various "blocking characters" that try to keep the young man from the girl he loves. But of course love triumphs in the end and the boy gets the girl, just as in our own cinematic

---

Seneca the Younger (Lucius Annaeus Seneca, c. 4 B.C.– A.D. 65) came from a wealthy equestrian family from northern Spain. His father was Seneca the Elder, a historian and rhetorician, and his nephew was the epic poet Lucan. His only son predeceased him. Seneca came to Rome as a teenager and began to study rhetoric and then philosophy with Stoic teachers and the Cynic philosopher Demetrius. After a sojourn in Egypt, he survived shipwreck on his way back to Rome, where he became a quaestor, a government official in charge of various financial duties. Seneca became one of Rome's most famous orators. According to one story, his brilliance offended the emperor Gaius and nearly cost Seneca his life. Under the emperor Claudius he was banished to Corsica for adultery. He was recalled by Nero's mother Agrippina and appointed praetor, a high official that presided over criminal courts and oversaw public games, among other duties. Agrippina also made Seneca the tutor of Nero, and he became Nero's adviser when Nero was named emperor in 54. As Nero grew into his famous degenerate character, however, Seneca's influence over Nero began to wane. Seneca eventually withdrew from public life, spending his time in philosophy and writing. In 65 he was forced to commit suicide for his alleged involvement in a conspiracy against the emperor.

romantic comedies, which Menander's plays resemble.

Drama in ancient Rome was strongly influenced by Greek models, which nonetheless fused with native theatrical traditions. No Latin tragedies have survived apart from fragments, including those from the plays of **Pacuvius** (220–c. 130 B.C.) and **Accius** (170–c. 86 B.C.), both of whom dramatized incidents and figures from Roman history and adapted stories from Greek myth. The nine tragedies of the younger **Seneca** (c. 4 B.C.–A.D 65.), the Stoic philosopher and tutor of Nero, are more literary than theatrical, indebted as much to earlier Roman poetry as to Greek tragedy. Their most striking feature is an extravagant violence that later influenced European Renaissance theater, as can be seen in the plays of Shakespeare, Marlow, and Ben Jonson.

The only Latin comedies to survive are the twenty plays of **Plautus** (c. 250–184 B.C.) and the six of **Terence** (b. 193 or 183–159 B.C.). These were adaptations of Greek new comedy, livened up with scenes and gags designed to appeal to a Roman audience. Like their Greek models, these plays involve stock characters, hidden treasure, mistaken identity, and romantic plots in which the boy gets the girl in the end. The plays of Plautus were known in the Renaissance, and his influence can be seen in works such as Shakespeare's *Comedy of Errors,* an adaptation of Plautus's *Menaechmi,* which is about twins separated at birth.

Even after the creative force of ancient drama was spent, theater continued to be an important public art form in the

Greco-Roman world. Numerous festivals revived the great Athenian tragedians, much as Shakespeare continues to be staged today. Actors were organized into powerful guilds that brought theater to the farthest reaches of the Roman Empire and even beyond. Athenian tragedy thus became a force for spreading Hellenic values.

PROSE FICTION

Prose narrative does not appear in classical literature until the first century A.D. Nine Greek novels, summaries of two others, and substantial fragments have survived, enough to give a good indication of what this genre of literature was like. A more accurate description of these works would be "romances," for there is little of the realism that we expect from the novel: that is, these works are largely devoid of the documentary detail of ordinary social and psychological life such as we can find outside our doors. Instead, the Greek romances focus on love, adventure, exotic locales, and occasionally fantasy. The typical plot centers on a good-looking boy and girl who fall in love, get separated, undergo numerous adventures and hardships such as imprisonment and shipwreck, but are finally reunited in the end. The focus on erotic attachment is reminiscent of other Hellenistic genres, such as epigram and comedy. The style is highly rhetorical, with finished speeches and descriptions of works of art, allusions to other literary works, and displays of geographical learning.

Probably the most famous and influential Greek novel is *Daphnis and Chloe* by **Longus** (second century A.D.), which combines the Greek romance with the pastoral world of Theocritus. It tells the story of two foundlings, Daphnis and Chloe, who are raised by shepherds and whose love is challenged by rivals, pirates, and the nearby world of the city and its temptations. In the end, however, even after discovering their aristocratic origins, Daphnis and Chloe return to the countryside to live as shepherds. Along the way Longus spends much time describing their sexual awakening and the charms of the rural world. Anyone familiar with Shakespeare's comedies, such as *As You Like It*, will see the influence of Longus's romance, which has been translated five hundred times since the sixteenth century.

Two works of Roman prose fiction survive: the *Golden Ass* of **Apuleius** (A.D. 125–c. 170) and portions of the *Satyrica* (more often called the *Satyricon*) of **Petronius** (first century A.D.). In the *Golden Ass* a young man tells the story of how, while dabbling in magic, he is turned into a donkey and undergoes a series of adventures. There are several side stories related to the main plot; the most famous of these is the story of Cupid and Psyche. A striking development in the novel occurs when the narrator is transformed into the author.

A more significant work for the development of the novel is the surviving section of Petronius's earlier *Satyrica*, often called "Dinner at Trimalchio's." The story concerns the adventures of a homosexual couple, Encolpius and Giton. Encolpius, stricken with impotence by the sex-god Priapus, has to defend Giton against numerous rivals—a plot that seems to parody the typical situation of the Greek romance.

The Dinner at Trimalchio's is a banquet the heroes attend at the gaudy, hideously vulgar mansion of a self-made millionaire named Trimalchio, an ex-slave. Many features of prose narrative and other Roman genres appear: complex narrative devices, side stories, erotic intrigue, parodies of Greek romance and philosophical works such as Plato's *Symposium*, and, most importantly, satire. In fact, the *Satyrica* anticipates the realist novel particularly in its documentation of social reality and its presentation of characters like Trimalchio, whose individuality transcends the broader stock types of Greek romance. At times Petronius's brutal satire of nouveau riche pretensions and moral decay brings to mind *The Great Gatsby* and the novels of a Balzac or Dickens.

LITERARY CRITICISM

The widespread role of poetry in ancient public life ensured that thinking critically and systematically about the mechanics and purpose of poetry became an important intellectual activity. A long-lived critical concept that first appears in the work of **Plato** (c. 429–347 B.C.) is that of imitation ("mimesis"), the idea that poetry creates imitations of situations and emotions. Plato thought this was a bad thing, for he believed that witnessing certain sorts of feelings created them in the viewer and made them more acceptable. Thus art, for Plato, has a moral and practical effect, helping to create the right and wrong sorts of people through what it imitates.

The *Poetics* of **Aristotle** (384–322 B.C.) established several ideas about literature and particularly theater that would later influence the Renaissance. We have already encountered his idea that tragedy's imitation of events arouses "pity and fear" in the spectator and leads to the catharsis of these emotions. Thus, contrary to Plato, who distrusts the depiction of such emotions because they will inspire the real thing, Aristotle sees a therapeutic value in the arousal and vicarious discharge of these emotions. Other important ideas from the *Poetics* include that of *harmatia*, the tragic flaw or error that inflicts a reversal ("peripeteia") of fortune on a basically good person, and Aristotle's proposition that poetry is more philosophical than history, since the former is more universal and treats of things that could be rather than merely those things that are.

Another Greek treatise of lasting influence is *On the Sublime*, which is attributed to **Longinus** (c. first century A.D.). Longinus goes beyond the discussion of mechanical correctness in writing to explore the "sublime," the experience of delight and awe that overcomes a reader in the presence of genius. Thus Longinus gives its due to the emotional experience of literary beauty, which he illustrates with analyses of passages of Greek poetry and prose. After the publication of a French translation of Longinus's work by Nicolas Despréaux-Boileau in the seventeenth century, the sublime became an important concept both in literary appreciation and in philosophy.

Perhaps the most influential work of ancient literary criticism is the *Ars poetica* of Horace, a verse letter addressed to two brothers named Piso. In this poem Horace sets out with wit and charm the rules for good poetry. That a poem must be a unified whole, its language appropriate to its theme, and its style suited to its subject matter are just a few of Horace's rules that influenced later poets such as Alexander Pope. The influence of the *Ars poetica* can be seen in the many now-famous terms and phrases it contains: the "purple patch," a phrase that is unnecessarily florid; *in medias res*, the need to start a story in the "middle" rather than all the way back at the beginning; "even Homer nods," the acknowledgment that even a master will sometimes make a mistake; and most importantly, the idea that literature should "delight and instruct," that is, please us aesthetically as well as provide philosophical or moral insight.

Unfortunately, we have only a small portion of all the literary scholarship that flourished in the ancient world. We can only imagine the value of lost works like Aristotle's treatise on comedy, Eratosthenes' work on the same subject, or the Epicurean Philodemus's *On Poems*, to mention a few. And we should note as well the many scholars and grammarians who studied literary texts, most of whose work is lost or survives only in fragments. These scholars tried to establish correct texts, compiled bibliographies and dictionaries, produced commentaries on authors, and devised principles of interpretation. [1] But enough ancient literary criticism and scholarship has survived to indicate that among the ancients the study of literature and language was a complex and sophisticated discipline, one that set the terms for the subsequent study of literature in Western culture.

---

[1] These commentaries, explanations, and critical notes written on ancient manuscripts are called "scholia," and such scholars are known as *scholiasts*.

ORATORY AND RHETORIC

Formal public speech was an integral part of ancient political, artistic, and religious life. As we have seen, poetry of all sorts was usually experienced as a public performance. Political activity required public speeches delivered before bodies of fellow citizens in councils and assemblies. Trials and lawsuits were for the most part competitions between speeches delivered before several hundred jurymen, and those who could afford them hired professional speechwriters ("logographers"). The ability to speak persuasively thus was the sine qua non of a public career, and rhetoric, the formal study of the techniques and skills for doing so, was the object of intense study.

Numerous orations from the ancient world have survived, giving us an important window into the political, diplomatic, and social lives of the ancients. [1] An influential set of Greek orations (including three called *Philippics*) comes to us from **Demosthenes** (384–322 B.C.), who tried to rally the Greek city-states against the rising power and ambition of Philip, the king of Macedon and father of Alexander the

---

[1] Other important Greek orators include Isaeus (c. 420–c. 340 B.C.), Isocrates (436–338 B.C.), Aeschines (c. 397–c. 322 B.C.), and Hyperides (389–322 B.C.).

Great. These speeches became models for all those defenders of liberty who through the centuries have tried to warn and prepare their countrymen against the machinations of a despot whose ascendancy depended on the complacency or corruption of his victims.

Although less well known than the political speeches, those composed for court cases offer equally valuable information about daily life in ancient Greece, including such topics as inheritance, property, citizenship, marriage, adultery, and homosexuality. For example, a speech attributed to Demosthenes called *Against Neaira,* about a prostitute who posed as an Athenian citizen-wife, gives us important details about the role of women as citizens and wives and the values and behaviors expected of them. So too the speech of **Lysias** (c. 458–c. 380 B.C.) called *On the Murder of Eratosthenes,* defending a man who killed his wife's lover, opens a window into the private lives and domestic behavior of ancient Athenian families.

Roman oratory is dominated by the fifty-eight surviving speeches of **Cicero** (106–43 B.C.), which illuminate for us the history, politics, and social mores of first-century B.C. Rome. Some of these orations were composed for trials, such as the famous series of speeches delivered for the prosecution of Verres, the rapacious governor of Sicily, or the defense of Caelius, a lover of Catullus's mistress Clodia, who accused Caelius of trying to poison her. From such speeches we get important insights into Roman social history and the machinery of provincial government.

Likewise Cicero's political speeches give us numerous historical details about the death of the Roman Republic, events in which Cicero played an important role both as orator and politician. From his four speeches exposing the conspiracy of Catiline (63–62 B.C.) comes the famous tag, *O tempora! O mores!* ("Oh the times, Oh the manners!"). His attacks on Marc Antony, called "Philippics" after the speeches of Demosthenes, cost Cicero his life and bequeathed to us another model of a spirited public defense of republican freedom against tyranny. The survival of Cicero's works into the Middle Ages allowed his oratory to become a critical influence on later European culture and political discourse.

Given the importance of oratory, the technical study of rhetoric was a flourishing academic discipline. The *Rhetoric* of Aristotle is the most influential of surviving Greek rhetorical studies, treating subjects such as the difference between rhetorical and philosophical arguments, the psychology of listeners and techniques for playing on their emotions, and issues of style and figurative language. Aristotle bequeathed to the West the basic divisions of rhetoric that would prevail for centuries: "invention," the selection of words to suit the issue; "disposition," the division of the subject matter and organization of the parts; "diction," including style, figurative speech, etc.; "delivery," including gestures and pronunciation; and "memory," tricks for remembering speeches, which were seldom read from a prepared text.

The premier orator of Rome, Cicero, also wrote several rhetorical treatises that have survived. A few treat the more technical aspects of oratory such as invention, but the more important *De Oratore, Brutus,* and *Orator* present us with a picture of the ideal orator, someone who has not just mastered the techniques of rhetoric, but is "liberally" educated, a humanist conversant with literature, philosophy, and culture. These ideals would profoundly affect the Renaissance's views on humanistic education and character. [1]

After Cicero the huge *Institutio Oratoria* (*Oratorical Training*) of **Quintilian** (A.D. 35–90s) is the most important surviving work of Roman rhetoric. Quintilian begins with the orator as a child and hence is concerned with pedagogical issues such as the proper curriculum and what makes a good schoolteacher. Along the way he provides numerous examples of Greek and Roman writing and his judgments of their worth.

---

[1] The anonymous *Rhetorica ad Herennium* (c. 86–82 B.C.), is notable for its section on style, which gives examples of the Grand, Middle, and Plain styles.

LETTERS

Several kinds of letters survive from antiquity, apart from the verse letters discussed earlier. These include private and official correspondence that survived quite by chance in the sands of Egypt, public letters exchanged by cities and rulers, the collected letters of famous personages, letters used as a means of communicating with a larger audience, and fictitious letters attributed to well-known figures.

Much, of course, has not survived; the loss of Aristotle's correspondence, which was published by Artemon, is particularly unfortunate. As examples of the third category, letters designed for a larger public, we have the thirteen attributed to Plato, which detail his experiences with the Syracusan tyrants Dion and Dionysius. Though probably not actually written by Plato, the seventh one provides information about his life that is most likely accurate. The letter form was a particular favorite of philosophers who wanted to reach a larger audience. The most important surviving writings of Epicurus come to us in the form of letters. The most famous examples of letters used for speaking to a larger public are obviously those of Saint Paul written to the churches in Greece and Asia and collected in the New Testament.

From Roman literature the most important collection of letters comprises those written by Cicero to his family and friends, especially Atticus and Brutus, the assassin of Caesar. This extensive body of correspondence includes official letters and other communications intended for a wider public, as well as more informal letters revealing priceless insights not only into Cicero's life but also into the social and domestic life of ancient Rome. The political letters date from the decades of the 50s and 40s B.C., and so provide important information about this critical period in Roman history, which saw the rise and fall of Julius Caesar and the ascendancy of Octavian, as well as the breakdown of the Republic in the civil wars that ultimately resulted in Cicero's death.

Another collection of letters with valuable historical information is the ten-volume set of letters written by **Pliny the Younger** (c. A.D. 61–c. A.D. 113.). Pliny is self-conscious about the literary qualities of his correspondence and its value as a chronicle of his times. Especially useful for historians is the tenth book, which covers the years Pliny governed the province of Bythinia-Pontus, which is now in Turkey. These letters not only give us information about the workings of provincial government but also provide the earliest description outside the New Testament of Christian worship—along with a rationale for the persecution and execution of Christians.

As did Greek philosophers, Roman thinkers used the

letter as a forum for communicating their ideas. The younger Seneca popularized Stoic philosophy in his 124 *Moral Letters*. These are closer to what we would call essays and cover topics such as friendship, happiness, suicide, what constitutes the supreme good, and the fear of death. These letters also contain information about Seneca himself and his times, and so have historical as well as philosophical value. The letter on slaves, for example, offers us a glimpse of the changing attitudes about this universal institution. Seneca's advice that "the man you call slave sprang from the same seed, enjoys the same daylight, breathes like you, lives like you, dies like you"suggests that by the first century A.D.the moral basis of slavery was beginning to be questioned. This tradition of casting philosophical discussion in the form of a letter, reinforced by the model of Saint Paul's letters in the New Testament, especially flourished among Christian writers.

BIOGRAPHY

Stories about the lives of important people came in several different forms in the ancient world, from relatively accurate histories to near fictional encomia to scurrilous attacks. Poets and philosophers, because of their public presence, were popular subjects of "Lives" that portrayed a series of individuals to illustrate patterns of influence and development. Most of these works have come down to us only in fragments and quotations. The best surviving example of this style of intellectual biography is the *Lives of the Eminent Philosophers*, by **Diogenes Laertius** (third century B.C.), who probably synthesized the work of earlier biographers and compilers. Diogenes covers the major schools and philosophers from the earliest "sages" to Epicurus. Though at times Diogenes' reliability is questionable, as he depends on earlier sources who themselves often got their information second- and third-hand, his work nonetheless is invaluable for the anecdotes it preserves about famous philosophers and for the extensive quotations it provides from their works, many of which are now lost.

The works of **Xenophon** (c. 430–c. 354 B.C.) contain several different styles of biography. His *Memorabilia* records

the conversations of Socrates on various topics, from friends
and family to education and virtue, while at the same time
providing charming anecdotes about the philosopher and his
interactions with others. The *Cyropaedia* is a quasi-historical
account of the founder of the Persian empire, Cyrus the
Great. Xenophon combines useful information about the
Persian empire with an almost novelistic treatment of Cyrus's
rise to power; he also includes long asides and dialogues
about leadership. Finally, his *Agesilaus* is a naked encomium
of the fourth-century Spartan king who battled both the
Persians and Sparta's various Greek enemies. To Xenophon
he is the paragon of all the virtues necessary in a good and
great man.

The most influential biographer of the ancient world
is **Plutarch** (c. A.D. 50–120). His "parallel lives" match
nineteen famous Greeks and Romans whose careers were
similar, including an additional four lives that stand alone.
Plutarch, like Xenophon and other earlier Greek biographers, is concerned to demonstrate the development and
effect of virtue and vice in the lives and characters of great
men. Thus, for Plutarch the purpose of biography is not
merely to provide the history of a life, but to deduce moral
and ethical lessons from that history. It is thanks to Plutarch
that we have so much information and so many anecdotes
about the great leaders and events of antiquity (though at
times his reliability can be challenged). Plutarch's influence
on European culture since the Renaissance has been enor-

mous, as can be seen in the poetry of Shakespeare, who knew Plutarch through the translation of Sir Thomas North.

The remains of Roman biography are as scanty as those of Greek biography, but what has survived gives us important information about Roman history. Famous men or their friends wrote defenses and justifications of their careers, such as the lost work of Cicero extolling the Republican martyr Cato, which Caesar answered with his *Anticato*, also now lost. An important example of this genre is the *Res Gestae* or *Achievements* of **Augustus** (63 B.C.– A.D. 14), creator of the Roman Empire, in which he defends the constitutional legality of his extraordinary power and position and the support he enjoyed among his people. Despite the obvious self-interest of Augustus's interpretation of his career, the *Res Gestae* nonetheless provides important historical details pertaining to this critical period of Roman history.

The earliest surviving Roman biographer to not merely apologize for his subjects' lives is **Cornelius Nepos** (c. 110–24 B.C.). From his *On Famous Men*, which covered four hundred lives, have survived the biographies of famous foreign leaders, along with biographies of Cato the Elder and Cicero's friend Atticus. Nepos for the most part praises his subjects and derives ethical lessons from their lives.

The justification and defense of a great man and his deeds are a consistent theme of ancient biography. Among the works of the historian **Tacitus** (c. A.D. 56–c. 118) is a laudatory biography of his father-in-law Agricola, who served as the governor of Britain from A.D. 77 or 78 to 84. Tacitus's praise of Agricola's life is developed in the context of an attack on tyranny, specifically the emperor Domitian. A spicier and more fascinating exposé of the Roman emperors, though at times an account that is highly unreliable, is the *Lives of the Caesars* by **Suetonius** (c. A.D. 70–c. 130). Suetonius also wrote a series of biographies of famous men, including poets, orators, and philosophers, but the only substantial surviving lives are those of rhetoricians and grammarians. His lives of the twelve Caesars from Julius Caesar to Domitian, however, have had a sizable impact on our perceptions of the early Roman emperors. Suetonius organizes his biographies around the subject's characteristics and accomplishments, and his narratives are illustrated with anecdotes. The biographer thus measures each emperor against the same set of expectations his Roman readers presumably held for their rulers. Suetonius is also famous for including descriptions of the sordid sexual practices and other vices of the emperors, which he exposes with relish. Suetonius provided the model for the *Historia Augusta,* a series of imperial biographies covering the years A.D. 117–284 that was composed by six different anonymous authors. [1]

---

[1] Another surviving biography from antiquity is the *Life of Apollonius of Tyana* by Philostratus (third century A.D.). Apollonius was a holy man and wonderworker, and Philostratus's biography gives us impor-tant information about pagan religiosity. Philostratus also wrote the *Lives of the Sophists,* brief descriptions of public speakers giving speeches.

Since the ancients thought that history resulted from the deeds of great men, and that these deeds in turn reflected a man's character, biography was a crucial historical genre. Accurate or not, the details of the lives of the Greeks and Romans portrayed in ancient biography have created for us much of our picture of the ancient world and its leaders. The popular conception of Cleopatra, for example, derives for the most part from Shakespeare's reworking of Plutarch's biographies of Caesar and Antony.

HISTORY

Before the Greeks, history (from a Greek word mean-ing "inquiries") was little more than a chronicle, a list of achievements or events associated with a great man like the pharaoh or the king. It was the Greeks who first self-con-sciously recorded events and information with a view to explaining their meaning or causes rationally, systemically, and critically, that is, without reference to the gods or other supernatural forces. The earliest Greek historians, who emerged during the late sixth century B.C., were known as "logographers" or "writers of prose." The most important among them was **Hecataeus** (c. 500 B.C.). Hecataeus wrote on genealogy, mythology, and geography, but only a few fragments of his work have survived.

Because of the loss of earlier historians' work, the title of "Father of History" passes to **Herodotus** (c. 490–c. 425 B.C.), whose *Histories* sets out to record and explain the wars fought between the Greeks and Persians in 490 and 480–79 B.C. Along the way Herodotus also describes the cus-toms, history, religions, and geography of Greece's neigh-bors, particularly Egypt. Although his critical powers some-times lapse, Herodotus is noteworthy for a rational approach to the evaluation of evidence and for his desire to find meaning in events rather than just to record them. Thus he interprets the Greek victories over the Persians as partly the result of their unique cultural values, particularly their love of political freedom.

The next important Greek historian—one of the great-est historians of all time is **Thucydides** (c. 460–455–c. 399 B.C.). His *History of the Peloponnesian War* fought between Athens and Sparta during the last half of the fifth century B.C. remains one of the most penetrating analyses of a con-flict between states ever written. His concern for accuracy, his insights into human nature and political psychology, his realist's acceptance of the tragic nature of human affairs, his refusal to admit supernatural causes, and his overall fairness (though we can tell whom he admires and whom he detests) all set the standard for subsequent historical writing as a sincere, painstaking effort to get at the truth of things and so produce what Thucydides called his own work, "a possession for all time."

Thucydides' history stops abruptly a few years before the war's end. The story of those critical subsequent years is provided by Xenophon's *Hellenica,* which traces events down to 362 B.C. Though nowhere near the historian Thucydides is, Xenophon's account nonetheless provides valuable information about the period dominated by Sparta until its defeat by Thebes at Leuctra in 371 B.C. Another important work by Xenophon is his *Anabasis,* which concerns an expedition of ten thousand Greek mercenaries, including

Xenophon, to fight for Cyrus, pretender to the Persian throne. After Cyrus's defeat and death, the Greeks had to make their way from deep in Persian territory to the shore of the Black Sea in order to get home. It is a rousing adventure story as well as an illustration of the strength of Greek cultural values under severe stress.

The next noteworthy Greek historian is **Polybius** (c. 200–c. 118 B.C.), who was deported to Rome after the defeat of Achaea, a league of city-states that tried to resist the Romans. In Rome Polybius became a friend of Scipio, the Roman general who would defeat Carthage. Thus, Polybius witnessed firsthand the triumph of Rome over Carthage in the Punic Wars and the rise of Roman power throughout the Mediterranean. Five books of his original forty-book history of Rome's remarkable conquest of the whole Mediterranean have survived, along with summaries and excerpts of others. Polybius's aim as a historian is to present the facts with as much accuracy as possible, which in turn demands exacting research on his part. Moreover, Polybius is concerned to explain the causes of events, particularly the deci-sions that themselves are the result of various factors. Polybius's discussion of the Roman "mixed constitution," which blended elements of aristocracy, oligarchy, and monarchy, was immensely influential on later political thought, especially that of the American founders.

One more historian writing in Greek who should be mentioned is **Josephus** (born c. A.D. 37–c. 100), a Jewish aristocrat who witnessed the fall of Jerusalem and wrote histories of the Jewish war and the Jewish people, including a description of the triumph celebrated in Rome after Judaea was conquered. A defender of his people and their history, Josephus is an important source of information for the decisive first century A.D. [1]

Roman history tended to focus more than did Greek history on the attempt to shape behavior and values in the present; thus, the past is presented in ways that reinforce the writer's didactic intent. This approach can be seen in the work of **Sallust** (86–35 B.C.), who wrote histories of the Catilinian conspiracy and the Roman war against the North African king Jugurtha. In both cases he reveals the corruption of the noble class and its falling away from traditional values as the cause of political and social disorder.

Many Roman historians were themselves men of action who had participated and shaped the events of their times. Most famous of these is **Julius Caesar** (100–44 B.C.), who wrote commentaries on his campaigns in Gaul (modern-day France) and his battles in the civil war against Pompey. The former commentary, despite its subtle ratio-

---

[1] Other surviving Greek historians include Diodorus Siculus (active c. 60–30 B.C.); Dionysius of Halicarnassus (c. 30 B.C.); Appian (c. A.D. 160); and Cassius Dio (c. A.D. 150–235) who all wrote about Roman history; and Arrian (b. A.D. 85–90), who wrote about Alexander the Great. Important historians who survive only in fragments include Ephorus (fourth century B.C.), who wrote a history of the Greek city-states in Greece and Asia Minor, and Theopompus (c. 376–c. 323 B.C.), who like Xenophon continued Thucydides' history and wrote another on Philip of Macedon.

nalizations of Caesar's sometimes constitutionally question-able behavior, nonetheless provides valuable insights into Roman war practices and generalship, as well as the cus-toms, geography, and religion of the Celtic peoples inhab-iting Gaul and Britain.

The moralizing purpose of history has been best ex-pressed in the work of **Livy** (59 B.C.–A.D. 17), who wrote, "Studying history is the best medicine for a sick mind," since it offers examples of noble and fine behavior to imi-tate and corrupt actions to avoid. His *History of Rome from the Founding* (*Ab urbe condita*) in 142 books traced Rome's rise from a village on the Tiber to world dominion. Roughly twenty-five books survive, as do short summaries or ab-stracts of the others. Surviving books describe significant episodes in Roman history, such as the Carthaginian Hannibal's march through the Alps and his devastating vic-tories that nearly destroyed Rome. Livy's purpose is to iden-tify the morals and values that made Rome great and that, once corrupted, led to the disorder and violence of the civil wars. Many of the famous stories from Roman history that appear in later Western literature and art, such as those about Romulus and Remus, the rape of Lucretia, and Horatius's defense of a strategic bridge, are found in Livy.

The last great Roman historian is **Tacitus**, (c. A.D. 56–120) who wrote the *Histories* and the *Annals*. The *Histories* cover the years A.D. 69–96, but only four of probably four-teen books survive. The *Annals*, like Ennius's epic inspired by the public record of the year's events, covered the years A.D. 14–68—the reigns of Tiberius, Caligula, Claudius, and Nero. Roughly two-thirds of a probable sixteen books survive. Tacitus's strength is his understanding of human character, which like most ancients he considered the engine of history, and the consequences for the empire of having emperors who were corrupt or weak. Like Livy, Tacitus thought the historian's purpose was to celebrate virtue and condemn vice: "This I regard as history's highest function, to let no worthy action be uncommemorated, and to hold out the reprobation of posterity as a terror to evil words and deeds." Tacitus's imperial history was continued by another Roman historian, **Ammianus Marcellinus** (A.D. 330–95), who was a Greek writing in Latin. Of the thirty-one books of his history, the last seventeen have survived. [1]

Ancient Greek and Latin historical writing marks the earliest attempt of people to understand themselves and their times through a perception of the past shaped not by divine powers or impersonal forces but by the actions, values, and characters of human beings. As such, ancient history is as much a humanistic enterprise as is ancient poetry or philosophy. It is always concerned with what Thucydides called "the human thing."

---

[1] Other surviving Roman historians include Valerius Maximus (early first century A.D.), who compiled *Memorable Deeds and Sayings;* Curtius (first century A.D.), who wrote a history of Alexander; and Eutropius (fourth century A.D.), author of a ten-book survey of Roman history.

THE CLASSICAL HERITAGE

The works discussed in this brief guide are just the highest peaks of ancient literary achievement. Numerous other kinds of writing have survived that, while not of the brilliance of the best, are nonetheless important sources of information about ancient life and culture, and so are important areas of study in classics. Many ancient scholars produced compendia of other authors that we call "epitomes." These were summaries and abridgments of longer works. For many ancient authors, only epitomes of their books have survived. Various other anthologies have come down to us in which authors and quotations survive that otherwise would have been lost. The *Greek Anthology* is a collection of four thousand poems spanning a period from the seventh century B.C. to the sixth century A.D.; its loss would have left a gaping hole in our understanding of ancient Greek poetry. Likewise, many fragments of tragedy and comedy as well as other literary works are preserved in the "Selections" and "Anthology" of **Stobaeus** (early fifth century A.D.), who arranged his selections by subject matter.

In addition, there are extant works that cannot be placed within any standard category but are crammed with anecdotes and quotations from literature otherwise lost.

The *Deipnosophistai* or "Scholars at Dinner" of **Athenaeus** (c. A.D. 200) contains in its fifteen books (twelve survive) a treasure trove of quotations, excerpts, and anecdotes from ancient literature. Similarly, the twenty books of the *Attic Nights* of **Aulus Gellius** (c. A.D. 130–180), a series of essays on a wide range of topics based on his reading of Greek and Latin literature, preserves much valuable information and numerous quotations. Finally, the *Moralia* of Plutarch is the title of an extensive collection of treatises on moral philosophy covering an astonishing range of topics, from "Advice to Married Couples" to "Flatterers and Friends." As well as providing illustrations of ancient values and morals, the *Moralia* influenced the essayists Francis Bacon and Montaigne, and through them shaped the modern essay. Many of these works perhaps make for tedious reading today, but for scholars they are priceless repositories of anecdotes, quotations, information, and examples of ancient habits of thought.

The literature of the Greeks and Romans is infinitely more interesting, sophisticated, and wide-ranging than any brief survey can capture. In the record of their encounters with the world, and in their analyses and depictions of human nature, the classical authors have bequeathed to us the means we still use today to express and make sense of ourselves and our experiences. To study the language, literature, and culture of the ancient Greeks and Romans is to do more than just master a discipline. It is to learn what we are, what we have been, and what we can become.

FURTHER READING

The state of the profession of classics and the central importance of Greek and Roman civilization for Western culture are addressed in E. Christian Kopff, *The Devil Knows Latin: Why America Needs the Classical Tradition* (ISI Books, 1999); Tracy Lee Simmons, *Climbing Parnassus: A New Apologia for Greek and Latin* (ISI Books, 2002); Victor Davis Hanson and John Heath, *Who Killed Homer?: The Demise of Classical Education and the Recovery of Greek Wisdom* (Encounter Books, 2001); Victor Davis Hanson, John Heath, and Bruce S. Thornton, *Bonfire of the Humanities: Rescuing the Classics in an Impoverished Age* (ISI Books, 2001); Bruce S. Thornton, *Greek Ways: How the Greeks Created Western Civilization* (Encounter Books, 2000); and Bernard Knox, *The Oldest Dead White European Males* (Norton, 1993). Two classics of scholarship discuss the influence of Greek and Roman literature on later Western literature: Gilbert Highet, *The Classical Tradition: Greek and Roman Influences on Western Literature* (Oxford University Press, 1949); and Ernst Robert Curtius, *European Literature and the Latin Middle Ages,* trans. Willard R. Trask (Princeton University Press, 1953).

For a general overview of Greek and Roman history, culture, and literature, students should start with *The Oxford History of the Classical World,* ed. John Boardman, Jasper Griffin, and Oswyn Murray (Oxford University Press, 1983). For classical literature more specifically, see the essays in *The Cambridge History of Classical Literature* (Cambridge University Press, 1982–85). A good place to look for translations of Greek and Latin authors not listed here is in the Loeb Classical Library, published by Harvard University Press.

Greek Literature. The most accurate translations of Homer remain those by Richmond Lattimore, both of which remain in print: the *Iliad* (University of Chicago Press, 1962), and the *Odyssey* (Harper & Row, 1967). Probably the best literary translations are those by Robert Fagles: the *Iliad* (Viking, 1990) and the *Odyssey* (Viking, 1996). The introductory essay by Bernard Knox included in Fagles's translations is the best introduction to Homer available. See also Seth Schein, *The Mortal Hero: An Introduction to Homer's Iliad* (University of California Press, 1984). Hesiod and the *Homeric Hymns* have been translated by Apostolos N. Athanassakis (Johns Hopkins University Press, 1976).

For tragedy see the *Complete Greek Tragedies,* edited by Richmond Lattimore and David Grene (University of Chicago Press, 1992). Two collections of essays by Bernard Knox are invaluable for approaching Greek tragedy: *The Heroic*

Temper: Studies in Sophoclean Tragedy (1964; reprint, University of California Press, 1983); and *Word and Action: Essays on the Ancient Theater* (Johns Hopkins, 1979). To get the most accurate translations of other Greek poetry the best bet is to look in the five volumes of *Greek Lyric Poetry,* ed. David A. Campbell, Loeb Classical Library (Harvard University Press, 1982–93). See also *The Greek Anthology and Other Ancient Epigrams,* trans. Peter Jay (1973; reprint, Penguin, 1981). Also useful is *Early Greek Lyric Poetry,* trans. David Mulroy (University of Michigan Press, 1999).

For Aristophanes' comedies the translations by Jeffrey Henderson for the Loeb Classical Library are dependable. Two excellent introductions to Aristophanes and comedy are Donald M. MacDowell, *Aristophanes and Athens* (Oxford University Press, 1995), and K. J. Dover, *Aristophanic Comedy* (University of California Press, 1972). For *The Voyage of the Argo* see *The Argonautika: The Story of Jason and the Quest for the Golden Fleece,* translation by Peter Green (University of California Press, 1997). Theocritus has been ably translated by Thelma Sargent, *The Idylls of Theocritus* (Norton, 1982); see the valuable study by Thomas G. Rosenmeyer, *The Green Cabinet: Theocritus and the European Pastoral Lyric* (University of California Press, 1969).

As for historians, see Herodotus's *Histories* translated by David Grene (University of Chicago Press, 1987); *The Landmark Thucydides: A Comprehensive Guide to the Peloponnesian War,* ed. Robert Strassler (The Free Press,

1996); two translations of Xenophon in the Penguin Classics, both by Rex Warner: *A History of My Times* (New York, 1978) and *The Persian Expedition* (Baltimore, 1961, 1967, 1972); and for Polybius, *The Rise of the Roman Empire,* trans. Ian Scott-Kilvert (Penguin, 1979).

English poet John Dryden's translations of *Plutarch's Lives* are still in print with the Modern Library. A nice introduction to Greek oratory, with a selection of speeches, can be found in *Greek Orations: 4th Century B.C.,* trans. W. Robert Conner (1966; reprint, Waveland Press, 1987).

Roman Literature. There are numerous translations of Catullus available, but I am fond of C. H. Sisson's *Poetry of Catullus* (Viking, 1966). More recently, David D. Mulroy provides an excellent translation with a good introduction in *The Complete Poetry of Catullus* (University of Wisconsin Press, 2002). Other solid introductions to Catullus include Kenneth Quinn, *Catullus: An Interpretation* (New York, 1973) and T. P. Wiseman, *Catullus and his World: A Reappraisal* (Cambridge University Press, 1985).

A good translation of Lucretius's *Nature of Things* is by Frank Copley (Norton, 1977).

For Virgil's *Eclogues,* see the translation by Barbara Fowler (University of North Carolina Press, 1997); for the *Georgics,* see L. P. Wilkinson's translation (Penguin, 1982) and his study, *The Georgics of Virgil* (Cambridge University Press, 1969); and for the *Aeneid,* see Allen Mandelbaum's translation (Bantam, 1971). For modern work on the *Aeneid* see the essays in *Oxford Readings in Virgil's Aeneid,* ed. S. J. Harrison (Oxford University Press, 1990). An excellent reading of Virgil in the context of Homeric heroic ideals is Katherine Callen King's *Achilles: Paradigms of the War Hero from Homer to the Middle Ages* (University of California Press, 1987).

Tibullus's poetry is available in the translation of Constance Carrier, *Poems* (Indiana University Press, 1968). For an introduction to Tibullus and his poetic milieu see F. Cairns, *Tibullus: A Hellenistic Poet at Rome* (Cambridge University Press, 1979).

Propertius has been translated by J. P. McCulloch in *The Poems of Sextus Propertius* (University of California Press, 1972). See too J. P. Sullivan, *Propertius: A Critical Introduction* (Cambridge University Press, 1976).

Horace's work is available in two volumes from the University of Chicago Press: *Satires and Epistles of Horace,* trans. Smith Palmer Bovie (1959), and *The Odes and Epodes of Horace,* trans. Joseph F. Clancy (1960). A good brief introduction is *Horace,* by David Armstrong (Yale University Press, 1989).

For Ovid, see *Ovid's Amores,* trans. Guy Lee (Viking, 1968); the *Metamorphoses,* trans. Mary M. Innes (Penguin, 1955); *The Erotic Poems,* trans. Peter Green (Penguin, 1982; Green's introduction is valuable as well); and *Ovid's Fasti: Roman Holidays,* trans. Betty Rose Nagle (Indiana University Press, 1995). For a general introduction to Ovid see *Ovid,* by Sara Mack (Yale University Press, 1988).

A good selection of Martial's epigrams can be found in *Selected Epigrams,* trans. Ralph Marcellino (Bobbs-Merrill, 1968). For Juvenal see *Satires,* trans. Rolfe Humphries (Indiana University Press, 1958). And for Petronius, see William Arrowsmith, *The Satyricon* (University of Michigan Press, 1959).

As for Latin prose: Cicero's voluminous works are most accessible in the Loeb Classical Library. A good selection from his works can be found in *Selected Works,* trans. Michael Grant (Penguin, 1960). Two other influential works are *On the Good Life,* trans. Michael Grant (Penguin, 1971), and *On the Commonwealth,* trans. George Holland Sabine and Stanley Barney Smith (Bobbs-Merrill, 1929). Caesar's commentaries are available in two volumes: *The Civil War,* trans. Jane F. Gardner (Penguin, 1967), and *The Conquest of Gaul,* trans. S. A. Handford (Penguin, 1951). The surviving books of Livy's history are available from Penguin under the titles *The Early History of Rome, The War with Hannibal, Rome and Italy,* and *Rome and the Mediterranean.* For Tacitus, see *The Complete Works of Tacitus,* trans. Alfred John Church and William Jackson Brodribb, ed. by Moses Hadas (Modern Library, 1942). Sallust's histories, translated by S. A. Handford, appear in *The Jugurthine War and the Conspiracy of Catiline* (Penguin, 1963).

打开一扇窗户，看看大学的专业

教授带你"逛"专业

由 130 多位浙江大学的老师和 30 多位学生一起完成，给将要成为大学生的学生们的书。

采用问答的方式，通过"身在专业"的名师大家和同学的生动经历，引领大家"逛"专业，帮助年轻人打开大学的窗，了解认识大学的专业。

希望这本好看、好懂、好用的"专业指南"，能在你选择未来发展方向时，助上一臂之力。

步入学科堂奥的台阶，通向开放未来的知识桥梁

人文社会科学基础文献选读丛书

浙江大学相关学科具有较高学术水平和丰富教学经验的教授和博导，几经筛选、精心校译，帮助读者面对浩繁的文献和有限的时间，以最短的时间、最少的阅读量、最可靠的方式，准确地掌握相关学科最重要的内容。

第一辑（已出）：

《西方哲学基础文献选读》 包利民 编选

《历史学基础文献选读》 包伟民 编选

《社会学基础文献选读》 冯 钢 编选

《经济学基础文献选读》 罗卫东 编选

《政治学基础文献选读》 郎友兴 编选

《管理学基础文献选读》 张 钢 编选

第二辑：

《文艺学基础文献选读》（已出） 徐 岱 沈语冰 编选

《语言学基础文献选读》（已出） 施 旭 编选

《传播学基础文献选读》（即出） 李 岩 编选

《心理学基础文献选读》（即出） 王重鸣 编选

《法学基础文献选读》（即出） 夏立安 陈林林 编选

《教育学基础文献选读》（即出） 徐小洲 编选

《宗教学基础文献选读》（即出） 王晓朝 编选

图书在版编目（CIP）数据

文学·经典：汉英对照／（美）杨，（美）桑顿著；高睿译．—杭州：浙江大学出版社，2015.5
（学科入门指南）
书名原文：A student's guide to literature;a student's guide to classics

ISBN 978-7-308-14253-3

Ⅰ.①文… Ⅱ.①杨… ②桑… ③高… Ⅲ.①文学—指南—汉、英 Ⅳ.①I-62

中国版本图书馆 CIP 数据核字（2014）第 303725 号

浙江省版权局著作权合同　登记图字：11-2014-337 号

学科入门指南：文学·经典
（美）R.V.杨　（美）布鲁斯·S.桑顿　著
高睿 译

————————————————————————————————

策划编辑　葛玉丹
责任编辑　陈佩钰（yukin_chen@zju.edu.cn）
封面设计　项梦怡
出版发行　浙江大学出版社
　　　　　（杭州市天目山路148号　邮政编码310007）
　　　　　（网址：http://www.zjupress.com）
排　　版　杭州立飞图文制作有限公司
印　　刷　临安市曙光印务有限公司
开　　本　889mm×1194mm　1/32
印　　张　8.625
字　　数　230千
版 印 次　2015年5月第1版　2015年5月第1次印刷
书　　号　ISBN 978-7-308-14253-3
定　　价　28.00元

————————————————————————————————